"You loo̶̶̶̶̶̶̶̶̶̶̶̶̶̶̶̶̶ dead man, Geoff."

Something flickered in his eyes and he studied her peculiarly. "Lady, my name is *not* Geoff."

Devon's jaw dropped, but she ignored him and forged ahead. "I want a divorce. If you'd come home after the accident instead of disappearing, we might have worked out our problems. But…"

"But what?" His tone sounded almost too civil. "What the hell is your name, anyway?"

"Are you telling me you honestly don't remember? My name is Devon Grayson."

"Grayson…" he echoed. "You're a very attractive woman, Devon Grayson. I still don't have a clue who you are, but I concede that it is possible that you're my wife. And, if you are, I'd like to get to know you better. So, no, I won't agree to a divorce."

Dear Reader,

Happy holidaze! The holiday season always does pass in a bit of a daze, with all the shopping and wrapping and partying, the cooking and (of course!) the eating. So take some time for yourself with our six Intimate Moments novels, each one of them a wonderful Christmas treat.

Start by paying a visit to THE LONE STAR SOCIAL CLUB, Linda Turner's setting for *Christmas Lone-Star Style.* Remember, those Texans know how to do things in a *big* way! Then join Suzanne Brockmann for another TALL, DARK AND DANGEROUS title, *It Came Upon a Midnight Clear.* I wouldn't mind waking up and finding Crash Hawken under *my* Christmas tree! Historical writer Patricia Potter makes a slam-bang contemporary debut with *Home for Christmas,* our FAMILIES ARE FOREVER title. Wrongly convicted and without the memories that could save him, Ryan Murphy is a hero to treasure. Award winner Ruth Wind returns with *For Christmas, Forever.* Isn't this the season when mysterious strangers come bearing…romance tinged with danger? Debra Cowan's *One Silent Night* is our MEN IN BLUE title. I'd be happy to "unwrap" Sam Garrett on Christmas morning. Finally, welcome mainstream author Christine Michels to the line. *A Season of Miracles* carries the TRY TO REMEMBER flash, though you'll have no trouble at all remembering this warm holiday love story.

It's time to take the "daze" out of the holidays, so enjoy all six of these seasonal offerings. Of course, don't forget that next month marks a new year, so come back then for more of the best romance reading around—right here in Silhouette Intimate Moments.

Seasons Greetings,

Leslie J. Wainger
Executive Senior Editor

Please address questions and book requests to:
Silhouette Reader Service
U.S.: 3010 Walden Ave., P.O. Box 1325, Buffalo, NY 14269
Canadian: P.O. Box 609, Fort Erie, Ont. L2A 5X3

A SEASON OF MIRACLES

CHRISTINE MICHELS

Published by Silhouette Books
America's Publisher of Contemporary Romance

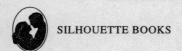

SILHOUETTE BOOKS

ISBN 0-373-07900-1

A SEASON OF MIRACLES

Printed in U.S.A.

CHRISTINE MICHELS

is a chronic daydreamer with a vivid imagination. Since her day job as an accountant provided little outlet for her creative inclinations (creative accounting being frowned upon in professional circles), Christine turned to writing. She is now an award-winning author of futuristic, historical and contemporary romances. Christine lives on the Canadian prairies near Lloydminster, Alberta, with her husband of twenty-three years, their fourteen-year-old son and a small menagerie of pets, consisting of a finicky Pomeranian, two imperious cats and a hedgehog with a very prickly personality.

This one's for all of you, my readers.
I wish you peace, prosperity and many, many years
of fascinating reading.

Chapter 1

This was it: Geoff's place.

Devon Grayson stared uneasily at the charming stone and cedar facade of the rustic cabin. Red and green Christmas lights decorated the window frames and porch railing, while warm yellow light spilled from the front windows to pool on a veranda that stretched the entire width of the cabin. On a cool December evening like tonight, it looked warm and welcoming.

If only she could expect a comparable greeting from its occupant.

Turning off the Jeep and extinguishing the headlights, she closed her eyes briefly, drew a deep breath and suppressed the urge to run away. She couldn't. There was too much that remained unfinished between them. Too much at stake for her. Finding the core of righteous anger buried deep within, she used it to gird herself to face him.

The least he could have done was call.

Buttoning her jacket against the cold, she hooked the strap of her purse over her right shoulder, opened the door of the Jeep, and quickly walked up the slush-covered walk. At the base of the veranda steps, she paused, lifted her face briefly to the cold caress of softly falling snowflakes, and drew one last deep fortifying breath.

Then, releasing it in a cloud of condensed moisture, she forced herself to step up onto the porch. The sound of a creaking board beneath her feet, as loud as a gunshot in the cool stillness, splintered her fragile composure, but she managed to propel her quaking legs forward. Completing the short distance to the door, she knocked before she could change her mind.

Standing there staring at the steel-clad door with its small sunburst window, at the Christmas wreath hanging there, she suddenly pictured herself poised at the fork of two roads in her life path. She sensed that this was one of those moments that could forever change the course of what came after. Frightened of the consequences and events she was putting into motion, she actually turned away. The urge to run was as powerful as it was illogical. But before she had taken a step, the door opened and she froze, trapped by the swathe of light like a doe paralysed by the headlights of an oncoming vehicle.

There was no going back now. She turned to face him.

Geoff, wearing black chinos and a black turtleneck sweater that hugged the muscular contours of his chest and upper arms, stood in silhouette against the bright, warm light of the room at his back. Her heart stuttered and then slammed against her chest wall in a reaction that had very little to do with fright.

"Hello, Geoff," she managed, in a voice that she hoped didn't sound as choked as it felt. "Surprised to see me?"

In the second of silence that followed, she sensed his gaze moving over her before he spoke. "Is this some kind of joke?"

"Joke?" The shadows concealed his facial expression. She had no idea what he meant, but she couldn't allow him to throw her off balance so quickly. "If there is one thing I'm not, Geoff, it's in the mood to joke, believe me." *Why hadn't he called?* Instead, he'd disappeared after the accident, allowing himself to be officially "presumed dead" for more than two years. *How could he have done that?* But she said none of that. Not yet. "I have just driven the entire day through a snowstorm to get here.

Now, do you want to discuss our private business out here, or are you going to invite me in?''

Although shadow still eclipsed his features, she sensed the frown in his expression as he considered her. A second later, he stepped back. "Come in." For the first time, she noted that his voice was altered. Once his voice had been all black velvet and Irish whiskey. Now it was silk-on-sandstone and cognac. Different but, unfortunately, just as appealing. She wondered what had happened to change it. The accident?

As he turned slightly to grant her entrance and the light fully illuminated his features, Devon's breath caught in her throat. Her gaze clung to him as she stepped into the house. She'd forgotten how handsome he was. Every inch of his six-foot-two-inch form was more attractive than she remembered. She felt as though a man-sized fist had reached into her chest to squeeze her heart. But there were subtle changes in his appearance, too. Changes wrought during a period of time when he had cut her out of his life.

A line furrowed the flesh between his thick black brows, drawing them together over olive-hued eyes that were definitely more intense than she recalled. And, his hair was subtly altered. Although still thick and black and wavy, a few strands of premature silver streaked the temples. He wore it longer now than he had in the past; medium-length waves on top and on the sides, but it brushed his shoulders in the back. A narrow white scar dissected his left brow, skirted his temple and disappeared into his hairline. The small disfigurement pulled the crest of his brow up slightly, granting him a perpetually satirical expression.

Devon's fingers tingled with the peculiar urge to trace that scar, to soothe the hurt that had caused it, and she rubbed them against her jean-clad thighs. She longed to erase the unwelcome urge as easily as she eliminated the sensation, but it was useless. Emotion rose in her throat as she stared at him: hurt, caring, anger and...oh, yes, as hard as it was to admit, *desire*. A tangle of feeling impossible to separate. She refused to consider the possibility that *love* might still be embroiled in there somewhere, too. Taking a deep breath, she subdued the absurd yearning to throw herself into his embrace.

She was engaged to another man. She no longer had the right to feel these things for Geoff.

Bracing herself to face his anger, she lifted her gaze to meet his.

Everything within her went still. There was no anger in his eyes. The expression in those dark green depths was uncaring, as cold as the December blizzard she'd braved to come this far, and somehow...empty. Despite everything she and Geoff had once shared, a shiver of apprehension traversed her spine. She felt as though she was looking into the eyes of a stranger.

The impression stayed with her even as he began to study her in return. "You saw me on television last night?" he asked as he wordlessly offered to take her coat. His tone expressed only mild interest; a man voicing an observation that meant nothing to him.

"Yes." Setting her purse down on the floor, she handed him her jacket. She felt confused. Almost frightened. There was something about Geoff that wasn't...wasn't Geoff. Her instincts clamored a warning of danger, but that was pure absurdity, and she ignored it. This *was* Geoff, and he would never hurt her no matter how angry he might be, no matter how much he wanted his anonymity. Still, a small part of her couldn't help remembering just how isolated this cabin on the shores of Deer Lake truly was. It was a good three miles to the northern British Columbia town of Northridge, maybe more.

As he turned to hang up her coat, Geoff looked at her over his shoulder. "And you thought you recognized me?"

"I didn't *think* I recognized you. I *recognized* you." Devon searched his face for the reason behind his cryptic comment, but his countenance gave nothing away. Although Geoff had made it very clear the previous evening that he had no interest in speaking to the reporters, a cameraman had managed to capture a full frontal image of him for a brief moment before Geoff had turned away. "Did you think I wouldn't know you?" Devon asked.

"You are still my husband, after all, Geoff. And you haven't changed that much."

His eyes locked on hers. Was that startlement she saw in their depths? In the next instant he blinked and the expression was gone. "Right," he drawled with a slight nod, but there was a disbelieving tone to the word that Devon failed to understand. He continued to regard her strangely, and the silence grew oppressive.

To ease the strain, Devon spoke again. "The Noralco foreman you pulled from the building is extremely lucky you were there. Do they know yet what caused the explosion?"

His silent, penetrating scrutiny continued. Devon felt her stomach clench. And then, just when she began to believe he would not answer, he responded, "No."

Devon cleared her throat. "Well...hopefully they'll find the cause soon."

He nodded almost curtly, then, seeming to come to some sort of decision, he asked, "Would you like some coffee?"

"Yes, please. That would be nice." She bent to unlace her ankle boots. Despite everything that was between them, Geoff's reaction to her presence was...unlike Geoff. She had expected him to be more vocal; she'd anticipated more rancor. Where was his passion? The Geoff she knew had been passionate in everything he did, the volatile Latin temperament he'd inherited from his Italian mother readily apparent. That was what was missing in him now. Passion.

She straightened, toed off her boots and bent to retrieve her purse.

Geoff led her through one end of a rustic cedar-paneled living room with a cathedral ceiling that soared into shadow overhead, creating a feeling of spaciousness often lacking in cabins. She just had time to note cognac-colored leather chairs and a matching sofa before they entered a country-style kitchen.

Geoff waved one hand in the general direction of the table and its four arrow-back chairs. "Have a seat while I put on a fresh pot of coffee."

"Thanks." She swallowed, feeling a bit awkward and uncomfortable, and took the time to study the room before moving toward the table.

Three of the kitchen's walls were eggshell white while the fourth was a cedar feature wall. The blue tones of a set of hand-painted delft plates hanging on the feature wall were carried forward to the ceramic countertop and used as an accent color in the cream linoleum flooring. The cabinets, table and chairs were wood—probably oak, Devon decided. A crystal vase of delft-blue silk blooms occupied the center of the table.

A woman's touch? she wondered.

Devon chose a chair at the rear of the table because it allowed her an unobstructed view of the room and, hence, of Geoff. He still had the powerfully muscled body and flat stomach of the construction worker he'd been when they'd first met, when both had been working to put themselves through university. She couldn't deny that he still fascinated her; he was still very attractive. But, Geoff was a part of her past now, and she was determined to move forward.

The coffee began to hiss and gurgle its way into the carafe, and Geoff carried a pair of cups to the table. "So," he said, "what can I do for you?"

Startled, Devon stared at him incredulously. "What can you *do* for me?"

He made no response to her exclamation, merely watched her with a slightly probing expression, and waited. For the first time in her life, Devon felt the urge to slap him.

"Well, for starters, you can tell me why you took an alias and dropped off the face of the earth two years ago, Geoff. You can tell me why you let everyone who cared about you think you were dead." She knew her voice was rising with the force of the outrage that was once again tightening her chest, but she couldn't help it. "You look awfully darned healthy for a dead man, Geoff." Her gaze raked him heatedly. "And then, I'd really like to know who this Jack Keller is that you're pretending to be."

Something flickered in his eyes and he studied her peculiarly. "Lady, my name is *not* Geoff. I'm afraid you've got the wrong guy."

Devon's jaw dropped but no words came out. If there was any response she'd been expecting, it was not this one. He was going to pretend he didn't know her. The absolute gall of the tactic floored her. "Oh, no you don't, Geoff. You are not going to do this. I want a divorce, and you are damned well going to give me one. Do you hear me?"

"Divorce!"

Well, it seemed that she'd been able to elicit an emotional response after all, even if it was only surprise. "Yes, Geoff, a divorce. If you'd come home after the accident instead of using it as a means to disappear, there might have been a chance for us to work our problems out. But..." She shrugged and allowed her voice to trail off as her gaze slid away.

"But what?" He didn't sound angry. Even the inflection of surprise was gone. In fact his tone was almost too civil.

"But, I refuse to allow you to make me part of this deception you've engineered—for whatever reason. I have somebody else in my life now. We want to get married."

Geoff turned to the counter for a moment to retrieve a sugar bowl and pitcher of milk to place on the table. At least he looked a bit thoughtful, Devon mused as she stared absently at the small pitcher. When had Geoff begun using cream and sugar? she wondered. Or, had he already forgotten that she drank her coffee black?

"Lady...." Geoff's voice drew her sharply back into the present. "What in blazes is your name anyway?" A trace of exasperation burned in his eyes as he stood looking down at her.

Devon froze, staring at him. What was her name? Had the accident affected his memory? "Are you trying to tell me that you honestly don't remember my name?" He didn't respond, merely waited with a very familiar stubborn set to his chin. Devon knew that characteristic well enough to know that, whether he honestly didn't remember her or was just being obstinate for some obscure reason, if they were going to get anywhere, she'd have to play along. "My name is Devon, you jerk. As if you didn't know."

"Devon...?"

"Devon Grayson." Devon bit the words off sharply.

"Grayson," he echoed. Confusion flared briefly in his eyes, and then, abruptly, he winced as though from a sharp pain and grasped the bridge of his nose between thumb and forefinger. For a long silent moment, he simply stood there. The coffee machine gurgled its last and he seemed to focus on that with almost single-minded deliberation. Retrieving the carafe, he poured the brew into the two waiting cups.

Weary after her daylong drive and, for some indefinable reason, suddenly near tears, Devon studied him as he joined her at the table. Taking the seat on her right, he avoided her gaze. Neither of them touched the cream and sugar. *Why is he doing this?* The question reverberated in her mind as she sipped her coffee. His lack of acknowledgement was worse by far than the churlishness and sarcasm she'd more than half expected.

She observed his lean-fingered hands as they closed around the cream-colored cup. The flex of a biceps muscle beneath the clinging fabric of his black turtleneck. The movement of his chest with each breath he took. And gradually, inexorably, her gaze rose to his closed face.

Geoff was eyeing her silently over the rim of his coffee cup. The frown line between his brows had deepened, and there was a tenseness about his face that hadn't been there scant minutes earlier. Slowly, he replaced his cup on the table. "Do you have any identification?"

Devon set her cup down so abruptly that coffee sloshed over the edges. "Pardon me!"

His lips stretched into a parody of a smile, but there was no warmth in the gesture. "Identification," he repeated. "Anything to prove that you really are who you say you are."

"Who else would I be?"

He shrugged. "I don't know. Right now, I don't care. I am getting a King Kong headache, and if it holds true to form, we have about ten minutes to finish our business here, while I can still think. Unless you have identification, this visit is over."

Feeling more and more as though she'd somehow stepped through a looking glass into an alter world where nothing was what it seemed, Devon reached blindly for the purse she'd set on the floor by her feet. Did he truly not know her? How was that possible? An injury from the accident? But, she'd heard on a talk show once that injury-induced amnesia—differentiated from memory suppression caused by emotional trauma—rarely lasted for long, and seldom amounted to more than a few lost days or weeks. Complete amnesia was so rare that most physicians never saw an actual case in their entire lives.

But rare meant unusual, extraordinary even, not impossible.

Numbed by the chaotic thoughts careening through her mind, she blindly extracted her wallet and handed it to him. If he wanted to see identification, then she'd darned well show it to him because there was no way she was going to let him shove her out the door until she had the divorce agreement she'd come for.

He snapped open her wallet and began sorting through her credit cards. When he came to her driver's license, he stopped for a moment, studying it carefully. Then he began sorting through the photos she kept: the kids' school pictures, the most recent photo of her parents, a ten-year-old grad picture of her brother, Winston.

Geoff returned to the pictures of the children. A moment later he raised his gaze to hers. ''Yours?''

''Of course they're mine,'' Devon snapped in frustration. ''They're also yours.''

He made no response to that, instead asking, ''How old?''

Devon wanted to scream. ''Geoff, I've had about enough of—''

''How old, dammit?'' He didn't raise his voice but bit the words off abruptly, forcefully, as his eyes flashed with something cold enough to send a shiver down her spine.

Devon stared at him, for the first time beginning to entertain the notion that this man really was *not* Geoff. She'd heard it said that every person in the world had a twin. Perhaps this man, Jack Keller, was Geoff's. She glanced at the picture he held. ''Britanny is nine now,'' she managed to say. Her daughter was a beautiful, intelligent child with a clear peaches-and-cream complexion, Devon's translucent gray eyes and Geoff's thick, midnight black hair.

Without taking his eyes from the photo, he nodded.

Who was this man?

The Geoff she'd married had been a loud and happy man. The kind of man who would bellow, "Come in! Come in!" to any visitors who appeared on his doorstep whether they'd been expected or not. He'd been demonstrative and affectionate. Discounting their last six months together, she couldn't recall a day of her marriage when she hadn't received a bear hug and a kiss as part of her morning fare. And, he'd been a kind but firm father.

It was only in their last few months together that Geoff had changed, withdrawn. Not simply from her, but from the children as well. And they'd all been hurt by his sudden uncharacteristic distance. Gone was the boisterous gaiety that had been so much a part of who Geoff was. Gone was the affection. And worst of all, gone was the time he'd always made for his children. It had been as though something preyed on his mind so completely that there hadn't been room for anything else. And yet he'd refused to talk about it. When she'd questioned him, begged him to confide in her, he'd shouted at her, "Just leave me alone, goddammit! Stay out of things that don't concern you." And then he'd slammed out of the house.

For six months, she'd hung on—living with his sullenness, his withdrawal, and his quick temper if someone dared to disturb him—all in the hope that she'd eventually rediscover the man she'd married. It hadn't happened.

And now, in yet another incarnation, it seemed, Geoff had entered her life again. Or rather she'd entered his. And this Geoff seemed like another man entirely. She couldn't imagine this man boisterously inviting anyone into his home any more than she could imagine him raising his voice in anger or slamming doors. He was too reserved, too controlled, too lacking in all the Italian passion that had made the man she'd married who he was. She sensed a coldness at the core of this Geoff that she wasn't certain could ever be thawed.

''And the boy?'' he demanded, jerking her out of her thoughts. ''What's his name?''

''Tyler. He's twelve,'' Devon murmured. Her son was tall, almost as tall as she was, with arrow-straight dark brown hair and his father's olive green eyes although they didn't show up well in the photograph. Unfortunately though, something else did.

''The kid has an earring,'' Geoff observed as he rubbed his forehead in a rhythmic gesture that seemed almost desperate.

Devon nodded. ''Yes.'' She hadn't wanted Tyler to get the earring, but as in so many things since his father had passed away...or *left* them...Tyler had ignored her wishes. But she refused to explain all that to this man. If he *was* Geoff, he'd lost the right for explanations a long time ago. If he wasn't Geoff, then he'd never had that right.

''There's no picture of anyone who looks like me in here.''

''Like a lot of men, Geoff didn't like to bother with having his picture taken, especially a studio picture. We only had two family portraits done in the twelve years we were together.''

''Geoff?'' he echoed. His eyes flashed with something like triumph as he flashed her a humorless smile that bared too many teeth by far. ''You're considering the possibility that I'm not him.''

Devon shrugged as she realized what she'd said. ''You look like him. *Exactly* like him. But, your personality is different somehow.''

''Maybe I've had reason to change.''

Devon stared at him. ''What are you saying?''

He rubbed his forehead harder. It was beginning to redden from the force of his ministrations. ''Hell, I don't know what I'm saying. Look, if you want to finish this conversation, I think you'd better come back tomorrow.'' He rose from the table so quickly that his chair scooted back, rocking precariously on its rear legs before slamming noisily back onto all fours.

''Geoff—''

''Goodbye, lady. You'll have to see yourself out.'' With those words he began walking unsteadily from the room. In fact, had

Devon not been there, she would have assumed he was drunk, his senses clouded by booze. His senses were clouded, she realized abruptly, but by pain not drink.

She retrieved her wallet from the table surface where he'd dropped it and, after stuffing it haphazardly back into her purse, followed him uncertainly from the room. There wasn't much sense in forcing her company on a man incapable of carrying on a conversation. But she certainly couldn't head home. Not yet. Not with so many unanswered questions buzzing around in her mind like angry bees. She'd get a room in Northridge for the night and come back in the morning.

By the time she made it to the living room and front entrance, her reluctant host was already out of sight. The sound of numerous falling objects succeeded immediately by a curse drifted down from the upper level of the cabin. It sounded like he'd dropped an entire bottle of pills into the sink. Devon surveyed the balcony overlooking the living room for some indication of which room he was in. Her eyes fastened on one doorway from which light spilled, pooling onto the gallery.

Devon hesitated. "Geoff, are you all right?" she called.

No answer.

"Geoff—"

Silence. She hesitated, uncertain whether she wanted to invade this man's privacy or not. He might look like Geoff, but his personality, his reactions, were those of a stranger.

And then she heard a thud. A very *loud* thud. She pictured him falling, his strong body felled by a type of pain she didn't understand and hoped never to know, and she knew that even were there some small chance that this man was not Geoff, she had to help him if she could.

She headed toward the stairs at a run. "Geoff—" she called once more.

Nothing.

When Devon rounded the corner of the upstairs washroom, she froze. It was worse than she imagined, for what she'd imagined might have been kinder. Rather than lying still and unconscious on the floor, Geoff was literally writhing in pain. He was on his knees, clutching his head in both hands as though he sought to keep it from exploding.

And she had no idea what to do for him. No idea how to help.

An empty prescription bottle lay on the floor by his side. Had he managed to take anything? She took a step toward him. "Geoff," she said. "Can you hear me?"

There was no response.

Noting a facecloth hanging above the vanity, she scooped as many of the small white pills out of the sink as possible and ran the cloth under a stream of cold water. After hastily squeezing the excess moisture from it, she went down on her knees at his side. Somehow, she had to get him to turn over.

She placed a hand on his shoulder. "Geoff, can you hear me?" This time she was rewarded by a groan and a very earthy curse.

"I have a cold cloth for your forehead. Can you turn over?" She pressed back as far as possible to give him space in which to maneuver. The room was of average size for a bathroom, but Geoff's big body took up most of the floor space.

With another groan, he fell over onto his side, pressing his back up firmly against the porcelain finish of the tub. His eyes were tightly closed, and he didn't seem inclined to roll over any farther, so it would have to do. At least she had access to half of his forehead now.

Devon gently pressed the cloth into place. "Is there anything else I can do?"

A moment of silence. "Pills," he croaked. "Need two."

"All right." Devon turned slightly toward the vanity and maneuvered her arm up to grope for a couple of pills from the small mound she'd scooped out of the sink. She was about to hold them out to him when she realized that he didn't appear as though he'd be particularly amenable to the idea of releasing the pressure on his head. "Open your mouth," she said.

The muscles in his jaws leapt spasmodically as though he was gritting his teeth, girding himself, and then he finally complied and Devon was able to give him the pills. He swallowed deeply, his throat muscles working in a manner that suggested even that small action was an effort.

"Would you like me to help you move somewhere more comfortable?" Devon asked.

The only response she received was a male grunt that was impossible to interpret. Since he didn't make any effort to move, however, she took his response as a *no*. Not knowing what else to do, she simply stayed at his side. Gradually the twitching movements of his body lessened, his breathing grew slower and more regular, and he released the death grip he had on his head. Devon heaved a sigh of relief. Whatever the medication was that had been designed to control such a debilitating headache, apparently it was strong enough to force him into the oblivion of sleep.

She observed him a moment in frustration. She didn't want to leave him sleeping on the cold, hard floor, especially since she didn't know how long the medication would keep him out, but she didn't have much choice. He was much too big and heavy for her to move. She *could* make him as comfortable as possible however. On the heels of that decision she rose to go in search of a blanket and pillow.

Standing in the doorway of the room just to the right of the bathroom, she explored the wall with her hand until she found a light switch. The room revealed by the illumination was a stark masculine bedroom. A homemade quilt fashioned of dark tweeds, rusty reds, and navy blues covered the bed. The dresser contained only a comb and a lint brush. A set of four books rested on the bureau. Geoff had certainly become more tidy since she'd last seen him.

Despite her reluctance to intrude on another's privacy, as a curious tension invaded her, Devon found her feet carrying her toward the bureau. When she was close enough to read the titles, she heaved a sigh of relief. Mysteries and thrillers. Dick Francis and Dean Koontz. The same type of novel that Geoff always read. It might not mean much in the vast scheme of things—a lot of people read the same type of novel—but the discovery made her feel better. Turning back to the bed, she quickly removed a pillow and the quilted spread and left the room.

Geoff had stretched out a little more fully in her absence. His turtleneck sweater had ridden up to expose an expanse of taut belly dusted lightly around the navel with dark hair. Devon was preparing to spread the blanket over him when her gaze shifted over that exposed patch of flesh one more time.

The mole!

Everything within her went still. She'd almost forgotten about the mole that Geoff had had a couple of inches above his navel. Where was the mole?

With an anxious glance at his face to ensure that he remained soundly asleep, Devon squatted on her heels to raise the edge of Geoff's sweater just a little higher. Where once a mole had been, Devon ran her finger over a jagged three-inch scar.

She sighed in disappointment. It proved nothing. Whatever injury he had sustained could easily have removed any trace of the small dark mole.

Rising, she covered him and gently placed the pillow beneath his head. Then, she went downstairs to sit on the sofa in the deeply shadowed living room and think while she waited. Questions careened through her mind. Was this man Geoff, or wasn't he? If so, why was he calling himself Jack Keller? And why had he insisted that his name was not Geoff? What reason could a man have for taking an alternate identity? Could he have done something against the law? But as soon as the possibility presented itself, she discarded it. Geoff may have been passionate and impulsive, even volatile at times—he'd loved to rant and bluster—but he'd never been violent, and he would never break the law.

No matter how much she thought the situation through, she only came up with more questions, and no answers. Even the incredible concept of amnesia provided only a partial answer to her many questions. Maybe she should just forget the divorce and go home. After all, if she'd never seen Geoff on television, she would have married David quite happily, never suspecting that her first husband was still alive. And, she was no longer so certain that the man upstairs was the man to whom she'd been married. There was something very different about him.

How could a man be, at once, so familiar and yet so much a stranger? It didn't make sense.

At some point during the tense hour that followed, the strain of the long drive combined with the stress of the situation took its toll and she slumped down on the sofa to sleep despite the chaos in her mind. But it was not a restful sleep for she was plagued by dreams. She dreamed of running down a corridor attempting to catch up with countless Geoffs all moving away from her. Each time she thought she'd caught the right one, she placed her hand on his arm to halt him, to turn him to face her, and found herself looking into a familiar face with the eyes of a stranger. In another, she dreamed of the memorial service they'd had for Geoff, only this time when she left the funeral parlor she was certain she'd seen Geoff hovering in the shadows. Watching her.

"Devon—" The voice came from a great distance, pulling at her. It was Geoff's voice, and yet it too was different.

"Devon, wake up."

She opened her eyes, confused for a moment by her unfamiliar surroundings.

"Are you all right?"

She looked over her shoulder and saw him crouched beside the sofa. Geoff! Now she remembered. "Yes, of course. Why wouldn't I be?"

"You seemed to be having a nightmare."

"I did?" She searched her mind for fragments, but came up blank. "I don't remember." Then as the fog of sleep continued to clear, she recalled that it had been he who had been in need of aid earlier. "What about you? Are you all right now?"

He nodded and his gaze slid away from hers almost self-consciously. "Yeah. Thanks."

Devon swung her legs over the edge of the sofa to settle her feet on the floor. "You're welcome." She twined her fingers together in her lap and glanced at her watch. It was just approaching 1:00 a.m., which meant she couldn't have slept much more than three hours. "So," she said, as she watched Geoff rise and take the chair nearby, "what now?"

He stared at her, his eyes expressionless and indifferent. "What you really mean is, am I ready to talk about this divorce you want so badly. Isn't it?"

She looked at him. "Yes. I guess it is."

His gaze swept over her in a brief but penetrating scrutiny. When his eyes once again lifted to meet hers, there was something new in their depths. Something intense and a bit feral. Something that made her breath catch in her throat. "You're a very attractive woman, Devon," he said. "I still don't have a clue who you are, but I concede that it is possible that you *are* my wife. And, if you are, I think I'd like the chance to get to know you a bit better before I agree to a divorce."

Devon stared at him, her shocked mind unable to grasp the meaning behind his words. "What are you saying?"

"I'm saying that I won't agree to a divorce. Not until I get to know you and my kids again. Not until I see if I can get my life back and—" He broke off and swallowed convulsively. Were it not for the expressionlessness of his tone, the coldness in his eyes, Devon might have thought that he was struggling with strong emotions. Then, without waiting for a response, he rose and stalked from the cabin leaving Devon to stare numbly at the closed door.

I don't have a clue who you are, but...it is possible that you are my wife...I won't agree to a divorce... The words echoed in her mind. Stunning. Inconceivable. *Until I see if I can get my life back.* Was this stranger who looked like Geoff now telling her he wanted to reclaim a life with *her*—with her children—in it? Devon shook her head. This was not going the way she'd planned it at all!

Chapter 2

Jack shoved his hands into the pockets of his chinos and hunched his shoulders against the crisp night air. He'd forgotten to put on his jacket, but he'd be damned if he'd go back and get it. Not yet.

He took a deep breath and absently watched his exhalation condense into mist as he wondered what the hell had happened to him in the last few hours. He felt as though he'd been swept up in a tornado. His emotions were spinning out of control until he didn't know which way to move, what to think or do. Was this woman...this Devon, his wife? He felt no sense of recognition, but after almost two years of existing in limbo, he wasn't willing to discount her claim too readily.

When she'd initially shown up on his doorstep calling him ''Jeff'' and talking to him as though she knew him, Jack had relegated her visit to one of two possibilities. One, it was an interesting case of mistaken identity. Or, two, she was a cop playing an elaborate game of entrapment. Ever since he'd accidentally been caught on camera the previous night, he'd been plagued by the worry that the authorities would find him.

He visualized the scrap of now-yellowed newspaper that lay in the drawer of his dresser. That single scrap of paper, in large part, had defined the course of his life over the past two years. He'd read it so many times, wondering if he was doing the right thing, searching for clues as to what was behind it, that he no longer had any need to see it to replay the exact words recorded there.

Missing Plane Found Amid Rumors Of Fraud

The light plane that disappeared in rugged north country almost three weeks ago was found yesterday by a bush pilot just one week after the seemingly futile search had been called off. Rescuers were immediately dispatched to the scene, however it now appears that there are no survivors. Due to the condition of the bodies, a positive ID will have to come from the coroner's office. However, identification discovered at the site leads investigators to believe that the remains of the two victims found in the downed plane are those of Geoffrey Grayson and Holly Loring. The third passenger of the plane, Spencer Loring, remains missing, but is presumed dead.

"Given the state of the craft, it would have taken a miracle for anyone to emerge with anything less than life-threatening injuries," says Chief Investigator Sergeant Marett. "Factor into the equation the passage of time and the harshness and remoteness of the country in this region, and the situation becomes very bleak."

The search for Spencer Loring's remains will continue, but investigators are not particularly optimistic. The ruggedness of the terrain will make any exploration difficult at best.

Even should he, by some miracle, have survived the crash that took the life of his wife, it is entirely possible that Spencer Loring may not want to be found. In a curious twist to this story, this reporter has learned that rumors of fraud are surfacing in a number of quarters in connection with

Loring's company, Fort Knox Security, although no details have yet been officially released. However, anonymous sources suggest that, if there is any substance to the accusations taking shape, Spencer Loring may prefer to remain missing rather than return to face a criminal trial and possible jail term. More on this will be forthcoming as details are disclosed.

Jack had never seen any other articles, but he hadn't felt he needed to. Until now.

The front door opened and he tensed. Not yet, dammit! He wasn't ready to deal with her and the chaos she'd brought into his life.

"Geoff—"

He exhaled and slowly turned to face her. She stood in the center of the porch. The bulkiness of her silhouette told him she'd donned her jacket, but the darkness prevented him from seeing her clearly. Still, the powers of observation he'd used earlier stood him in good stead for he knew exactly what she looked like. About five foot six, she was slim, perhaps a little more curvy than current fashion dictated, and definitely more than passingly attractive. She wore her straight sable brown hair in a shoulder-length style with bangs. Her eyes were a bit on the small side, but they were a clear luminous gray that made them seem larger. Her features were delicately boned, almost fragile, with high cheekbones and a narrow nose that was neither too long, nor too short. She had full kissable lips and a set of orthodontic-perfect teeth. The scarlet red of the sweater she wore made her fair complexion appear almost translucent. Although she wasn't beautiful in the fashion-model sense, he could certainly understand what he had seen in her. *If* indeed he ever had.

But Jack didn't trust her completely. In fact, he was feeling distinctly paranoid. "Yeah?" he asked in response to her call. His tone was more abrupt than he'd intended.

"I...I'm confused."

He barked a laugh, but there was no humor in it. "You think *you're* confused." Who the devil was he? Geoff Grayson? Spencer Loring? Or some other person whose name had not yet surfaced? Or, would he maintain the Jack Keller persona he himself had invented in a rash attempt at self-preservation?

"Are you saying—?" She broke off and raked her fingers through her hair, setting the bangs on end. The gesture had the earmarks of a habit that emerged when she was stressed or looking for words. "Do you have amnesia?" The words came out in a rush.

He considered her, wondering if she would accept his explanation or reject it as fiction. "Yes." He offered her nothing more. He didn't trust her enough yet to share the birth of Jack Keller with her.

Jack Keller had come into existence in an old recluse's cabin near Great Beaver Lake in northern British Columbia a few short days after he'd awakened to the glare of a pair of vibrant, piercing blue eyes set in a grizzled face topped by a thick mop of white hair. It had been a rather frightening and intimidating countenance when beheld from the viewpoint of a man who found himself barely able to speak and as weak as a baby. The image of those eyes gleaming down at him, studying him with an air of detached curiosity, was as clear in his memory now as it had been on that day. However, the first words out of the crusty old codger's mouth had served to lessen his trepidation.

"Hurry up and get well so you can get out of here and leave an old man to his privacy, will ya, Spence?"

Spence?

The name had rung no bells; come with no sense of belonging. And that was when Jack had found himself floating on a sea of anonymity. He had no idea who he was, where he had come from, or where he was going. And the old man—who introduced himself as Bill Johnson—knew little more, for the man carrying Spencer Loring's identification was a stranger to him. He'd discovered him wounded and hypothermic in the woods nearby, and so hoarse he was almost mute. Bill surmised that he'd ruined his voice by shouting for help.

"How bad is it?" Devon asked, startling Jack back to the present. She moved toward him, and for the first time he noticed that she carried something in her hands. In the next instant, she draped his sheepskin jacket over his shoulders and tugged it close around him before backing away to a comfortable distance. For some reason, her gesture warmed Jack in a way the jacket itself could never have done. He hadn't been a monk in the last two years by any means, but he'd found that most women tended to be reserved around him. Wary. The caring little courtesy that Devon had just extended was not something that he'd received often.

Was it something she'd done for Geoff? he wondered. Had they shared a loving and demonstrative relationship? In the next instant, he dismissed his musings as pure fancy. Their relationship couldn't have been as wonderful as all that or she wouldn't be seeking a divorce.

"Geoff?"

"Yeah?"

"The amnesia." As he watched her, Devon raised clasped hands to her chin and closed her eyes for a moment, appearing almost as though she was praying. Then she said, "I asked you how bad it is," in a voice scarcely above a murmur.

Not in the mood to discuss his situation, he purposely misunderstood her question. "It's amnesia. It's bad."

"That's not what I meant." Lowering her hands, she took a step closer to stand directly in front of him so that she could look up into his face. "How much have you forgotten, Geoff?"

Her movement brought her into the multi-hued illumination created by the Christmas lights that lined the porch railing, and he stared at her for a moment, searching for some genuine concern *for him.* But he read only confusion in the depths of her dove gray eyes. He decided to make his response quick, and, hopefully, painless. "I have no personal memories."

"None?"

"None," he confirmed. "Not even my own name."

"Oh, God." Once again she raised her hands to her chin in a praying gesture. "Oh, Geoff, I'm sorry. These last two years must have been horrible for you, too. I never considered anything like this. It's so...unbelievable." She concluded on a choked sound, suspiciously like a sob. And, avoiding his gaze, exhaled a sigh on a cloud of steam into the chill night air.

Jack knew what she meant. Amnesia was the stuff of novels, not life. That made it unbelievable. Hell, if he wasn't living it, he wouldn't believe it either.

The silence stretched and Devon hugged herself against the cold air. Then slowly she looked back at him. "So you had no clue whatsoever as to your identity?"

Jack shook his head. She probably didn't want to believe the amnesia angle and he couldn't blame her. It was pretty inconceivable. "Do you remember a man named Spencer Loring?" he asked.

"Of course I remember Spencer. He was your best friend. You often did business together." Abruptly, Devon broke off as her gaze raked his face in consideration. "Do *you* remember him?"

He didn't respond at once. He had believed that he *was* Spencer Loring. A man who for some reason had run afoul of the law. Knowing he couldn't defend himself against criminal charges when he had no memory of the situation from which they'd arisen, he'd taken an alternate identity and silently mourned the loss of a wife whom he couldn't remember.

Jack shook his head. "No, but it was his identification I was carrying when I was found."

She frowned thoughtfully and stared out at the snow-draped cedars. "That's possible. You both carried your wallets in your jackets. The weekend your plane crashed, you were both wearing denim jackets. If you had taken the jackets off at some time during the flight, then you could have grabbed the wrong one when you put yours back on. Especially if, when you put it on, you were disoriented after the crash."

She stared thoughtfully out at the yard for a moment and then she continued in a musing tone, as though thinking aloud. "It wouldn't have been the first time you two accidentally switched jackets. It actually happened a couple of times before, because you were the same size and had much the same taste in clothing. But..."

"But what?"

She looked at Jack. "Spencer's driver's license would have had his picture on it." The statement doubled as a question, and Jack knew what she was asking.

"I thought it was a bad picture."

"Spencer had very dark brown hair and brown eyes."

Jack shrugged. "Like I said, I thought it was a bad picture. Other than those two small details, it looks like me."

Devon considered him thoughtfully and finally conceded. "There were some people who used to think you were brothers. But I don't understand, if you thought you were Spencer, why are you going by the name Jack Keller?"

Jack studied her intently as a fragment of the paranoia engendered by his amnesia returned to haunt him. But he'd already told her more than he'd ever told anybody. "The old man who nursed me back to health following the accident brought a newspaper to the cabin after one of his trips to town. There was an article in it that suggested that Spencer was in big trouble with the authorities."

Devon slowly nodded. "I remember it," she said. "I think there were even some rumors concerning Future-Tech for a while. Future-Tech sold Fort Knox Security many of the security systems that Spencer installed. As far as I know, nothing came of it. Dad handled it and, as usual, refused to worry me with the details. But, from what I understood, all the charges against Future-Tech were dropped. I think some companies are still in the process of suing Spencer's estate for damages though."

Abruptly, she shivered and rubbed her arms. "I'm freezing."

Jack studied the woman standing before him. He'd understood less than half of what she'd just said. Future-Tech? What had a company called Future-Tech to do with them? How had her father *handled* it? And what damages had been incurred?

But in the next instant, as his mind took a different tack, he dismissed his questions for they seemed distant and unimportant.

It was incredible to him that this attractive woman could be his wife. That he could have had two children with her. That they would have undoubtedly shared a number of years together.

And yet he could remember not the slightest thing about her. She was a stranger to him.

He looked out over the snow-frosted landscape. In moments of weakness, he'd sometimes longed for a way to reclaim a life with meaning, with people around him who cared. But he'd relegated his longing to the realm of a dream that would never be realized and resigned himself to this new existence. And now...now Devon had shown up on his doorstep and he no longer knew what to think.

His initial inclination had been to doubt her. But, when she'd said her name was Grayson, he'd begun to question. Was it possible that, for some reason, he'd been carrying another man's ID? Was it possible that he *was* Geoff Grayson? That he had no reason to avoid the law because he'd never run afoul of it in the first place? That he had a life somewhere?

Turning away from Devon, he squeezed his eyes closed and took another deep breath of the mountain air. When he'd awakened on the floor of the bathroom, he'd gone over everything that had happened. It hadn't taken him long to realize that if he gave Devon the one thing she asked of him—a divorce—it would mean relinquishing any claim he might have to a past life. He wasn't prepared to cast that stake away lightly.

In the next instant he'd been furious with her, hating her for offering him the possibility of a life, a *real* life somewhere with friends and family who cared, but not wanting him in it. She'd driven all day to find him, not because of some great love for him, but because she wanted a divorce. She wanted to cut him, officially, out of her life.

"Who is he?" Jack asked aloud.

There was a second of silence as she sought to follow his train of thought. "My fiancé?"

Jack nodded. He needed to know who the man was who had her love now. Who was the man she wanted to raise his children in his stead? *His* children. The words echoed in his mind, bringing a lump to his throat.

"David Randolph," Devon replied. "You may remember—" She broke off abruptly at her poor choice of wording, and then resumed. "He's a lawyer in my father's law firm. We were planning on being married this summer, but...well, now that I know you're still alive that won't be possible until we finalize a divorce."

The silence grew. Finally, Jack reiterated his position. "There's not going to be a divorce until I get a chance to try to reclaim my life. I want to get to know my kids."

What had their names been? Oh, yes. Britanny and Tyler. He searched the black void of his mind for any hint of their presence in his life, but again came up empty. The doctors had long since given up hope that he would regain his lost memory. *It's been too long,* they said. *The longer it takes the less likelihood there is of a full recovery.* Still, Jack refused to despair. He had lived for a reason. He had to believe that. And maybe his children were the reason.

Kids needed two parents. He had a beautiful daughter to raise and to protect from unscrupulous males. A daughter to draw pictures with and teach to cook. And he had a son to take fishing and sailing. A son to teach how to be a good and decent man. His heart swelled.

"Geoff, you don't need to be married to me to reclaim your life. You're welcome in the children's lives, and Future-Tech is still alive and kicking although it's not quite as profitable as it was when you were running it."

He ignored her argument in favor of divorce and focused on her second statement. "This Future-Tech you keep mentioning was *my* company?"

She nodded. "A production and design company, Future-Tech Manufacturing."

"What did I design?"

"Computer hardware components, security systems, that kind of thing. You did a bit of the software programming too, but not much. Primarily you hired programmers to meet those needs."

Jack thought about that, and wondered if that knowledge would come back to him. Or, perhaps he'd never lost it, but it hadn't surfaced simply because he hadn't called upon it. That's how most of his knowledge had returned to him, with the single exception of his personal life. He resolved to put the theory to the test as soon as possible. Reclaiming his career would be an important step in reclaiming his life.

"And there were rumors of Future-Tech being involved in the same fraud as Fort Knox Security?"

"Yes, but like I said, Dad took care of it."

"He's a lawyer." It was a statement, but he threw it out for confirmation sake.

"Mmm-hmm."

Jack considered that but didn't know what conclusions to draw.

Devon hugged herself against the chill and looked out at the night. "What do you do now?"

"Pardon me?" He looked down at her in confusion.

"For a living?" she clarified. "What do you do now?"

"I manage the resort here." He nodded in the direction of the lake.

"Oh." The silence stretched, and Jack wondered if she was somehow disappointed by his reply. But when she spoke again, she was on a different tack all together. "So, if you didn't know me when I arrived on your doorstep, why did you let me in?"

Jack shrugged. "You talked as though you knew me, and, for someone in my position, that alone was intriguing enough for me to want to hear more. I was a bit suspicious, too, though. I thought you might be a cop."

She frowned thoughtfully. "Because of the article about Spencer?"

He nodded. "I didn't really think they'd go to that extent to get him, but I couldn't totally dismiss the possibility."

There was a long moment of silence as they stood together.

Abruptly Devon spoke. "Geoff...I've got a million questions, none of which I can put into words right now. I feel like I've been dropped into a movie-of-the-week. I need to think about this for a while." She turned and took a couple of steps away from him, then stopped as an afterthought gripped her. Without turning, she said, "I'm sorry for thinking the worst of you,

Geoff. You didn't deserve that.'' On that note she walked quickly away and reentered the house.

Jack stared after her, confused by the real emotion he'd heard in her voice.

Did she still care for him? Did he want her to?

He didn't have time to analyze his own feelings more deeply before she reappeared with her purse over her shoulder. Alarm shot through him. She was the only link he had to a past that had eluded him; he couldn't let her go. ''Where are you going?'' His tone was more confrontational than questioning and, the instant the words emerged, he wished he could recall them.

She stopped in her tracks. In the faint illumination spilling through the small sunburst window on the door, her eyes met his. Challenging. Determined. Wary. The manner in which a woman might look at a stranger whose reactions she didn't trust. Jack felt something clench in his gut. He ignored it. Clearing his throat, he tried a more conciliatory tone. ''I'm sorry. I didn't mean to bark at you. This has been a bit much for me, too. Won't you stay? Please? I have questions, too. A lot of them.''

She stared at him, a peculiar expression on her face as though for the first time tonight she truly did not recognize him. And then she shook her head. ''I don't think now is the right time, Geoff. I'm confused and tired and feeling a little—'' she shrugged slightly as she searched for and found the right word ''—raw. I need some sleep. Can you just give me directions to a good hotel?''

His lips quirked at the absurdity of her question. ''This is Northridge, Devon. We don't have any classy accommodations. There's only *one* hotel and it's not exactly the kind of place I'd recommend for a woman. The best place in town is probably Eva Wright's Bed-and-Breakfast, but you won't be able to get in there this late.''

Jack hadn't been afraid of much for a very long time, but he was afraid to let this woman leave. If she walked out of here tonight, she could walk out of his life. Disappear as suddenly as she'd appeared. And he knew nothing about himself yet. He knew almost nothing of her. Or his family. And, despite her request for a divorce, he realized that deep down he harbored a small hope that maybe—if he and this woman could learn to care for each other again—*maybe* he dared dream of going home. Maybe he dared dream of reclaiming his life in its entirety.

"I have a guest room," he said. "Why don't you stay the night?"

She considered him silently. "I don't think that's a good idea, Geoff."

"Why? It's not as though people will be able to talk—we're already married. Right?"

The hint of a smile touched her lips for the first time, and then she shook her head. "I just don't think I have the strength to try to make sense of this situation tonight."

He held up his hands in a gesture of surrender. "You can go straight to sleep if that's what you want. We won't talk tonight. I'll take some time off tomorrow, and we can discuss everything then." She had looked down as he talked, avoiding his gaze, and he stepped forward, lifting her chin with his finger, to look into her eyes. They were wide, confused, and...vulnerable.

He didn't want to see that. Not yet. He wasn't ready to open himself up, to trust her. So, mentally taking a step back, he clamped the lid on his emotions and smiled in a manner he hoped was reassuring. "Agreed?"

She looked into his eyes for endless seconds as though searching for something. Finally, she nodded. "All right. I'll need my case from the Jeep."

"Good." Noting that a portion of her bangs still stood on end, he reached to smooth them down. A few of the fine strands clung to his calloused fingers and, as he struggled to arrange them without pulling, his knuckles brushed her temple. He was unprepared for the jolt of sensual awareness that transmitted itself from her soft warm skin. Like a lightning bolt, it shot through his body to center somewhere in the region of his groin, a hot, glowing coal of awareness. Tamping it down, he backed away. "If you'll give me your keys, I'll get your case."

A moment later he carried her suitcase up onto the veranda where she stood waiting. He wished now that he hadn't made such a sweeping promise to avoid discussion. As he opened the cabin door and they reentered the house, he had to ask. "May I ask you just three questions, Devon?"

A hint of apprehension entered her eyes, but she nodded.

"What's my full name?" He set down her case in the entrance and turned to close the door. "How old am I? And...where did we live?"

She smiled softly, relief evident in her expression despite the aura of strain that clung to her. "Your name is Geoffrey Hunter Grayson. You will be thirty-six years old this summer. Your birthday is July twelfth. And, we lived together in the house we designed in Kelowna. The kids and I still live there. I couldn't bear to leave it."

"We designed?"

Devon nodded. "I'm an interior designer, and you always had a knack for design. A natural extension of your mother's Italian passion and creative genius, I guess. She's a wonderful artist, so you come by it honestly."

His chest felt suddenly tight. He had a past: a wife, kids, a home, a mother, and a career. He was *somebody*. It was the best Christmas present he could have received. "Thank you," he murmured around the constriction in his throat.

He glanced at the clock over the fireplace. One-thirty. Memory struck like an electric shock, ruining the moment. He was supposed to be picking up Marissa in fifteen minutes. Turning to Devon he said, "I'll show you up to your room in just a second, all right? I just have to make a quick call to cancel a date."

Devon's eyes widened. "Isn't it kind of late for a date?"

"She works in a bar," he said by way of explanation.

"Well, please don't cancel on my account. I wouldn't want to cause you any trouble."

Jack studied her. Was there a trace of tension in her voice? He was absurdly pleased by the idea that some part of her might actually be jealous, although there was no need. His friendship with Marissa was platonic; he simply enjoyed her company. She was one of the few women in town who had befriended him without expectation. Then, deciding he must have imagined

Devon's reaction, he shook his head and responded, "No trouble." Stepping into the living room, he reached for the phone.

Though she'd turned away to afford him some privacy, her disinterest was only feigned for Devon found herself holding her breath and straining her ears as Geoff began to speak, apologizing to the woman on the other end of the phone. She had no right to be eavesdropping, yet she couldn't have stopped if she'd been paid.

She was inexplicably but undeniably relieved to discover that Geoff seemed more concerned about Marissa obtaining an alternate ride home than about missing their date. Once that was taken care of, the conversation changed course. "Friday?" he said in his slightly grainy baritone. "Oh, damn, I forgot." Leather creaked as he dropped down onto the cognac-colored leather sofa beside the phone. "I'm not sure that I'll be able to make that either.

"He did, did he?" Geoff asked in a tone that was almost teasing. A pause. Then, "All right, why don't you go with him then. If I do make it, we'll have a dance." Silence for the space of a few seconds and then, "Bye, Rissa." There was a soft clunk as he replaced the receiver.

He looked at Devon. "There, that's taken care of. I'll show you to your room now." He lifted her case and crossed the room to the staircase.

"Thanks," Devon said as he deposited her case on the bed.

He nodded and turned to leave the room. "Good night, Devon," he said as he started to close the door and then he caught himself in midgesture. "Oh, if you need anything, just ask. And feel free to make yourself at home."

Devon stood alone in the guest room, listening to Geoff's footsteps as he moved downstairs. And then there was silence. She held her breath, almost afraid to move in the sudden stillness that enveloped the cabin. Afraid to think or examine her feelings concerning the one-sided conversation on which she'd blatantly eavesdropped. Afraid that, despite her plans and intentions, she was going to be hurt all over again.

The sound of the television coming on below released her from her paralysis.

Feeling strangely numb, and welcoming the desensitization for she suspected it protected her against feelings she wasn't yet prepared to examine, Devon moved toward the window. Dripping evergreens draped in heavy wet snow blocked her view of the neighboring cabins, but to her left she had a good view of the lake. The snow had stopped falling, and an enormous nearly full moon bathed the snow-blanketed ice in pristine radiance. Beyond the pine trees marking the edge of the property on the right, the lights of the town glowed in the distance. Northridge. And somewhere there, a woman for whom Geoff had feelings. Maybe not strong feelings, but feelings nonetheless. Had he slept with Marissa? she wondered.

Sitting down, supporting her head on her hands, Devon leaned on the desk to stare thoughtfully from the bedroom window, her thoughts haunted by the nebulous image of a woman named Marissa.

Who was she? What did she look like?

A picture of Kim Basinger solidified in her mind and she thrust it away.

She was surprised by the strength of the jealousy gnawing at her. Why should she care if Geoff was seeing another woman? She was in love with another man. Two years ago, when Geoff had disappeared, they'd already been on the verge of divorce. Or rather, she'd threatened him with it in the hope that it would force him to talk to her, to tell her why he'd grown so distant. For her to feel this way now just didn't make sense. But the sentiment was there and she found herself incapable of reasoning it away. It seemed that time had not tempered her emotions. The idea of Geoff with another woman, kissing her, touching her, making love to her...hurt enough to provoke thoughts of homicide.

Her contemplation drove her from her chair and she began to pace the room. The only illumination was that coming through the window from the moon, but it was enough. The cabin bedroom was simply furnished with a double bed, night table, dresser and phone desk, and could be easily negotiated in the semidarkness. Shoving her hands into the pockets of her jeans, she asked herself for the hundredth time since learning of Geoff's condition what her next move was. Nothing came to mind.

What she wanted to do was escape. Go home and forget this entire incident. Forget that she'd ever seen him on television. Forget the unpredictable and illogical emotions that assailed her when she was near him. She wanted to forget him and marry David.

But, she wasn't a quitter; she never had been. And she'd invested too much emotion already to just give up and go home. She had to talk to Geoff, discuss the situation rationally, and arrive at a course of action that would satisfy both of them, allowing him to reclaim his old life, if that was truly what he wanted, while granting her and their children a sense of security that had been sadly lacking lately.

But, if this new strange Geoff was interested in *her* as part of the life he wanted to reclaim, he was going to be disappointed. No matter how attractive she still found him, she'd be damned if she'd simply take him back into her life as though the last twenty-eight months—and the difficult months before that—had never happened. She had David in her life now. And, she still didn't understand what had torn Geoff and her apart in the first place.

Something had pulled Geoff away from her, from their family, during their last six months together, and that something had all but destroyed their marriage. Whatever it was, only Geoff knew, or had known.

And yet, he seemed to want to be part of her life again. *That* was something she couldn't chance.

Without knowing what had been at the root of their difficulties, she wouldn't be willing to risk her heart again, or her children's fragile sense of security. Eventually Geoff would remember whatever problem had so preoccupied him, and it would wrench them apart again, putting them right back where they'd started. She didn't think she had the strength to fight all those battles again.

The stairs creaked slightly and she turned toward the door, listening to the sound of Geoff climbing the stairs. Shaking free the fetters of reason, her imagination took flight. He would stop at her door under some pretext or other. She would answer his soft knock, opening the door to him. Then, they would stare at each other wordlessly, as they had so many times in the past. In a single long gaze, they would communicate all their needs and wants, their desires and love.... Love?

Oh, Lord. Devon's breath caught in her throat. She didn't still love him. She didn't! But belying the words in her conscious mind, butterflies began hatching out of their cocoons in droves to swarm through her abdomen. And she stared at the door suddenly paralyzed by the knowledge that she didn't know what she'd do if he really did knock at her door. But, in the next instant, his steps moved on and seconds later she heard the door to the other bedchamber close.

Realizing that she'd been holding her breath, she released it on a sigh. Her heart hammered erratically in her chest as she tried to find an explanation for the strange sense of dejection that besieged her. She wiped her sweaty palms against her thighs and rolled her head in an attempt to release some of the tension in her neck. "I'm going crazy," she murmured. Her irrational response to this man terrified her.

She desperately wanted to escape. To go home, forget all the emotional upheaval of this meeting, and get on with her life.

Somehow she suspected that getting over this Geoff would be even more difficult than it had been the first time. On some level, he intrigued her in ways the Geoff she knew, the Geoff she'd married, had never done. And that frightened her to death.

"You're really doing it, Devon," she murmured. "You're losing your flippin' mind."

After tonight, she wouldn't stay in this house. She couldn't. Not with him just a few steps away. She'd stay in town a couple of days in an attempt to work out the details of their divorce with this new Geoff. Hopefully that would be long enough to arrive at a course of action. In the morning, she'd move into the bed-and-breakfast he'd mentioned—provided it had a vacancy.

In the meantime, she had to try to get some sleep. As she opened the case resting on the bed and withdrew her nightgown and wrap, she had the terrible feeling that it was going to be a very long night.

Chapter 3

Jack stared into the darkness. Night cloaked the room in shadow while sleep teased at the edges of his mind like a seductive wraith, desirable but elusive. He wondered how long it would take for him to start thinking of himself as *Geoff*. It wouldn't be easy; he'd been Jack Keller for a long time already. Yet, he was already feeling...different. Although the thread was tenuous at this point, for the first time in memory he was beginning to experience a sensation of being connected.

He tried to imagine himself as Geoffrey Hunter Grayson. What had his life been like before he'd disappeared from Devon's life? What had it felt like to know that he belonged with her? To know that she belonged with him and would be a part of his life? To come home after a day's work to an attractive wife and two wonderful kids?

But, once again, his mind remained obstinately blank. He substituted a television sitcom family picture—the only family that came to mind—and wondered if his own family had been anything like it. A knot formed in his throat, and he swallowed against it. Family life. It was the life he'd wanted for himself but believed he could never have. He wanted it again. If not with Devon, then with someone else. He just wished he could remember what it had been like the first time he'd lived it.

And Devon wanted a divorce. The thought infuriated and frustrated him. Not because he loved the woman; he didn't even know her, but because he felt that she was trying to deprive him of his life. A life he wanted back.

Life in Northridge had not been bad, by any means. He had a job here and he'd made some casual friends. The kind who didn't pry. Even so, his existence here had somehow seemed...empty. Like a plant struggling to grow in dead soil, he felt inhibited. As though he was only partially alive. And now, he refused to ignore the possibility, however slim, that his previous life might return a sense of wholeness to his existence.

A career, family, friends...they were worth fighting for. If there was one thing he'd learned when he discovered himself an island in a sea of interconnected people, it was that. Perhaps, if he'd not believed that he was a wanted man, a criminal, he would have allowed himself to become closer to the new friends he'd made. He might even have fallen in love with another woman and begun a new life. But he hadn't been able to allow himself to trust enough to do that. And so, he'd remained an island.

How, now, could he give up the chance to regain a real life?

The answer was simple. He couldn't. Not yet. But that left him with the task of convincing a woman who no longer cared for him—for reasons he couldn't even remember—that she should take the time to reintroduce him to the life he'd once had. His only hope of doing that lay in refusing her the divorce she wanted so badly until she'd complied with his demands.

And, truth be told, he wasn't averse to spending more time in the company of Devon Grayson. She was an attractive woman.

What had happened to them? he wondered. He wished he could recall something that would give him some clue as to why she wanted a divorce. But he knew the wish was useless. On a personal level, it was as though he'd been born two-and-a-half years ago.

He rolled the name *Geoff* around in his mind. There was no

spark of connection. Sighing in defeat, he once again closed his eyes against the blackness of the room, seeking sleep. He was just beginning to doze when the sound of a stair creaking startled him and his eyes flew open. For an instant he stared at the night-darkened room in confusion.

Devon! She wouldn't be leaving, would she? Sneaking away?

Rising quickly, he moved silently to the door and opened it a crack. Devon, clad in a peach satin nightgown and wrap, was making her way stealthily down the stairs.

Well, at least it didn't look as though she was trying to leave. "Is something wrong?" he asked before he'd fully contemplated the effect his voice coming out of the darkness would have.

Devon gasped, jumped, and barely managed to catch herself as she turned to face him. "Wh-what?" she gasped.

He winced mentally. If he hadn't been naked he might have rushed out to steady her but, at the moment, that simply wasn't an option. "Sorry about that," he murmured through the crack in the door.

She nodded, but her hand was still hovering over her chest as though to contain her leaping heart. "It's all right," she returned. "What did you say? Before, I mean?"

"I asked if something was wrong?"

She shook her head. "No, I just couldn't sleep and I thought I'd heat up some milk, if you don't mind?"

"Of course not. Go on down. I'll join you in a moment." Jack closed his bedroom door and paused, staring into the darkness as he contemplated the sight of Devon in her peach satin nightclothes. "Very nice," he murmured, and then he flicked on the light and dressed.

Devon had just put a small pot of milk on the stove when she glanced up to see Geoff leaning against the kitchen doorway watching her. "Hi," she said with a faint smile.

He nodded slightly but said nothing as his gaze swept her from head to toe, lingering on her bare feet for so long that she felt the urge to try to hide them beneath the hem of her robe. Then slowly, torturously, his gaze moved back up her body until his eyes met hers and locked. She swallowed. There was so much heat in the dark green depths of his irises that they positively smoldered. And, for the first time in a very long time, Devon felt...beautiful. More than beautiful. She felt irresistible and seductive, though she'd certainly not had seduction in mind.

She swallowed nervously, very conscious of the fact that somehow she had to break this spell. Clearing her throat, she gestured vaguely toward the pot on the stove. "Did you want some?" she asked a bit huskily.

"Want some?" he repeated.

She indicated the pot on the stove more pointedly. "Some warm milk?"

"Oh. Yeah, sure. Thanks." And he moved into the room with a lazy stride. "I'll get some cups. Do you want some chocolate in yours?"

She frowned slightly. "No, thank you. Chocolate has caffeine in it, doesn't it? At least that's what I was told."

He shrugged. "The little bit of caffeine it may have doesn't bother me as much as the idea of warm milk without some flavoring does."

"Oh." She smiled. She could have told him that he used to drink it without flavoring on occasion, but saw no point.

A minute later she poured warm milk into the two cups Geoff had set on the counter, and then he carried the cups to the table. It felt strangely familiar to sit with him like this, and yet at the same time somehow awkward. Rather like two friends who had grown apart over time and no longer knew what to say.

He sipped his chocolate. "So," he said a second later, "since we're up anyway, would you be averse to a little conversation?"

She considered him and all they had to discuss. "No, I guess not. As long as we don't talk about anything contentious until I've had a good night's sleep."

"All right. I guess I can agree to that." He offered her a fleeting smile that, for an instant, totally transformed his hard features. But, all too soon, it was gone. "Tell me about Kelowna and Future-Tech. Why did I start the company there rather than in Vancouver?"

Devon considered. "Cost primarily, I guess. The shipping is a bit more expensive, I suppose, but commercial property was more reasonably priced. At least it was at the time that we bought." She went on to describe the company he'd built, the people he'd hired, and the dreams he'd once had of eventually breaking into the U.S. market with his security systems. "You were even looking at manufacturing systems for the home security market, designing smart houses and that kind of thing."

Geoff stared frowningly into his cup for a moment. "It's a lot to digest."

"Yes. I suppose it is."

He lifted his shoulders slightly as though shrugging off the concerns associated with a company he didn't remember. "What about the house we designed? Tell me about it."

She sipped her warm milk. "It's a two-story on a hillside overlooking the city and, in the distance, Lake Okanagan. It has a beautiful cedar deck in the back, lots of trees on a large lot, and a studio for me to work in just behind the garage. Actually, if I had it to do over again, I'd make the studio larger because, as it is, I've ended up using a good portion of the garage as well. But...I love the house the way it is."

She shrugged, seeking the words to continue. How did you describe *home* to a man who no longer remembered it? "Inside...well, it's not perfect by any means. I've never been a perfect housekeeper. And the children certainly aren't perfect little angels. They're just kids." She smiled, remembering. "You used to come in the door from work almost every day and call Tyler to pick up his coat and hang it in the closet, yet he never learned. Even now, he tends to just throw it on the floor in the entrance when he comes in.

"Britanny loves to make popcorn, but she sometimes forgets to watch it closely enough so that there are often fluffy white pieces of popcorn someplace on the kitchen floor. Both kids' rooms look as though they've been burglarized, but, in complete contrast to Tyler, Britanny can find anything in her room in seconds. Tyler's room is more like a black hole. I'm sure it sends socks to another dimension."

Geoff smiled. Encouraged, Devon continued. They talked of inconsequential things, things that made a family a family, and then Devon stifled a yawn.

"It looks like the milk's working," he commented.

She nodded and checked her cup. It was empty. "I think I'd better go back to bed while I feel tired."

"Sure, you go ahead. I'll see you in the morning."

Jack watched her leave the room and then drained the dregs of his hot chocolate. He still didn't know why Devon wanted a divorce, and her demand that they avoid discussing anything contentious had prevented him from asking. What confused him was that he couldn't see himself wanting to divorce her unless there was a side to her he hadn't seen. She was beautiful, intelligent, and interesting. Still, he didn't know everything yet. Hell, he supposed when it came down to it, he didn't know much of anything. Yet despite the fact that he felt a bit overwhelmed by all he had heard, he was not put off. Not discouraged in the least.

And not tired. Dammit!

Still he knew he'd need his sleep so, after setting their cups in the sink, he made his way up the stairs, past the closed door of the guest room, and into his own room once more.

Yet back in bed, he found himself staring into the darkness of his room again. Thoughts careened through his mind, delving obstinately into the memories of his recent past as he searched for clues to his present predicament.

Bill had never said much about the period of time he'd cared for Jack before he'd regained consciousness. Jack had always assumed he'd been unconscious the entire time. But, now he couldn't help wondering...what if he'd said something in his sleep? Maybe that something could help him piece together the fragments of his past.

Had Bill ever said anything?

Jack frowned into the darkness, remembering. It had taken an entire month of care after he'd regained consciousness in Bill Johnson's mountain cabin, before he had recovered to the point where he could actually leave Bill to his privacy. During that time, he discovered very little about Bill, and even less about himself. Bill had been a veterinarian at one time. It was his expertise in that area that had prompted him to decide that Jack had a better chance of survival staying put than he would have being bounced and jounced over miles of mountain road in an attempt to reach a town with medical facilities. Thankfully, he'd been right. Beyond that, Jack knew almost nothing about the taciturn old man.

When it came to himself, Jack had come to realize he remembered more about the world around him than he recalled about his personal life. He knew guns and how to use them although he didn't particularly enjoy hunting. He loved to fish though and was fairly accomplished at it. He even knew how to hammer a nail and repair a leaky faucet. Neither had it taken long for him to regain the ability to argue environmental and conservation issues, politics, and religion, and he'd done so, at times, from morning to night. But as far as he could recall, Bill had never mentioned him saying so much as a single name while he was unconscious, nothing that could have given him a sense of identity. And, knowing his situation, surely the old man would have said something if there'd been anything to tell. He'd retained only one tiny fragment of personal memory, and that had been of the attractive blond woman whose picture Bill had found in his wallet when he'd discovered him.

Holly Loring. The feelings associated with Holly had been especially strong.

Jack scowled into the darkness as he was left wondering now about the depths of those feelings. He'd thought them the legitimate feelings of a man for his wife. Now...he didn't know. Had he been having an affair with his best friend's wife? Was that, perhaps, the root of the trouble between Geoff and Devon?

Until today, the back of the photograph in Spencer's wallet had seemed to reinforce his feelings, for the words *All my love, Holly,* had been inscribed on the flip side in a neat feminine hand. Now, of course, he knew those words had not been meant for him, but for Spencer.

Nevertheless, Holly haunted his dreams and his thoughts on a regular basis; her picture flashing into his mind without warning.

Holly laughing, trying to snap him with a tea towel while they did dishes together. Holly crying as she stood at his side while they watched a coffin being lowered into the ground. Holly in her wedding gown, smiling, her eyes sparkling with happiness as she faced him. He had thought the wedding had been *theirs*, assumed her to be his wife. Now he realized he must simply have been remembering fragments of Holly's wedding to Spencer.

Abruptly the memory he most hated sliced into his thoughts with the piercing impact of shrapnel. A vision of Holly as he believed he had last seen her: her blond hair streaked with blood; her beautiful green eyes sightless and lifeless; her lips cold and blue. She stared at him accusingly from the shadows of his own mind.

Jack bolted upright to click on the bedside lamp as his chest swelled with agonizing pain. The urge to fight, to crush something became almost unbearably strong. ''Dammit to hell!'' He dragged his hand down his face and then rubbed his scalp with both hands, closing his fists around clumps of hair, tugging on them as though inducing pain there could lessen the pain in his heart.

Then, with a sigh, he opened the drawer of his bedside table and withdrew her picture. A smiling, happy Holly stared back at him.

There was one thing he knew for certain: he had loved Holly Loring. Her death still hurt, after all this time. Whether that love had been the platonic love of friendship or something more, he didn't know.

What did that mean for him? For his future?

What if *he* had been responsible for Holly's death? For Spencer's? Had the crash occurred through some fault of his? Perhaps it wasn't the blow to his head that had caused his loss of memory as the doctors concluded. Maybe he couldn't remember because some part of him couldn't bear to remember.

His thoughts skittered away from the idea, looking for someone or something else to blame for his suffering. But, it was like looking into a void, for there was no one there. No name. No face. No memory. With the exception of old Bill Johnson and the fragmented memories of Holly, he had no recollection of anyone that he had known prior to his arrival in Northridge.

Needing to move, to dispel the awful restless tension within him, Jack rose, heedless of his nakedness, to pace the room. Sleep would be a long time coming this night.

It was eight o'clock the next morning when Jack awoke to the smell of fresh coffee and bacon. Late for him; he was usually up at six. After a hasty but bracing shower, he was about to head downstairs the way he always did in the mornings: barefoot and shirtless, wearing nothing but his jeans, when he remembered his guest and paused long enough to shrug on a shirt and don a pair of socks. Halfway down the stairs, it occurred to him that, if they had been married, his concession to modesty was probably unnecessary; Devon had undoubtedly seen him wearing much less.

The thought was a bit disconcerting.

When he reached the kitchen, he halted in the doorway to observe Devon. She was wearing the same peach satin wrap and nightgown she'd worn earlier. Her face was completely devoid of makeup and her long hair was slightly mussed from her night's sleep. Yet, she looked...delicious.

Turning to grasp the egg carton that she'd placed on the counter, she caught sight of him and jumped slightly. "Oh! Good morning. Um..." She flushed slightly in apparent embarrassment, and Jack found her heightened color intriguing. "I hope you don't mind me making myself at home. I woke up and couldn't get back to sleep so I came down to make coffee and I saw the bacon, and, well, I was hungry."

Jack shook his head. "I don't mind." He wondered why she was so nervous. "I told you to make yourself at home."

She nodded. "Good. Um, I'm sorry I'm not dressed. I was going to go for a quick shower and get dressed as soon as I got the bacon broiling, but when I looked upstairs you were using it, so...I'll just go after breakfast if that's all right."

"Sure, that's fine." He moved into the kitchen to pour himself a cup of coffee and then leaned back against the counter to observe her. Why would she think he'd care if she wasn't dressed? Were the truth to be told, he liked that peach wrap of hers better than a pair of jeans any day. It didn't reveal any more—probably less—but it was softer. Sexier. He noticed a nervous pulse pounding in her throat, and, as she mixed up the eggs for an omelette, her hands trembled. "You want to tell me what's bothering you?" he asked.

Releasing the fork with which she'd been beating the eggs, she dropped her hands to the countertop and closed her eyes long enough to take a deep breath. Then, crossing her arms protectively over her chest, she turned to look at him. "I'm sorry, Geoff. I'd hoped it wasn't obvious, but...this is just so awkward for me. I keep forgetting that, to you, I'm a stranger. I mean it seemed pretty natural for me to come down and start breakfast this morning...until I remembered that you don't know me anymore. And then I started wondering how you'd feel about it and other things, and...I don't want to be presumptuous, so—"

"Devon—" He interrupted her rapid flow of words.

"Yes?"

"I understand. Don't worry about it. Yes, you are a stranger to me, but that will change. And, as far as breakfast is concerned, I certainly don't mind not having to eat my own cooking. Just relax. Okay?"

She sighed and some of the tension left her shoulders. "I'll try."

"Good. I'll make some toast to go with the omelette," he said, changing the subject.

Jack followed Devon's lead, speaking only of inconsequential things as they enjoyed a companionable breakfast—Devon's omelette was delicious. Having cleared the table and started a fresh pot of coffee brewing, he was just about to broach the subject of their marriage when there was a knock at the door.

Devon tensed. "Oh, heavens! If you're getting company already I'd better get upstairs to shower and dress." And, before Jack could think of anything to say, she was gone.

The knock came again. Frowning slightly, wondering who it could be this early in the morning, Jack answered it. He was stunned to see one of the local Mounties standing there. He knew him by sight as Sergeant Tom Kane, but they'd never spoken. Jack normally avoided cops, although he *had* spoken to one of Kane's colleagues the night of the explosion. In that instance, it had been unavoidable.

In his early-to-mid-thirties, Kane was tall, with Nordic blue eyes, sun-bleached blond hair and an athlete's physique. The kind of guy women got all flustered around and men wanted with them, not against them, in a brawl.

"Jack Keller?"

Jack nodded shortly. In a fraction of a second, all his paranoia returned. Maybe he *was* Spencer. Maybe Devon, if that was her real name, *had* come here to entrap him. Maybe the two years he'd spent avoiding any and all association with the law had been for naught, and this man was here to arrest him.

"I'm Sergeant Kane. I was wondering if I could speak with you for a moment?"

As a result of the chaotic suspicions tumbling through his mind, Jack's tone bordered on hostile when he replied. "What about?"

"The warehouse explosion."

"I told you people everything I could the other night."

"I'd like to go over it with you again if it wouldn't be too much trouble."

Jack studied the cop on his doorstep. He considered refusing, but that would probably just arouse the man's suspicions. He didn't need that. "Sure." He stepped back and allowed the Mountie into the cabin.

Moments later they entered the kitchen. "Would you like a cup of coffee?"

He was surprised when Kane accepted. Much of Jack's opinion of cops had been colored by television, and two years of avoiding all contact with them. On television, he'd rarely, if ever, seen a cop bridge the boundary between cop and civilian by accepting an offering. Still, he found he couldn't quite let go of the suspicion that continued to seep out of that deep dark hole where his memory should have been.

"So," he said, as he set their coffee on the table, "how can I help you?" He was immediately stuck by a sense of déjà vu and realized that he'd said very similar words to Devon just the previous evening. He hoped Kane's visit didn't prove as detrimental to his equilibrium as Devon's had.

"We received the arson investigator's preliminary report on the warehouse explosion this morning." Kane spoke in a low, serious tone.

"And?"

"It was no accident." He paused, studying Jack thoughtfully with an astute blue-eyed gaze that saw everything while giving away nothing. "We've got a couple of things to look into, but I wanted to ask you if you remembered anything more, Mr. Keller? Anything else on that vehicle you saw leaving as you pulled in?"

Jack frowned in concentration and grimly sipped the hot black coffee. "Nothing that I can think of. Like I said the other night, I only saw the guy in profile. Didn't recognize him or his truck at the time, but I didn't think anything of it until later. When I drove through the gates, I went straight to the warehouse to meet with Wiseman for coffee like I always do on Tuesdays. That's the day I pick up the week's maintenance supplies, and I was getting some lumber to repair the picnic shelters that particular day. It looked quiet. I didn't see anybody else in the yard at all." He shrugged. "I guess because I was a bit later than usual. I remember wondering if I'd caught the guys on their break or something because I'd forgotten about the shift change." He shook his head. "That's about it. If anything else comes to me, I'll let you know."

"Why were you late?"

"I had a flat tire to get repaired."

Kane nodded his acceptance of the explanation. "And were you and Wiseman friends? Did you see him often?"

Jack studied the cop's expression. "Aside from Tuesdays when I picked up supplies, I'd go by for coffee every couple of days. Sometimes, if his wife was away, he'd stop by here for a beer on his way home from work. That's about it."

Kane nodded, cast his gaze around and then asked, "Do you know of any reason why someone would want to kill him?"

Jack shook his head. "He didn't talk about himself much." Neither of them had. That's what had made it a comfortable friendship. The Noralco foreman was a man he'd had numerous dealings with since arriving in town, and he was the closest male friend Jack had in Northridge.

Kane nodded, sipped his coffee and changed course. "Do you think you'll recognize the man you saw leaving if you see him again?"

Jack shrugged. "I can't be sure."

"A local?"

Jack frowned, trying to bring into focus a face he'd seen for only seconds. "Possibly." He knew all the locals by sight, but this person had been in profile.

"You still think the truck was a dark blue or dark green Dodge?"

Jack shook his head. "I said Ford, not Dodge. An older model. And yeah, as far as I can recall it was dark-colored." He met Kane's gaze. "How is Wiseman?" he asked.

Kane sipped his coffee before replying. "He'll live, thanks to you. But it'll be a long time before he's ready to go back to work."

Jack nodded. "I'm glad he'll make it."

Kane drained the dregs of his cup. "Listen, Mr. Keller, I was wondering..."

Jack tensed. "Wondering what?"

"Would you mind physically going through the motions you made that afternoon? Kind of a reenactment for me? It's been my experience that, simply by putting themselves back into a situation people can remember details they otherwise wouldn't."

This was beginning to sound distinctly like he was under suspicion, Jack mused. As though Kane wanted to see just how many times he'd tell the story the same way. Then again, maybe he'd just been watching too much television. "You want me to drive to the lumberyard and explain everything again?"

Kane nodded. "If it wouldn't be too much trouble."

With a mental grimace, Jack looked hopefully toward the doorway. Devon still hadn't reappeared, however, so he really had no excuse not to do as Kane asked. Besides, if he didn't do it now, the cop would probably appear at an even less opportune time to ask again. Finally, he shrugged and said, "As long as it doesn't take too long. I'll just leave a note for my houseguest."

As she closed the bedroom door, Devon wondered at herself and the peculiar motivations surfacing within her. She'd applied her makeup with particular care and styled her hair with an eye for perfection because—for some reason—she wanted to be...*beautiful* today. She tried to tell herself that it was only a desire for self-confidence motivating her, because she always felt less confident when she wasn't at her best, but intuitively she knew it was something more. And, as a result, she was more than a little nervous as she dressed to face the day...and the stranger who was still her husband. But it turned out that she needn't have worried. When she descended the stairs ten minutes later, Geoff wasn't there. A note propped conspicuously against the silk blooms in the center of the table read:

Devon,
I had to run out for a while. Be back by noon so that we can talk. Make yourself at home.

Jack

The large bold lettering and almost vertical style were familiar, but the signature threw her. Oh, she knew he thought of himself as Jack and probably would continue to do so for some time. But somehow, for the first time, it really brought home the brutal truth of Geoff's situation, and the severity of the problems facing them. What were they going to do?

No answers were forthcoming.

She poured herself a cup of the still-hot coffee from the carafe, wincing a bit at its strength, and walked to the patio door behind the table to stare out at the lake. The first thing she had to do

was get out of this house before proximity to Geoff engendered
more problems. Problems with which she knew she was not prepared to deal.

What had been the name of the woman who owned the bed-
and-breakfast? Devon massaged her left temple as though the
action could stir the memory to the surface.

Eva Wright! That was it!

Setting her half-finished coffee on the table, she went in search
of a phone book. She hoped the bed-and-breakfast had room.

It did. She reserved a room for herself and then asked directions.

"Do you know where Deer Lake is?" Eva asked.

Devon hesitated. "Yes," she responded slowly.

"Well, we're on Lake Shore Drive," Eva said in her slightly
breathless voice.

Lake Shore Drive was Geoff's address. The road stretched all
the way from Northridge to the lake and had a number of larger
properties along it.

A premonition began to worm its way into her mind and
Devon stretched the phone cord to its maximum length as she
craned to see out of the living room window. But it was no use,
the fir trees blocked any view she might have had of Geoff's
neighbors.

Eva continued, "From Northridge, you just turn north on Lake
Shore and follow it around—you'll end up heading west—and
we're about halfway down on the left. You can't miss us. It's a
big old Victorian-style house with a bed-and-breakfast sign in
the front yard."

Now that she thought about it, Devon vaguely remembered
passing a large Victorian house just before turning into Geoff's
drive. She hadn't noticed a sign, but then she hadn't been looking
for one. "I see," Devon responded, feeling a little dazed. It was
a trifle closer than desirable, but at least she'd be out of Geoff's
house until they worked things out between them.

"Do you think you can find that?" Eva sounded a bit concerned.

"Oh, yes," Devon murmured. "I'm sure I can."

"Good. We'll see you this afternoon then. Bye-bye."

Devon had just poured herself a fresh cup of coffee and was contemplating the idea of packing her things when she heard the front door open and close. Her heart stuttered and then started up again in double time. The clumping sound of boots dropping to the floor was followed by the rattle of hangers in the closet.

And then, Geoff entered the kitchen.

Catching sight of her standing near the patio door, he stopped in midstride. His gaze swept her quickly from head to toe and back again. And then, their eyes locked. Hers wary and vulnerable; his hard and expressionless. "Hi," he said in that slightly rough tone she still hadn't gotten used to. "Sorry I had to leave you alone, but one of the local cops wanted to go over some things at the Noralco site with me."

"Hi." The word emerged as a hoarse whisper and Devon cleared her throat to find her voice. "It's okay."

He nodded and his gaze roamed her features. Reminding herself that this was not the Geoff she knew, Devon sought out the differences in his appearance. Then, realizing what she was doing, she broke the strange magnetic pull of his attractiveness and sipped her coffee. Still, he didn't move. The fabric of the silence grew taut with strain.

Lifting her head once more, she saw an emotion she didn't recognize in the olive green depths of his eyes. And then, in a flash, it was gone.

"Do you want some lunch?" he asked.

She shook her head. "No, that's fine."

He glanced at the clock. "It's noon," he said. "We might as well eat while we talk. Come on. I'll take you out for lunch."

Devon hesitated, all her senses on high alert. In that moment, she detected the subtle scent of his aftershave. Noted the way his chambray shirt fit his broad shoulders. Even heard the faint ticking of the clock on the wall. "I'm really not that hungry," she lied. "And I should pack my things."

"Pack?" he echoed, his tone both questioning and adversarial.

She nodded. "Yes. I'm moving into Eva Wright's Bed-and-Breakfast this afternoon."

She saw the tension leave his shoulders. "That's really not necessary. You can stay here."

"No, I can't."

He studied her a moment, then nodded. "All right. But you have to eat." Picking up her purse from the countertop where she'd left it sitting, he handed it to her and took the coffee cup from her hand, setting it carelessly on the table. "Come on," he murmured, grasping her arm in a firm hand to lead her from the room.

Once again, Devon resisted. She really wasn't prepared to spend time with him...socially. She wanted to talk about all the things that needed to be talked about between them, and then escape. She was going to have to call David soon, too. He'd be worried. She should have called last night.

Geoff stopped. "Look. Unless you want me to pick you up bodily and carry you, you'll come."

She stared at him. "You wouldn't!" The idea of being carried by him was...too damned appealing. The last thing she needed was a potent male assault like that on her already muddled senses.

His expression was uncompromising. "I would," he replied.

Devon believed him. "All right," she murmured. "I'll come."

He flashed her a grin that disappeared all too quickly. The boyish gesture revealed, for a fraction of an instant, a softer side to this hard, too-serious man. Her heart did a cartwheel. Oh, Lord, what had she risked by coming here?

Chapter 4

As Geoff closed the cottage door behind them, his imperturbable stranger's facade was once again solidly in place, and the brief glimpse at a lighter side to this intense man might never have been. Devon felt a peculiar wariness creep into her soul that she had never expected to feel in Geoff's presence. The Geoff she had married had been exactly what he seemed: a friendly, outgoing man who loved good company, good food and life in general. This man, on the other hand, seemed so reserved and unreachable that discovering his true personality might be more akin to peeling away the layers of an onion. She sensed something cold and hard at his core, but she wasn't certain she wanted to know him well enough to learn what it was.

Could a head injury change a man that much? Or had something else altered the man she knew?

Geoff held open the door of his Bronco for her to enter, and then moved around the vehicle to get in the driver's side. "There are three restaurants in Northridge," he said as he put the keys in the ignition. "The Diner, The Gold Dragon, and the Union Hotel restaurant. The Diner has good old-fashioned burgers, or roast beef. The hotel restaurant has the same, plus a few Italian dishes and take-out pizza. And the Gold Dragon is, of course, Chinese food though I think they serve a few burgers too. Take your pick.''

Devon stared at him. ''You used to hate Chinese food.'' She added one more small item to the growing list that proved this man was not the Geoff she'd known.

Geoff flashed her an unreadable look as he started the engine. ''I did? Why?''

She shrugged. ''I have no idea. Too much MSG maybe. You were always very health conscious.''

He seemed to consider that as he put the vehicle in reverse. ''What do you mean by health conscious? Did I jog?''

Devon nodded. She found having to tell him about himself disconcerting. ''You jogged five mornings a week for half an hour. You lifted weights three days a week. And whenever you could find time, you sailed, fished or hiked.''

He nodded thoughtfully. ''I still do most of those things.'' Then he added, ''But I don't hate Chinese food. In fact, I rather like it. You want Chinese?''

Devon shook her head. ''Actually I think I'd like something lighter. Soup and salad would be great.''

He nodded. ''The Diner it is.''

''That's where I stopped last night to ask for directions to your place,'' she offered.

''I figured that must have been how you found me.''

They fell silent for a few moments as Geoff drove the gravel road into Northridge with the speed and confidence of someone who traversed it often. Devon noted a carved cedar sign heralding Wright's Bed-and-Breakfast on her right and she studied the place with interest. The grounds seemed to occupy a good two acres. In the rear, near the lake, a large white gazebo was visible through the hanging boughs of evergreens. Since the house, which had been painted a pale banana yellow accented by bright teal green, was set back some distance from the road, a long narrow gravel drive looped through the front yard. Her interior decorator's mind kicked into gear and Devon craned her neck to get a better view of two large circular towerlike structures, attached to the rear corners of the imposing Victorian. She suddenly found herself eager to see its interior. Then they were past it, and she focused her gaze forward again.

"Tell me about the kids," Geoff said abruptly.

Devon looked at him, but he was staring at the road and she could discern no expression. "All right," she murmured neutrally. "I told you that Britanny is nine. She's in grade four and doing very well. Her favorite subjects are spelling and English. Tyler turned twelve in March. He's in grade six."

"Does he like school?"

Devon hesitated. "He used to, but...he's changed a lot in the last couple of years."

Two years. Since his father had disappeared from his life. It wouldn't take much for Geoff to read between the lines and make that connection. "You've been having trouble with him?" Geoff's words emerged as half statement, half question.

"Oh, yeah," Devon returned quietly. "We've had our problems."

Geoff looked over at her. "Tell me."

Her gaze slid away as she shrugged. "I wouldn't know where to start. Besides I'm not sure you really want to know." She smiled cautiously. "You might decide reclaiming your life isn't worth the trouble."

Geoff focused on negotiating a curve in the road before looking at her again. "It's worth it," he said simply. "Whatever happens, it's worth it."

Devon stared at him feeling slightly chastened by the intensity in his eyes, in his tone. What had he endured in the past two years? She swallowed and then focused on the conversation. "I wasn't kidding when I said I didn't know where to start. Tyler's misbehavior has become so constant that I don't even call him on the small stuff anymore. If I did we'd be fighting constantly."

"The earring?" Geoff asked.

"Small stuff," Devon returned.

He nodded. "Do you have any idea why it all started?"

"I've spent a lot of time thinking about that. I think he blames me for your disappearance from our lives."

Geoff shot her a startled look. "Why?"

"He heard me ask you for a divorce just a day or so before you disappeared. The day you told me that you'd invited Spencer and Holly to join us on the fly-in fishing trip that was originally intended for you and I to be alone together to talk about our marital problems. I was so angry that I refused to go, but—since you had business to discuss with Spencer—you went ahead with your plans. Anyway, Tyler heard our argument. Later, he raged at me that it was my fault you went away. I tried to explain the situation to him, but...I don't think he understood."

"So Tyler and I were close?"

Devon nodded. "Up until the last six months we were together. Then you withdrew from everyone, including Tyler."

Geoff shot her an impenetrable look. "Why did I do that?"

She shrugged. "You tell me. The reason I asked you for a divorce was because I was sick to death of living in the same house with a man who refused to communicate with me."

He seemed to be turning that around in his mind as they reached the outskirts of Northridge and he slowed for a stop sign. Devon took the opportunity to examine the small town since she hadn't had a chance the previous evening.

Judging by appearances, she'd say that Northridge probably didn't have a population of more than a couple of thousand people, if that. But it was a quaint little place, even when seen on a gray day after a December blizzard, she thought wryly. Geoff turned left on Juniper Avenue, and she spied the now-familiar pink neon sign advertising The Diner. Farther down the street she saw signs for Radio Shack, Jim's T.V. Repair, an Esso station, and a Safeway. Geoff braked to a halt in an angle-parking slot before the restaurant and wordlessly got out, coming around to open Devon's door where he grasped her elbow to escort her the few steps to the restaurant.

"Thank you," she murmured as he opened the restaurant door, holding it for her to precede him. As soon as she'd stepped past him, he placed his hand on the small of her back to guide her.

The contact, which once she'd been so accustomed to that she would scarcely have noticed, was now disconcerting, somehow too intimate.

"This way," he said, indicating that she precede him.

The Diner was redolent with the scents of French fries, hamburgers, and fresh coffee. The fluorescent lighting, made harsh by the unnatural gloom of the day, uncharitably illuminated the scarred tables, blue vinyl booth seats and sturdy chrome chairs. But appearance didn't seem to matter: The restaurant was crowded. And, if the meals were consistently as good as the late supper she'd had here the previous evening, Devon could understand why.

Geoff guided her toward an empty booth in an area near the rear of the restaurant where there were fewer people, obviously seeking privacy for the discussion he wanted to have. Only seconds after they'd taken a seat, a waitress wearing a name tag identifying her as Maureen arrived with a pair of menus and a carafe of coffee. Maureen was fortyish with short curly brown hair, worldly blue eyes, and the lined face of a heavy smoker. Before she even had a chance to so much as open her mouth in greeting, a man yelled from somewhere near the center of the diner. "Hey, Moe, bring me a piece of that apple pie, will you?"

Maureen didn't even turn to look at the caller. "Hold your horses, Harvey," she called over her shoulder. "Can't you see I'm busy?" Then she looked at Geoff. "Afternoon, Jack."

"Hi, Maureen," he said quietly, but he didn't smile. The lack of warmth in his greeting didn't seem to bother the waitress, however. She was probably used to it, Devon reflected. Maureen merely switched her gaze to Devon and, with a gesture of the carafe toward the coffee cup sitting upside down on a saucer on the table, asked, "Coffee?"

"Please." Devon automatically smiled slightly though she was too tense to feel much like smiling, and turned the cup over to accept the fragrant brew.

"You must be the lady that Tammy said she gave directions to last night?"

Devon smiled at the unabashed inquisitiveness inherent in the small town personality. "That would be me," she acknowledged. "I'm Devon Grayson."

"Maureen Hillaby," the waitress returned, and then with a glance in Jack's direction said, "I see you found him all right."

"Yes."

A second later, the waitress finished filling Geoff's cup, handed them each a menu, and moved away. Geoff stared at his coffee for a while, sipped it thoughtfully, and then lifted his gaze to meet Devon's. "I need to ask you something."

"All right," Devon said with a touch of wariness. This sounded serious.

He cleared his throat. "Do you think our marital problems in those last months might have been because—" He broke off, took another sip of his coffee, and allowed his gaze to slide away.

Devon frowned. "Because of what, Geoff?"

He didn't look at her. "Do you think I might have had an affair?"

Devon hesitated, considering his question. "I considered that actually. What woman wouldn't in that situation? But I decided it was pretty unlikely."

"Why?"

"Because I almost never had any trouble reaching you. If you weren't at home, you were at the office, and vice versa. It would have been pretty difficult for you to have an affair when there was so little time."

Geoff nodded, but the frown on his face told her that he still didn't totally accept Devon's evaluation of the situation.

"What made you ask?"

He shrugged. "I don't know. Just a thought." He took another sip of his coffee and, when next he spoke, seemed to be off on another tangent. "Were we close friends with the Lorings?"

"We were more than friends with the Lorings, Geoff. They were family."

"In what way?"

Everything within Devon went still. Oh, God! He didn't know. *Of course he doesn't know. He has amnesia.* She closed her eyes briefly, wishing there was an easy way to tell him.

"Devon?"

There was no easy way. "Holly Loring was your sister, Geoff. It was through you that she met Spencer."

Geoff set down his coffee cup with a slight clatter, and stared at Devon. Something fearful and intense smoldered in the depths of his olive green irises. "My sister?" he repeated.

Devon nodded.

His hand clenched on the handle of his coffee cup. "It was my sister who died in that crash?"

"Yes, Geoff. I'm sorry."

"But she didn't look anything like me," he protested. "There was a picture. She was fair...blond."

"That's true. Holly lightened her hair, and she inherited your father's skin tones. You take after your mother."

"Tell me—"

"So, are you folks ready to order?" Maureen asked as she approached their booth.

Geoff stared at the waitress blankly for a second, and then, with a frown, opened his menu and began to scan it quickly. Maureen looked in Devon's direction and raised a questioning brow. "I'll just have your soup of the day and a tossed salad with ranch dressing on the side," she said.

"Steak sandwich for me, please," Geoff said when Maureen had finished recording Devon's order on her pad and was once again looking in his direction. "And more coffee."

"Comin' right up."

When the waitress had refilled their cups and moved away again, Geoff continued as though there'd been no interruption. "Tell me about my parents," he said in a low tone. "Where do they live?"

"I never met your father. You told me that he passed away in an accident when you were sixteen. Your mother lives in Maple Ridge. She likes to be close to Vancouver where she can show her sculptures and paintings." Devon hesitated, and then plunged ahead. "For the last few years you two hadn't gotten along very well."

His gaze fastened on her face. "Why?"

Devon swallowed. "She remarried, Geoff. You didn't approve of her choice."

Geoff frowned, and the expression was somehow much more forbidding than she remembered. "Is she happy?" he asked.

"Oh, yes. Very happy. They do a lot of travelling together. He's an artist too, so they share many of the same interests."

"Then why didn't I approve?"

Devon swallowed, uncertain as to whether she should bring all of this up again now. But what was to be gained by waiting? "You were concerned that Robert was using your mother. He's about five years younger than she is, and not quite as successful as an artist yet, so most of the travelling they do is at your mother's expense."

Geoff considered that silently for a moment, then asked, "Can she afford it?"

Devon smiled. "Oh, yeah. I think so. She told me that her last sculpture sold for a very nice piece of change."

"If she can afford it, and this Robert makes her happy, then I don't see the problem." He shrugged.

At that moment, Maureen brought their meal and conversation waned although they continued to speak casually about the children and Devon's parents.

As they drove back to his place a short time later, Jack pondered all that he'd learned. And yet, no matter how much he learned, he was always left with more questions. The incredible sense of loss he felt whenever he thought of Holly Loring could definitely be explained by the fact that she'd been his sister. But, if he hadn't been having an affair, then what could have caused the problems in his marriage to Devon in those last few months? Something work-related? And, if it was something work-related, why hadn't he been able to talk to Devon about the problem? It didn't make sense.

He looked over at the woman who was still his wife. *His* wife. He liked the sense of belonging that word brought with it. And, so far, he liked Devon.

Oh, he knew that she still wanted a divorce. He sensed that she was just biding her time, humoring him, until she felt the time was right to broach the subject again. And she was probably right. Now that he knew his identity—even if it all still seemed a bit unreal—he could reclaim his life without trying to reclaim his marriage. But, he didn't want to give up the possibility of getting it *all* back. If he never came to care for Devon, if she couldn't learn to love him again, then *yes,* he would agree to a divorce. But it was much too soon to sign away that chance.

Damn, he wished he knew what had happened in those last six months of their marriage. A thought occurred to him. "You said that Spencer's estate is still being sued by a number of companies who had losses. Right?"

Devon looked at him and nodded. "Yes. Why?"

"So people have pretty much accepted the fact that Spencer was into something illegal?"

She frowned. "I don't know if I'd go that far. What's accepted is that the security systems installed by his company are at fault for the losses. Whether Spencer was into something illegal, or whether he was as much of a victim as the companies who had the losses hasn't been determined and I'm not sure it ever will be. The systems could have been tampered with before they were installed. But, since Fort Knox Security was liable for damages, I guess that liability has passed to the estate."

"But I thought you said he bought those security systems from Future-Tech."

Devon met his gaze. "That's right."

"So why isn't Future-Tech sharing in that liability?"

She shrugged. "You'd have to ask my father about that. I think he was able to prove that the systems were fine when they left the Future-Tech warehouse, but I don't know for sure how he handled it."

Jack considered. "Don't you think it's just a little odd that we started having problems with our marriage at the same time that all this was going on? Maybe I was involved in it in some way. Maybe that's what was bothering me."

Devon nodded. "I had thought of that, but I don't see how you could have been involved unless it was somehow accomplished against your will. You were simply too honest to have

done anything shady. And since I believed that both you and
Spencer were dead, I abandoned that course of thought as useless
because I didn't have any way to find out. Even now, we're not
any further ahead if you have no memory of those times.''

Jack stared stonily at the road ahead. ''Maybe it will start
coming back to me.'' He wanted to regain his memory. More
than anything. But he knew he was grasping at straws.

After making arrangements for Devon to return to his place
for dinner and then returning her to her Jeep so she could go
and check in to the bed-and-breakfast, Jack had gone through an
abbreviated version of his workday. It was a bit of a late start,
but winter workdays were short anyway. The first thing on his
agenda had been a meeting with his employers, George and Rita
Landes. Now officially retired, they had begun the Deer Lake
Resort more than thirty years earlier and despite their retired
status, still oversaw everything. Jack hadn't been quite sure how
they'd react to his precipitous request for a leave of absence, but,
one way or another, Jack was determined to return to Kelowna
with Devon. How else could he find out about himself, about the
man he'd been?

As it turned out, he needn't have worried about the Landeses'
reaction. In fact, Jack received the distinct impression that his
request for a minimum of a month's leave of absence was almost
welcomed by George, for it would give the old man an excuse
to get his hands dirty again.

With notice of his imminent departure taken care of, Jack had
made a quick security check on the cabins. That was when he'd
discovered the truck parked at the Scottses' cabin—a cabin that
was supposed to be sealed up for the winter while the Scotts
were in Arizona. And the truck had looked suspiciously like the
one he'd seen leaving the Noralco site the night of the explosion.

Damn! He'd have to notify the police.

It was three-fifteen when Jack pulled up to the small stone
building on Juniper Avenue that housed the local police detach-
ment. Tension coiled in his gut as he eyed the place. The last
thing he wanted to do was go in. After two years of avoiding

cops it was kind of hard to simply discard his ingrained caution. But...he didn't see that he had a choice. Setting his jaw, he opened the door of the Bronco and, thoughtfully, made his way up the walk to the police station.

When Jack entered the building, Sergeant Kane appeared to be in the process of making coffee. "You here to see me?" the six-foot-three-inch cop demanded before the door had even closed behind Jack.

Jack nodded. "I don't know if it's anything or not, but I thought I should mention it to you."

"Well then, Jack—" He halted. "May I call you Jack?"

Jack shrugged. "Sure. Why not?"

Kane smiled. "And you might as well call me Tom. Everyone else in this town does." He set a clean pair of cups out. "Anyway, as I was saying, you might as well join me for coffee. The afternoon's only half over, and I need an infusion."

A minute later, having prepared his coffee to his satisfaction, Kane handed Jack a cup of the hot black brew and grew serious. "So, did you remember something else?"

Jack shook his head. "No, but I did see a truck parked out at the lake today that looks a lot like the one I saw the other night." He sipped his coffee before continuing. "I thought you might want to check it out."

Kane nodded. "I appreciate that. Where can I find it?"

Jack gave Kane directions.

"If I come across a guy who fits the description of the one you gave me this morning, are you going to be around to come in and take a stab at identifying him?"

Jack nodded. "I should be around for a day or so anyway."

"Great. I'll call you if I need to talk to you then."

Fifteen minutes later, having finished their coffee and talked more about the prospect of the coming fishing season on Deer Lake than of anything else, Jack left the station. He was in the process of driving home to start his supper preparations for the evening ahead with Devon when he spied her going into the local Radio Shack and hesitated.

What was she doing? he wondered. Should he join her?

He was finding himself more and more attracted to her all the time, and it was happening so quickly that he wasn't sure he liked it. The one area where he preferred to maintain absolute command was over his emotions. So many things in his life had been beyond his control for so long that he'd taken solace in the fact that his emotions at least were manageable. Now, he found the idea that his command over his emotions was slipping, that it may indeed have been only an illusion all along, rather disturbing. He needed control.

But he also rather liked Devon.

His thoughts flitted toward her fiancé, and he wondered rather caustically how opposed the man was to a long engagement. Because Jack was in no hurry to sign away his right to an association with the wife he did not remember.

He wanted, *needed* to remember her, to recall the feelings he'd once had for her. He wanted to remember what it had been like to share in the birth of his children. He wanted to remember everything...their love...the cause of their problems in those final months together. And he wasn't about to let her out of his life until he'd given himself the chance to summon all those memories from wherever they were buried.

Why couldn't he remember? *Dammit!* He slapped the palm of his hand against the steering wheel as frustration sawed through him. But, as pain stabbed through his temples, the warning sign that another of his debilitating headaches was on the way, Jack realized that his frustration served no purpose. Reaching into the breast pocket of his shirt to extract a small container, he removed a pill and swallowed it quickly before the headache could get its teeth into him. One pill wouldn't knock him out, and if he caught them promptly enough, he could usually head off the type of agonizing episode that he'd had the night Devon had arrived.

That done, he put the Bronco back into drive and headed down Juniper Street to the Radio Shack. He had a legitimate excuse to go there after all. If Geoff Grayson was supposed to be some kind of computer expert, Jack needed to start testing that knowledge to see if any of his expertise would return to him. To do that, he needed a computer.

He could afford it. He'd saved a considerable sum of money since coming to Northridge and going to work at the resort, so that was no problem. He just wasn't certain he was ready to put himself to that particular test yet.

Parking in front of the store, he sat staring at the computer display in the window, hesitant to enter. Devon was in there. Was she trying to determine how to test his knowledge of those aspects of his life? Probably. What other reason could she have for going to a Radio Shack when she herself had said that her expertise with computers was limited?

What if he couldn't remember? What if this important part of his life, of who he had been, eluded him as determinedly as his personal memories? And yet he couldn't avoid putting himself to the test for much longer. Before he attempted to reclaim his life in Kelowna, he needed to know how much of his memory he could regain.

The bell over the door jangled as he entered and Devon, standing at the glass display case that doubled as a counter for the register, looked toward him. Her beautiful gray eyes widened slightly in surprise. "Geoff!"

Ralph Morin looked up. "Hi, Jack." And then he glanced at Devon and frowned. "Or should I call you Geoff?"

Jack shrugged. "Geoff's a nickname," he said, improvising. "Either will do."

Ralph nodded, obviously not understanding, but apparently judging the incident too unimportant to bother pursuing. "I'll be with you in a moment, Jack." With a distracted air, the proprietor returned to what he was doing: installing a new battery into the remote starter for Devon's Jeep.

So *he* hadn't been her reason for coming, Jack realized. He noticed her quizzical expression. "I thought maybe I should get a computer," he explained.

"Oh, of course. I thought..." Taking notice of an interested glance from Ralph as he followed their exchange, she broke off.

Jack studied the slight flush on her cheeks. She was flustered and he could almost read her thoughts. *I thought you'd followed me.* He had, but damned if he'd admit it.

"So...what kind of computer are you planning on getting?"

Jack thought about that but came up empty. He didn't know the first thing about them. "What do you suggest?"

Almost an hour had passed before Jack and Devon emerged from the store. The notebook computer he'd ordered would be in tomorrow morning, shipped by courier from a store in Vancouver. Taking Devon's advice into consideration, he'd decided not to purchase a desktop model computer. Since he didn't know what the next few days or weeks were going to hold for him, portability was a key feature. The notebook computer with docking station that Ralph had demonstrated looked as though it would have everything he needed and suit his requirements. He hoped.

"Are we still on for seven then?" Devon asked.

"Of course."

She nodded. The awkwardness was back between them. Two strangers, who shouldn't have been strangers, feeling their way along the path of getting to know each other. "Well, I'd best get back then. See you later."

"Sure." Jack got into the Bronco and watched her leave. He was looking forward to the evening more than he would have thought possible. Starting his truck, he glanced at his watch. Holy...! It was ten minutes to five! He had roughly two hours to get home, put together a decent meal, and take a shower before Devon got there. Thank God for microwaves. Just to be on the safe side though, he'd better stop at the supermarket and grab one of those bags of ready-made salad. He might not have time to concoct one.

Chapter 5

Devon pulled up at Geoff's place at five past seven. She'd planned to be a couple of minutes early rather than late, but she'd been stalled in the hallway of the bed-and-breakfast by one of the other guests, intent on conversation. Now she looked at the door to Geoff's cabin and tried to prepare herself for the evening ahead. As much as she would prefer to avoid contention, tonight would be the time for her to broach the subject of the divorce again. She needed to get home to spend Christmas with her family, and thus far she and Geoff had spent more time revisiting the past than they had talking about Devon's purpose in coming here in the first place.

She'd called home upon her arrival at the bed-and-breakfast, of course. The children, on Christmas break from school at the moment, were staying with her parents. It had been good to speak to them; she'd needed to hear their voices. She'd also told her parents and David about Geoff's situation. The conversation with David had been the most difficult.

He hadn't wanted her to come to Northridge in the first place. His suggestion had been for her to keep her distance and to simply have Geoff—alias Jack Keller—served with divorce papers. But Devon hadn't been able to do that. After more than thirteen years of marriage, she needed closure in her relationship with Geoff, and she couldn't have found that without a face-to-face meeting. The fact that she'd begun to wonder over the past hours if perhaps David hadn't been right, hadn't made it any easier to defend her position when she'd spoken with him.

David had made it very clear that he wanted her to come home immediately—with or without Geoff's agreement to sign the divorce papers. In fact, he'd been rather adamant about it. She understood his motivation. David quite naturally felt threatened and he was jealous. He didn't want her spending time with Geoff. And, to be truthful, were the situation reversed, she'd probably feel much the same. Still, remembering their rather tense telephone conversation, David's peremptory tone rankled. Partially due, no doubt, to her own illogical anticipation of the evening ahead.

And she *was* anticipating it. Despite the knowledge that her planned meeting with Geoff would undoubtedly include a good deal of friction, Devon found herself looking forward to it because…well, she didn't know *why* precisely but it had to do with the fact that Geoff was cooking, and Devon had always loved the break from eating her own less creative concoctions. That at least was familiar. He'd always loved to cook—usually fattening Italian dishes laden with cheese.

Now, she got out of the Jeep, smoothed the fabric of her black skirt and made her way to Geoff's door. A strange expectation coupled with pure nervous tension coiled in her abdomen. The feeling was strangely akin to the excitement and uneasiness one might feel on a first date, and yet this was not a date and could not be even remotely construed as one. The man she was meeting, although certainly a stranger to her in many ways, was her soon-to-be ex-husband. And her purpose here was not romantic. In fact, it was pretty much the opposite. So she didn't understand why she should feel this way.

But she did.

"Hi," she said, as Geoff opened the door in response to her

knock. He was once again wearing black chinos, but this time, instead of the black turtleneck, he wore a green silk shirt. And he looked…wonderful. Distressingly so.

"Come in," he said.

Devon thought maybe she should head for home as fast as the Jeep could take her. Instead, she smiled and stepped inside, allowing Geoff to take her coat before she removed her shoes. The cabin was warm and homey. A fire blazed in the fireplace and delicious smells wafted from the kitchen. "Mmm," she said, lifting her nose appreciatively. "What did you make?"

"Grilled chicken breasts with honey-mustard sauce, stuffed potatoes, and broccoli with cheese."

He was watching her intently, so Devon was careful to school her expression. "Well," she said, "it sounds like you're still a better cook than I am." The change, though, lay in the fact that Geoff had never cooked anything but Italian cuisine prior to his disappearance. Of course he wouldn't have wanted to subsist for two years on nothing but the Italian pasta dishes that had been his specialties, so it made sense that he'd learned to cook other dishes. She didn't know why she should feel surprised. "I guess you must have grown tired of fettucine and lasagna and bought yourself some cookbooks," she added with a smile.

Without returning her smile, he continued to study her intently for a minute, his olive green eyes seeking answers to questions not yet voiced. Then he said, "I used to cook a lot of Italian food, and that's what you were expecting tonight." It was more statement than question—a conclusion already drawn.

"Well, yes," Devon hedged, "but don't get the wrong idea. I'm not disappointed in the least. I'm not fussy. That's my problem." With a self-deprecating grin, she patted her hips.

He studied her a moment more, as though weighing the veracity of her statement, and then nodded. "Good," he said simply. "Because I didn't know I had an Italian mother, and I never tried cooking much in the way of Italian food. I'll have to give it a shot and see how much comes back to me." He paused. "Why don't you come on into the kitchen."

"Can I help with anything?"

He shook his head. "I've got everything under control. Just have a seat." He waved a hand vaguely in the direction of the table which already held a huge bowl of salad and a basket of fresh dinner rolls. "I'll join you in a moment."

As Devon watched him move about the kitchen, his darkly handsome countenance so much more solemn and intense than the man she remembered, she couldn't help but be reminded of the conversation she'd had with Eva Wright earlier in the afternoon when she'd asked Eva if Jack Keller was her neighbor.

"Why, yes, he is," she'd responded. "Do you know him?"

"We've met," Devon hedged, not wanting to go into explanations that would make no sense to a stranger in any case.

Then Eva grinned conspiratorially. "He's very handsome, isn't he? Though I must confess that he frightens me a bit."

"Really? Why?" Devon asked, although she had to admit that she herself had felt almost frightened, for a brief moment, in the presence of the new intense Geoff she'd encountered.

Eva shrugged, looking a bit uncomfortable. "He's just so big, with all those scars and everything. It makes him look so...violent."

"Scars?" Devon echoed. With the exception of the one on his eyebrow and the other on his stomach, she hadn't seen any scars.

"His back you know. It looks like he was pretty badly hurt at one time," Eva said with a delicate shiver. And then, before Devon could pursue the topic further, she had firmly changed the subject.

Studying him now, Devon cringed to think of the kind of pain he must have endured if his scars were as extensive as Eva had intimated. And, now that she thought about it, she couldn't help wondering how Eva had come to see Geoff's scars in the first place. Perhaps at the beach during the summer?

"Here we go," Geoff said, interrupting her thoughts as he placed a plate of delicious smelling stuffed potatoes surrounded by chicken breasts smothered in sauce and garnished with parsley sprigs onto the table.

Devon's mouth watered. "It looks wonderful."

The remainder of the evening passed relatively smoothly. They ate good food, drank good wine, and talked about the good times they'd once shared. Or rather, Devon talked and Geoff listened, occasionally asking questions.

Now, as the evening began to draw to a close, Geoff could tell that Devon had something on her mind and a curious tension began to tighten his chest. Devon had known the man she'd been married to so well that she had expectations on almost every level. And it seemed that, on most of those levels, Jack failed to meet expectation. More than once this evening she'd said to him, "You're so much more" *something,* "than you used to be." More serious and laconic. More willing to learn new things. And more dispassionate.

Since he couldn't very well argue her assessment, Jack accepted her statements. But, now he wondered if whatever was on her mind had to do with these perceived changes in his character. Finally, as the tension continued to mount, he decided he was going to have to ask. It didn't look as though she'd ever get round to broaching the subject on her own. "What's on your mind, Devon?"

She jumped slightly and her gaze flew up to meet his. Guilt? Whatever it was, she knew he wasn't going to like it. Must be the divorce subject again. She cleared her throat and rose from the table to look out the patio door at the snow-blanketed lake. "I spoke with David earlier today," she murmured quietly.

He expected that she would have. "And?" he finally prompted her when she didn't go on.

"He wants me to come home. Despite the extenuating circumstances surrounding your...um, condition, he feels that we can accomplish the divorce through a third party." She didn't look at him.

Jack rose to approach her, trying to see her expression. "And what do you feel?"

Her slender shoulders shrugged beneath the fabric of her teal blue blouse. "I don't know what to think anymore, Geoff. We need to come to terms on this."

"Didn't you offer to reintroduce me to my life—to our children—even if I agreed to a divorce?"

She nodded. "Yes. Yes, I did."

"We can't accomplish that through a lawyer. Can we?"

She turned to look at him and seemed surprised to see him standing so close. "No, I don't suppose we can. And I will still do that for you despite David's feelings on the matter. I feel I owe you that much. But, as I said before, Geoff, we needn't delay the divorce in order for me to do that. I need to get on with my life and...well...since finding you, I feel as though I'm stuck in limbo again."

Join the club, he thought. Aloud, he said, "The only thing I have that you want is the divorce, Devon. And I'm not prepared to give you what you want until I have what I want. If you can't accept those terms—" he shrugged "—well, I guess you'll just have to sue me."

Her eyes widened as she stared at him incredulously. "You don't trust me!"

"I don't trust anybody," he returned. "It comes with the territory."

She swore softly, despairingly, beneath her breath. "What is it, exactly, that you want, Geoff?" Her beautiful dove gray eyes, brimming with emotional anguish now, fastened on his face and he wanted nothing more than to enfold her in his embrace. To hold her and protect her from all misery. But he couldn't, and he didn't.

"I want my life back, Devon. The way it used to be, if I can get it back."

"With me in it?" she asked in a shocked tone.

"Maybe," he said quietly. "If there's anything left to reclaim between us, I want it. And if not, who knows—" he shrugged "—we might find something new."

"Oh, Geoff." She closed her eyes briefly, then turned back to the patio door, shutting him out as she stared blindly out at the night. "I've got David in my life now."

"Do you love him?"

"Yes...of course." But her answer had come too quickly, and Geoff sensed that she had been asking herself the same question. There was uncertainty in her voice.

He placed his hand on her arm, gently turning her to face him. When she looked up at him, her eyes luminous and wounded, her lips soft and trembling, something clenched deep in his gut and he knew he couldn't let her go. Not yet. "I've got news for you, Devon. You've got both of us in your life now. And I don't plan on getting out of it anytime soon."

Devon froze as Geoff raised his hands to her shoulders; she felt curiously fragile beneath his touch. His thumbs found their way inside the collar of her blouse to trace the contours of her collarbone, skin against naked skin. A tingle raced through her, tightening her nipples. Her breasts swelled. Her breathing quickened. She trembled and saw something primitive and triumphant flare to life in his eyes as her involuntary reaction communicated itself to him.

This couldn't be happening.

He moved his hands down her arms then, capturing her wrists and lifting them, wrapping them around his neck as he brought her body up against his. Devon swallowed. She should put a stop to this right now. She should grab her purse and walk away. She should go home. But a part of her wanted this moment more than she would have thought possible. A part of her revelled in the feel of Geoff's arms around her again. A part of her remembered the love she'd had for this man. And that errant piece of herself held reason hostage to desire.

He bowed his head then, to press his lips to hers, increasing the force gradually until, with a soft sound of protest and surrender, she opened to him. And then, as though her surrender was some sort of signal, his embrace tightened until she felt every ridge and plane of his hard chest against her swollen breasts. His kiss deepened until she felt consumed by its feral power. His hips rocked against her until she felt the evidence of his desire boldly pressing against her.

And yet, despite the intense sense of familiarity, the feeling of having come home, the strangeness of this Geoff made itself known even now. She felt a savagery at his core, as though the primal instincts of man's distant past were closer to the surface in this man than they had been in the husband she remembered.

They called to all that was female within her, commanding her body to life, inducing a primal passionate madness she felt helpless to resist, demanding her submission. She couldn't ever remember feeling quite this intense a loss of control. Not in Geoff's arms, and not in David's.

David!

She pulled out of Geoff's embrace, stunned that she'd forgotten her fiancé's existence for even so short a time. What was happening to her? She stared at this new strange Geoff, trying to perceive what it was about him that gave him such power over her. But whatever it was, it was camouflaged. "I have to go," she murmured. Turning away from him, she found her purse on the floor and draped its strap over her shoulder. "If you're not going to agree to a divorce no matter what I say, then I have no reason to be here."

"What about your promise to help me get my life back?"

She stiffened. "What about it?"

"I have a computer arriving tomorrow morning that may help me regain more of the memories I need, but I need your help, Devon. I need you to prompt my memory. Promise me you'll stay in Northridge one more day while I finish making the arrangements to leave," Geoff said behind her. "Please! On Thursday morning we can leave for Kelowna together. Then, with your help, I can start getting my life back."

"Thursday is Christmas Eve."

"I know. But...please. Think of it as your Christmas gift to me. I've spent two Christmases alone. I'd like to spend this one with my family."

Devon closed her eyes and sought the inner strength to refuse him. But this man was her husband. He had been through hell in the last twenty-eight months—they all had—and he needed her help. Slowly, she nodded. "All right. One more day. But..."

"But what?" he asked, his slightly rough baritone caressing her, intoxicating her with its magnetic power. Silk-on-sandstone and cognac.

She swallowed. "What was between us is over, Geoff. Please

let it go." Yet part of her knew that she was saying it as much as a reminder for herself as it was a warning for him.

There was a moment of silence, and she almost turned to face him though she knew it would have been a mistake. And then he said, "If it's over, why are you begging me to let it go? What are you afraid of, Devon?"

You, she almost cried. *Of who you are now. Of the stranger you've become. Of this peculiar attraction between us.* But she said none of those things. "I won't be unfaithful to my fiancé."

"But you'll be unfaithful to your husband. Exactly how many times have you slept with David, Devon?"

She whirled. "That's unfair! And, it's none of your business. I didn't know you were alive."

"You do now." His intense green-eyed gaze threatened to rob her of her equilibrium.

"And that's why I want a divorce."

"No."

She stared at him. He didn't even remember her, so he certainly couldn't love her. "Why are you being so stubborn about this?"

"Because I want us to have a chance to save our marriage." His intense gaze bored into her. "If after a while I don't get my memory back and I don't come to care for you, if you never come to love me again, then I'll agree to a divorce, Devon."

"It's not just a question of love, Geoff. It's not knowing what tore us apart the first time. What if you suddenly remember everything? What if you remember whatever it was and start acting the same way? I can't go through all that pain again, Geoff. I won't!"

He nodded. "Fine. So we'll find out what it was...together." He hesitated, and then seemed to soften. "Think about it, Devon. Think about all those good years and good times you were telling me about earlier. If you could get them back, what would it be worth to you?"

She stared at him. How could she answer that? Did he have any idea what he was asking of her? "I have to go," she said as she headed for the door. "I'll talk to you tomorrow."

Jack trailed after her to take her coat from the closet and help her on with it. She was about to open the door when he spoke, forestalling her. "Devon..."

"Yes?"

"Thanks for coming. I really enjoyed the evening."

Without turning around, she nodded. "I did too. Dinner was delicious."

The door closed behind her and silence, broken only by the crackling coals in the fireplace, blanketed the cabin. For a moment, Jack stood frozen in place, staring at the door he'd seen countless times in the last two years. Why did he want her so badly? Why did his life seem more empty than ever the minute she wasn't in the room? Why?

But there were no answers forthcoming.

An instant later the phone rang, jarring him from his musings. "Hello."

"Jack, it's Tom Kane. I've got a fellow here I'd like you to take a look at. Do you think you could come down to the station for a few minutes?" Kane must have sensed his hesitation for he immediately added, "If it's a bad time, we could do it tomorrow morning first thing."

Jack sighed inwardly. "No, that's fine. Sure I can come down. I'll be there in about twenty minutes." Why not? It would make the perfect ending for the perfect evening he'd planned that hadn't turned out so perfectly after all.

Do you know any reason why someone might want you dead? That had been Sergeant Kane's question to Jack last night after he'd talked to the man they'd arrested. Apparently the man had alluded to having received payment from a third party in order to *get some guy who was supposed to be at Noralco.* Since Jack was the only person Kane had discovered who had a regular schedule which would have placed him at Noralco at that time, Kane had speculated that the explosion may have been meant for him.

Jack frowned as he replayed the meeting in his mind. Sergeant Kane had to be mistaken, and that's what he had told the sergeant last night. He had made no enemies in Northridge. Heck, he'd pretty much avoided most people. The only person in town who knew he wasn't Jack Keller was Devon, and it had been the Noralco explosion that had brought her here. So, the scenario that someone had been trying to kill him just didn't add up. On any one day, a number of people would have a coffee at the Noralco Lumber store as they waited for their orders to be filled. If indeed the explosion had been geared toward anyone other than a Noralco employee, it had to be one of them.

"You're going to need some software." Devon's voice tugged him from his thoughts. She was browsing a wall of software titles while they waited for Ralph, the salesman, to bring Jack's new computer out from the back. "Do you know what you want?"

Jack shook his head. "No. What did I used to have?"

Devon shrugged. "As far as I know, you had a design program, a spreadsheet, and just basic word processing. Computers were one area where we did not have a lot in common, Geoff. I'm just barely computer literate."

"Well," he said, "I guess we'd better get Ralph to recommend some software then."

An hour later, they had Jack's new notebook computer set up on the kitchen table while they installed the software packages he'd purchased. It felt strangely comfortable to be sitting with Devon, allowing her to direct him as she read the instructions. He finished installing the design program he'd purchased and called it up. "This is the kind of program I used to design security systems?"

Devon hesitated. "It should be similar anyway. The computer system you used had a huge memory, so you probably had a much more extensive program than this one." She grimaced. "I did warn you that I wouldn't be able to help much with this."

Jack nodded and began manipulating the program. He *knew* this, or something very much like it. He'd seen it before.

Over the next two hours as Jack experimented, more and more came back to him. Given time, when it all came back to him, he was certain that there wouldn't be much that he couldn't accomplish with a computer. *This* was definitely part of who he was:

An electrical engineer majoring in computer architecture. An entrepreneur. A designer of corporate security systems. He felt rather than knew that computer system security had been his area of speciality, and Devon confirmed it. But he'd provided building security systems as well. Wireless security had been an area he'd been developing.

Devon made sandwiches for lunch. His sat on its plate untouched because he couldn't seem to take his hands off the keyboard long enough to eat. Besides, he wasn't really hungry. Devon resumed her seat next to him and began eating her sandwich—it smelled like egg salad. After a moment he noticed that she was giving him curious glances. He was about to ask her what was on her mind when she spoke, "Geoff?"

"Hmmm?"

"How is it that you can remember *things* when your memory is prompted, but not people?"

He shrugged slightly and glanced at her. "The way the doctor explained it was that there are apparently two types of memory— fact and task. Fact memory is the details of who, what, when, where, and so on, while task memory is just what it sounds like— the memory associated with performing tasks. I seem to be able to trigger my task memory fairly readily. But, I've lost most of my fact memory except much of what the doctor called my social memory recall. I don't know if that's a medical term, or just something he referred to it by."

"But what does it mean?"

He stopped typing and looked at her, then looked beyond her for a moment to the window and the evergreens beyond. "I guess it means that I can remember most things that are general knowledge, but not things that defined me as a person on a personal level. I remembered how to drive a vehicle as soon as I sat behind the wheel of one—task memory; and I remembered who was Prime Minister—social fact; but I couldn't remember Holly, no matter how long I stared at the picture of her that was in my wallet because that was a *personal* fact memory.

"I still don't really remember her as my sister except for the things you've told me. And those things have already become scenes in my mind, as though they're my own memories. It's strange.'' He looked back at Devon and shook his head. ''I can't explain it any better because I don't understand it myself. The doctor said they don't know enough about the way the brain works for him to attempt a more detailed explanation.''

Devon chewed and swallowed thoughtfully. ''I guess when you think about it that's the way it seems to be in most of the movies that have amnesiac characters. I mean people forget who they are and everyone associated with their identity, but they always seem to remember how to use a phone or a microwave.

''Do you often get headaches like the one you had the other night?'' she asked as her thoughts took a new direction.

He shrugged. ''Not as often anymore. At first I got them all the time. Now, they're mostly triggered by fatigue or stress, I think, and I've learned to manage them for the most part.''

Devon eyed him consideringly. ''Are they somehow responsible for your amnesia?''

He shook his head. ''As far as I know, they're just a lingering effect of the head injury I sustained in the plane crash.''

''So even if the headaches eventually go away all together, you may not get your memory back. Is that right?''

Jack stared at her, suddenly distracted by her beautiful dove gray eyes, her perfect oval face, her full kissable lips. God, he wanted her. ''Yeah. That's about right,'' he managed to say as he tore his gaze away, but his mind was no longer on the conversation. Neither was it on the computer.

Tomorrow he'd return with Devon to Kelowna. He'd enter her territory. Hers and David's. And that thought bothered him more than he cared to admit. He wanted the chance to hold her in his arms, to begin to test the theory that they might have something worth salvaging. He wanted the chance to get to know her *here*. And suddenly he remembered the town Christmas dance that was taking place that evening.

''Did we dance much?''

''Dance?'' She seemed confused by the abrupt change in topic. ''Um, yes, occasionally. I always liked dancing, and you really loved it at times.''

''There's a Christmas dance tonight at the community center. Would you like to go?''

Her gaze lifted abruptly, connecting with his. ''Oh, Geoff, I don't think that's a good idea.''

''It's a public dance,'' he argued. ''What harm could there be? Besides,'' he pressed, ''I think I should reexperience as many of the things we used to do as possible to try to recall the past. Don't you?'' It was an unfair gambit, appealing to her sense of fairness and responsibility in the hope that it would overcome her sense of obligation to David, but at the moment Jack didn't care. He was willing to fight dirty.

Chapter 6

Devon didn't know what had possessed her to agree to go to the dance with Geoff—it was foolhardy to say the least—but she had. He would be by to pick her up at eight. Since she hadn't packed with social occasions in mind, she'd had to run into town to buy a dress. The one she'd chosen was emerald green in a glossy, almost satiny, fabric with a fitted bodice, thin spaghetti straps, and a flared skirt that fell to just below her knees. It was much more dramatic than anything she usually wore, but then she hadn't been to a dance in a long time. Movies had been more David's style. And when she'd tried the gown on, she simply hadn't been able to resist it. It made her feel beautiful and she couldn't wait to put it on again. She'd already showered and put her hair up in a chignon, but before she finished getting ready, she had a call to make.

Eva Wright had given her a telephone message upon her return that stated simply, *Call David.* Terse and to the point, just as their last conversation had been. Devon grimaced. Maybe she'd call her mother first.

"Hello," Honoria Sherwood answered in her light, breezy voice.

"Hi, Mom."

"Devon, how are you? How are things going? Is Geoff remembering anything more?"

"I'm fine, Mom. Geoff is remembering some things, but not personal details. How are things there? Have you told the kids anything?"

There was a pause. "Well, no...not yet. I didn't want to get their hopes up if it didn't work out. Especially not at Christmas time. Is Geoff coming home with you?"

"It looks that way, Mom. He says he wants to try to get his life back." She hesitated, her confusion about his condition coming to the fore. "It's so strange the way some things seem to come back to him. I mean this morning he didn't even know if he knew how to use a computer. Then, after just a couple of hours on one, he was already manipulating programs like a pro. It's just so...odd."

Her mother commiserated and then asked, "When will you be getting home? You'll be here for Christmas, won't you?"

"Of course. We're leaving here in the morning, so we should be there by evening. I don't want to miss Christmas Eve with the kids. I know it's going to be tough Mom, but could you try to explain to the children that their father won't remember anything about his life with us before the accident."

"Of course, dear. I'll do my best. But there's something else you should be concerned about."

"What's that?"

"David's already assumed that you're coming home either tonight or tomorrow night. He's planning on being here to welcome you. And, under the circumstances, I don't think that is a good idea. Do you?"

Oh, boy! "I'll talk to him, Mom. I have to call him anyway."

"It's a good thing that he's planning on spending Christmas with his family this year, or Christmas day could have become really complicated."

"Yes, it could have."

"Well, I'll let you go then, dear. And drive carefully when you come home."

"I will." Slowly, thoughtfully, Devon hung up the phone. Given their attitudes toward each other, the one thing she did not want was to have Geoff and David in the same house with the children when they saw their father again for the first time in over two years. The tension and displeasure that David was feeling, and would undoubtedly exhibit towards Geoff, would surely communicate itself to the kids, and they didn't need that. They'd had a difficult enough time this last while.

She sighed. There was no sense putting it off any longer. Picking up the receiver, Devon dialled David's office number. If he had a client, it would go through to voice mail, otherwise he'd answer. She almost hoped it would be the former.

"David Randolph," David's voice came over the line, clear and businesslike.

"David, it's Devon."

"Devon! You're still in Northridge?"

"Yes. I'm leaving tomorrow morning." She explained the situation and asked David not to be at her parents' home when she arrived. "I just don't think it'll be good for the kids to have both you and Geoff there."

"I don't see why not," he argued. "I've certainly been more father to them in this last year than he has."

"Yes, but he was their father for a lot of years before that. To them, he will always be their father."

"Some father! I don't see why he has to come back here now. Doesn't he realize that everyone's lives didn't go on hold because his did?"

Devon hesitated. She'd never encountered this side of David before, and she didn't quite know how to deal with the petulant person he'd become since Geoff had reentered her life. He sounded like a spoiled child. "David, Geoff's return doesn't mean that the kids will love you any less," she said in an effort to reassure him. "It isn't as though we're each given a cup of love to use and the more people we love the less there is to go

around. All his return means is that you'll have to accept the fact
that they'll always love Geoff, too. Can't you do that?''

''I don't know.'' A pause. ''What about you?''

''What about me?''

''Am I supposed to share your love with him, too?''

Devon's jaw dropped. David's jealousy was getting distinctly
ugly. ''You're being ridiculous!''

''Am I? You said yourself once that, if Geoff had come back
and you'd been able to work out the problems in your marriage,
you wouldn't have pursued a divorce. Remember?''

''Yes, I remember. So what's your point?''

''My point is that maybe you've never stopped loving him.
Do you still love him, Devon?'' David's voice coming across
the miles of wire sounded accusatory and argumentative.

Devon rubbed her forehead to forestall a headache. This conversation was going nowhere, and she was tired. ''Geoff is a
different person now, David. He's not the same man.''

''That doesn't answer my question. Do you still love him?''

Devon's temper snapped. ''No! Yes! Maybe! I don't know!
Is that what you wanted to hear? I still have feelings for him.
I've been married to him for more than thirteen years after all,
and most of that time was happy. But I don't know if it's love
I feel. I hardly know the person he is now. Dammit, David, can't
we talk about this when I get home? This isn't the kind of conversation we should be having over the phone.''

''You want to break off the engagement, don't you?''

Devon went still. Her instinctive reaction was to scream, *no!*
But, she realized almost instantly that her reaction was engendered more by a desire for the protective shield of *being engaged*
than it was by fear of losing David. Being engaged forced her
to master and subdue her inexplicable attraction to Geoff. Being
engaged helped to keep her from plunging too deeply into a new
relationship with a man she no longer knew. Being engaged furnished an emotional buffer. But, she loved David. At least she
thought she did. ''Is that what *you* want?'' she asked.

''I won't play second fiddle to another man, Devon. But,
you're not going to turn this around on me. I asked you.''

''I don't have an answer, David. I honestly hadn't thought about it.''

''That pretty much gives me an answer, doesn't it? A couple of days ago, you wouldn't have had to think about it.''

That was true. Devon swallowed. ''Look, David, we'll have to talk about this when I get home.''

''Sure, Devon. Whatever you say. When exactly will that be?'' His tone was glacial and distant.

Devon closed her eyes in despair. ''You'll be home from your parents by Sunday afternoon, won't you? I'll come over to your place then, all right?''

''Why not? I don't have any plans.'' He hung up in her ear.

Lifting the receiver away from her head, Devon stared at it and then slowly replaced it on its cradle. Men!

Trying to dismiss the fact that a relationship she had relied upon was falling down around her ears, Devon went to the closet. The new dress hung before her, and she fingered it indecisively. She really shouldn't go to the dance. Not with her emotions in turmoil the way they were. But she had promised Geoff, and, to be honest with herself, she wanted to go. It had been a long time since she and Geoff had danced. She'd missed it. Would this new Geoff dance as well as the man she'd married? Would he lead with the same confidence? Hold her with the same gentleness? Or, would this be the area where this Geoff failed to live up to the expectations she held of the old Geoff?

Two and a half hours later, Devon's heart pounded erratically as Geoff led her through the steps of a dance, but its pounding was only partially from exertion. Having discarded his black suit jacket earlier, Geoff was excruciatingly handsome in black trousers and a snow-white shirt that accentuated his dark attractiveness to perfection. And she wondered how she could ever have doubted that her husband would, once again, meet her expectations.

Geoff danced as well as he always had, with an added measure of almost-menacing intensity, his eyes holding hers with unsmiling dynamism. He led her with the same confidence, and added a seductive quality of purpose. He held her with the same gentleness, but let her feel the unyielding strength in his arms and fingers. Devon swallowed as heat coiled in her lower abdomen. The changes in Geoff were subtle, but definite, and for the first time she admitted to herself that she found this darker, somehow more dangerous version of her husband almost unbearably attractive. He was seducing her. She knew it, and she was powerless to stop it, for his seduction was waged with his eyes and his soul rather than with words and touches. The sexual tension between them was so palpable that she was scarcely aware the music had stopped until Geoff drew her to a halt and offered her his arm.

"Would you like to get something to eat?" he asked. Tingles of awareness raced through her body in reaction to the caress of his slightly rough baritone voice. "The ladies usually cater a pretty good meal."

Devon glanced toward the colorfully decorated buffet tables. Apparently the tradition in Northridge was to leave the buffet in place most of the evening for people to help themselves. People who ate, drank less and they had fewer problems with inebriated citizens. As a result, the hall was organized in such a way that the dance went on in the center of the floor while people dined at the tables on the fringes.

Devon nodded mutely in response to Geoff's query. She wouldn't have been able to speak at that moment if her life had depended on it.

Geoff flashed her one of his all-too-fleeting grins. "Good, 'cause I have to confess I'm famished."

She was too, she realized. She'd just been so caught up in other sensations that she hadn't noticed. Devon managed to find her voice. "That's what happens when you're too wrapped up in your computer to even eat a sandwich. And I bet you didn't stop when I left either, did you?"

He shook his head. "I hooked up the modem and did some research on the Internet. Future-Tech has its own web page, did you know that?"

Devon frowned thoughtfully. "I don't recall anybody telling

me about it, but I could be mistaken.'' She looked at him. ''So, did you learn anything more?''

''I learned some things about Future-Tech that I needed to know,'' he said as he picked a plate from the stack at one end of the buffet. ''How many people it employs, management's stated commitment to ongoing research and development in order to turn out innovative products at competitive prices, some of the details about product lines—'' he shrugged ''—that kind of thing.''

Devon studied his profile. He seemed thoughtful. ''*You* are the one who had the commitment to research and development, Geoff,'' she said as she too picked up a plate. At Geoff's indication, she preceded him along the buffet table laden with food.

Minutes later, they found an unoccupied table and, after setting down his plate, Geoff left to get some wine for them. When he returned, they ate, shared half a bottle of the wine, and talked. Occasionally townsfolk would drop by the table to visit, wishing them a ''Merry Christmas!'' before bluntly asking ''Jack'' for an introduction to his companion. But they were unfailingly polite and welcoming, so Devon didn't mind the interruptions. She was simply enjoying the evening, basking in the accord that had developed between herself and Geoff, and trying not to contemplate their next dance. Geoff was so easy to be with. Too easy to be with. Because of that, because of her seesawing emotions for both David and Geoff, her own future was now up in the air. She could no longer contemplate the weeks and months ahead with any certainty. And yet, tonight, none of that seemed to matter.

''Where are the kids staying while you're here?'' he asked suddenly.

''With my parents.''

''Good,'' he said with a nod, and Devon realized that he'd been considering the possibility that she'd left the children with David. She almost smiled. Now *that* would have been funny. David was good with the kids—kind if not particularly demonstrative—but the thought of them in his neat orderly apartment where even the magazines were stacked in a tidy little pile on the coffee table was a bit like picturing a lively pair of Saint Bernard puppies in a china shop.

"I'm glad you're coming home in time for Christmas," she said, and then wasn't sure she should have. She didn't want him to misunderstand. "It'll be good for the children to have you back in their lives." She hoped that he'd be able to recapture the camaraderie he'd once had with them. She hoped that he never remembered whatever it was that had made him a stranger to them all, or that, if he did, this time he'd be able to deal with it.

Geoff nodded and then stared at her with something akin to horror in his eyes.

"What is it?" she asked.

He shook his head. "I don't know how I could have forgotten something so important."

"What?" she asked again.

"Presents!" he exclaimed. "We'll have to stop somewhere tomorrow so that I can get some presents."

Devon nodded. "Of course, if you like. But I'm sure the children will be happy simply to have you home."

"Kids need presents," he insisted.

They had just finished their supper and were planning their trip to Kelowna the next morning—Geoff had decided to follow her in his own vehicle since he'd need one when he got there anyway—when an exceptionally attractive blond woman approached their table. Devon estimated her age at twenty-five. "Hi, Jack," she said. She wore a short denim skirt, a fancy denim shirt decorated with sequins and metal studs, and high-heeled black sandals that showed far too much of her long, shapely legs as far as Devon was concerned.

"Marissa," Geoff acknowledged the woman with a nod and a faint smile. "You made it home all right the other night?"

She nodded. "If I hadn't, you would 'a heard about it," she said with a feigned pout. "Standing me up like that. I may never recover from the blow to my ego." Marissa's voice was deep and husky, a Kathleen Turner voice that was undoubtedly the envy of every woman in town.

"Uh-huh." Geoff didn't seem too concerned about the blow to her ego. "Marissa, I'd like you to meet my...friend, Devon Grayson. Devon, Marissa Grainger." His hesitation was so brief that it was barely noticeable. Was he beginning to think of her as his wife? Devon wondered. She found the idea inexplicably gratifying. But, of course, he couldn't very well introduce her as his wife without opening himself up to a million questions from everyone in Northridge who still knew him as Jack Keller.

Devon offered her hand and Marissa grasped it with a friendly smile. "Do you mind if I steal this gorgeous hunk of male for a minute, Devon? He owes me a dance and I mean to collect." She leaned forward to whisper in Devon's ear, "Not that it will do me much good. He seems to have appointed himself the big brother I never had ever since the first time I met him. But a lady has to try." She smiled and straightened, then continued in a normal voice, "I promise I'll bring him back."

"Of course," Devon said. Despite herself, she liked the unpretentious young woman. "Go ahead."

"You're sure?" Geoff asked her. When she nodded, he rose and moved out onto the dance floor with Marissa Grainger who, as fate would have it, looked remarkably like a slightly younger and more flamboyant version of Geoff's sister, Holly. No wonder Geoff had treated her like a sister. In some part of his mind, he must have felt the same protectiveness toward her that he'd always felt for Holly.

But even knowing that didn't keep Devon from feeling just a tiny bit jealous, for Geoff and Marissa looked wonderful on the floor together. His dark handsomeness was a perfect foil for her fair beauty; her flamboyant grace an interesting contrast to his restrained strength.

"Well now," a voice suddenly boomed at her side, "I can't leave an attractive lady sitting all by herself at a public dance. That would be a sin for sure." Devon looked up into the handsome face of a tall blond man. "I'm Tom Kane," he said, with a drop-dead gorgeous smile as he offered her his hand.

Devon grasped his hand and smiled. "Devon Grayson."

He nodded. "Merry Christmas, Devon," he said in a low voice. "May I have the pleasure of this dance?"

Devon hesitated, but Geoff was still out on the dance floor with Marissa. "Why not?" she said with a smile. Kane offered her his hand and she accepted, allowing him to lead her onto the dance floor.

Besides being breathtakingly handsome in a Slavic way, Kane was a smooth and accomplished dancer, Devon discovered. Yet dancing with him was comfortable rather than exciting.

"I understand you're in town visiting Jack Keller?"

Devon looked up at him. "Yes. Do you know him well?"

Kane shrugged. "It's a small town. Everyone knows everybody to some degree. So, how long have you known him?"

Devon hesitated. She didn't want to leave Geoff open to uncomfortable questions from his friends until he was ready to discuss their situation. "Not long," she said. She wasn't really being dishonest. After all, when she thought about it, she really hadn't known *this* Geoff long at all.

"Did you meet around here?"

Devon nodded. "At Deer Lake."

"Really?" Kane's eyes searched her face and Devon received the distinct impression that he didn't believe her, though why it should matter to him was beyond her understanding. "That's interesting."

She nodded, but offered him nothing more as the song came to an end and they separated. Devon looked across the dance floor to see Geoff escorting Marissa to a table on the other side of the hall. A handsome young Brad Pitt look-alike was already seated there, apparently awaiting Marissa's return. Her date, no doubt. Geoff said something to him, the two men shook hands, and then Geoff turned to make his way back to their table. That was when he caught sight of Mr. Kane with her.

His expression didn't change so much as it...froze in place, an unreadable mask. He veered toward them.

Kane smiled. "Hi, Jack. I was just about to escort your lovely lady friend back to your table."

Geoff nodded cordially, but he didn't smile. Then again, he

rarely did. Kane didn't seem to take it amiss. "No need," Geoff said. "I was planning on asking her to dance anyway."

Kane stepped back. "Well then, it was nice meeting you, Ms. Grayson. Thank you for the dance. Enjoy yourselves."

"Thank you. We will," she said. Geoff said nothing.

She turned to face him, stepping naturally into his arms as the music started up again. "Is something wrong?"

His gaze was still on Kane. "What did Sergeant Kane want?"

"*Sergeant* Kane?" she repeated.

He looked at her then. "You didn't know?"

She shook her head. "He introduced himself as Tom Kane."

Geoff studied her face for a moment as though seeking something. "Did he ask you anything in particular?"

"Just how long I'd known you. I told him not long. Why?"

He seemed to relax slightly then. "No reason I guess. Just my instinctive paranoia surfacing again." Then, with a fleeting smile, he said, "But, let's just forget all that and enjoy the dance, shall we?"

It was an invitation Devon couldn't refuse. She felt his large warm hand on the small of her back, felt his thighs brush against hers as they moved, and knew she didn't want this night to end. Tomorrow would bring with it so many uncertainties, so many decisions she wasn't prepared to make. For tonight, all she wanted to do was bask in the sensation of being in Geoff's arms again. Her limbs grew languorous and her blood thickened until it seemed to throb through her veins. Her breasts swelled and tightened, becoming sensitive to the slightest brush of contact with his chest. And her heart contracted as she drank in his handsome face with her eyes. How could she have forgotten how absolutely gorgeous he was? And what the hell was she going to do about her complete lack of resistance to his charm?

The music came to a stop and the musician spoke into the microphone. "Well, folks, for the second time tonight we have a couple standing right under the mistletoe. And a real nice couple they make too. Jack Keller, if you don't kiss that lovely lady you're with, I'll come down there and do it for you. With Angela's permission, of course." The speaker waggled his brows questioningly at a woman sitting on the sidelines who gave him a mock scowl and shook her head. ''Oops.'' He laughed. ''Guess you'll have to do it, Jack.''

As the crowd began to hoot and clap in good-natured encouragement, Devon cast a startled glance up. Sure enough, they'd ended the dance standing directly beneath the mistletoe. She felt the heat of a flush crawling up her cheeks. *Oh, boy! Now what had she gotten herself into?*

As she lowered her gaze to meet Geoff's she found herself gazing into smoldering green embers, and the sound of the crowd faded to a dull roar as blood rushed through her veins in response to the accelerated pounding of her heart. Without a word, Geoff lowered his head to press his lips to hers. It was a chaste kiss. The kind of kiss one bestowed amidst a crowd of people. But the contact was pure velvet heat and it robbed her of both breath and thought.

And then it was over, and the sound of the crowd rushed back in. ''Would you like a drink?'' Geoff asked.

Devon nodded. ''Yes, please,'' she replied in a tone scarcely above a whisper. She needed the opportunity to regroup, to gather her muddled senses.

It was getting late, and they'd danced most of the night. Geoff sighed inwardly—he'd actually begun to think of himself as Geoff again—and wished he could delay the inevitable end of the evening. Then, he looked down once more at the woman in his arms. God, she was beautiful. He couldn't seem to get enough of looking at her. Slowly, leisurely, he traced the delicate bones of her bare shoulders with his eyes wishing he could do it with his lips instead. Then, lifting his gaze to hers, he almost missed a step. For the sultry, hungry look in her eyes could mean only one thing: she was as attracted to him as he was to her. But in the next instant she blinked and focused her gaze beyond his shoulder, and he couldn't be absolutely sure that he hadn't simply imagined something that he very much wanted to see.

''Well folks, it's well past midnight and this will be the last song,'' the band's singer suddenly announced. ''Merry Christmas everyone! You've been a great audience, and we hope you enjoyed the evening.''

Oh, yeah! he had definitely enjoyed the evening, Geoff thought as the audience clapped their appreciation. And he still wasn't ready to let Devon out of his arms. Unfortunately, he wasn't going to have a choice in the matter. As the song ended, he released her with more than a twinge of regret. "I guess we'd better get going."

She nodded. "Yes. We'll want to be on the road by mid-morning at the latest." Did she too sound just a little bit regretful? He hoped so.

"I could have danced another hour or more," he mused.

She smiled. "It's been a long time, and it was fun."

They retrieved their coats, and left the hall. The night air was crisp, condensing their breath in small clouds of steam as they moved across the parking lot to the Bronco. Geoff unlocked the door and silently aided Devon in before moving around to the driver's side. After starting the vehicle and activating the heater, he turned to her. He could barely see her in the darkness—it was an overcast night—but he could smell her perfume. At odd moments throughout the night, he'd caught himself inhaling deeply in order to better appreciate its gentle fragrance. He would never grow tired of its subtle exotic flowery scent. "We still have some plans to make," he said. "Would you like to stop by my place for coffee?" The hall where the dance had been held was on Lake Shore Drive, beyond his place, so they'd have to pass his cabin on the way back to the bed-and-breakfast anyway.

He could feel her gaze on him in the darkness, and for the longest time, she didn't reply. Finally she murmured, "What kind of plans?"

"Where I'm going to stay in Kelowna, for one," he said. "When you're going to reintroduce me to the staff at Future-Tech and what we're going to tell them. What kind of role I'm to play in the kids' lives for the first while. That kind of thing." He shrugged. "I want as much as possible settled before we get there, and since we're driving down in separate vehicles, we won't be able to discuss it on the way."

He sensed more than saw her nod. ''All right, Geoff. But I can't stay for long.'' Her tone was wary. She probably didn't trust his motives.

Smart lady! Because he fully intended to seduce her, to make her admit that there was still something between them, while he still had the home advantage.

Chapter 7

Devon stared out the window at the blackness of the night surrounding them, isolating them. What the hell she was doing? Geoff might be a stranger to her in many ways, but she couldn't deny that some kind of chemistry was at work between them. And that chemistry was at least as powerful as the one that had gripped them when she'd first met Geoff so many years ago, perhaps even more so. Considering that, she was a fool to go to his place where, without the buffer of being surrounded by a couple of hundred townspeople, anything might happen. It was unfair to David, to herself, and to Geoff.

She had made a commitment to another man. Although technically she was still married to Geoff that didn't make him any less a stranger. He did so many things differently.

Would he make love differently?

Her breath froze in her throat as the errant thought rampaged through her mind wreaking havoc even as it aroused interest and provoked forbidden but oh-so-tempting images.

"Are you all right?" Geoff's much-too-sexy voice reached across the space that separated them to tantalize her.

She nodded, but it took her a second longer to find her voice. "Yes, of course. Why do you ask?"

"I thought I heard you gasp or something."

Had she made a sound? "I yawned," she lied.

Her answer seemed to satisfy him and she retreated into her thoughts once more. She shouldn't have agreed to stop at his place to talk. She didn't trust him.

Heavens! She didn't trust herself.

In the grip of the magnetism and fascination that raged between them, what would she do if he kissed her again? Probably keel over helplessly in the grip of her own lust, she thought in self-disgust. If only the sexual side of things between herself and David had been better, perhaps she wouldn't have felt so...needy.

She grimaced. Now, she was trying to blame her own weakness on David.

"Here we are," Geoff said as he turned into the drive.

Uh-oh! "Geoff...maybe this isn't such a good idea."

"What? Talking?"

His question made her feel foolish and she sought desperately for another reason why this was not a reasonable time for a discussion. "We have to get up early and be on the road," she protested weakly.

He nodded. "In separate vehicles. That's precisely why we need to talk now."

Devon sighed. Well, she would simply have to be strong—for all their sakes. That was all there was to it.

Minutes later, after hanging their coats in the closet, Geoff led her into the living room. "Have a seat," he said, indicating the cognac-colored leather sofa. "I'll just start the fire to take the chill out of the air and then go get us a couple of drinks."

The last thing Devon wanted to do was watch him start the fire. As he squatted down and began transferring wood from the bin to the fireplace, she couldn't help noticing how his trousers hugged his firm butt and muscular thighs. He reached forward, and his silk shirt grew taut across his broad back, defining the rippling power inherent in his torso. Her heart staggered and then righted itself, and she forced her gaze upward. But even that didn't help. Geoff's face in profile was about the sexiest thing she'd seen in a long time. She loved the bluish shadow of the whiskers that lurked beneath his clean-shaven jaw. She admired the bold blade of his nose, the arch of his cheekbone. And she itched to caress that perpetually arched eyebrow.

"Maybe I should make the coffee while you finish the fire," she suggested a little desperately.

He turned his head to look at her, and for an instant he said nothing as his intense green eyes held her captive. Then he favored her with that all-too-fleeting grin that did strange things to her insides, and said, "Actually I've been thinking I'd rather have wine. What do you think?"

Wine to fortify her sagging spine and bolster her dissipating resistance. That would be a good thing. She nodded. "Wine is fine. Do you want me to get it?"

He shook his head. "You wouldn't be able to find it. I'll get it in a second."

And so Devon had little choice but to stay where she was, but she kept her gaze fastened on the fire Geoff was starting, rather than on the man.

Half an hour later, most of Geoff's questions had been discussed and answers arrived at. He would stay with her parents until he could find an apartment to rent that was close to her place. She would reintroduce him to the staff at Future-Tech on the Tuesday following the Christmas weekend. They'd decided to tell the staff the truth about Geoff's condition, for there was nothing to be gained by dissembling. And, finally, they'd decided that Geoff should be involved in the children's lives on a daily basis if he so chose; it would be a relief for Devon to share with another person the responsibility for some of the dashing around to club meetings and music lessons.

When Geoff excused himself to go to the washroom, Devon sipped her wine, stared at the fire and contemplated how warm and pleasant it was just sitting there. But she really should finish her wine and get going. It was past one-thirty in the morning and they had a long drive to face in just a few hours.

A moment later, Geoff returned. "You didn't say anything

tonight about my dancing," he said. "I can't help wondering if I dance the same, or not."

Devon nodded. "You were always good at dancing. I didn't notice a change." *Except in the way you hold a woman,* she added silently. But that was one observation she would not make aloud.

He nodded and seemed relieved. "Did we ever dance to anything besides country music?"

She smiled, remembering. "Yes, actually. About six or seven years ago you dragged me off to some classes in ballroom dance. You wanted to learn the tango and salsa and I-forget-what-else." She shrugged. "Must have been the fault of your Latin ancestry."

"And did I learn?"

"Oh, yeah," she said wryly. "You excelled, although I can't say the same thing for myself. I'm not very accomplished in the natural-rhythm department."

"You know," he said as he rose and moved across the room to the stereo, "I think I have some ballroom music. I didn't really know why I bought it at the time." He extracted a CD from a small stack inside a cabinet. "Here it is." Within seconds, he'd turned on the stereo, put the disc in and programmed it to play the third song. Then, carrying the remote, he strode back across the room to Devon and extended his hand. "This one's a tango. Let's give it a try."

"Oh, no. It's been too long," she argued, shaking her head for emphasis as she resisted the compelling urge to take his hand. "I hardly remember how."

"Who cares? There's nobody here but us."

Devon swallowed. That was definitely a big part of the problem.

"Besides," he continued, "I need to find out if *I* remember." When she still didn't take his hand, he leaned forward to grasp her by the arm and tug her to her feet.

"Geoff, I—"

But he placed a finger over her lips to circumvent her argument. Then, looking deep into her eyes with his intense unreadable gaze, while her lips still tingled from the touch of his finger, he said, ''Please?'' in a husky tone that she was powerless to resist.

Wordlessly, she allowed him to lead her to the area behind the sofa which provided them with more space. It was about seven feet wide and the entire length of the living room. Still it did not have the proportions of a ballroom. ''There's not enough room to tango,'' Devon tried one last protest.

''We'll abbreviate,'' he responded, undeterred. With a flick of his wrist, he hit a button on the remote and then tossed it onto the sofa. The lively melody of a tango charged the air, the music itself seeming to swirl and dance around them. Geoff held her gaze with his, imprisoning her within his embrace as he began to move; his rhythm, as always, perfect; his movements fast, smooth and incredibly sexy. The minute stretched, absorbing the next until each minute ran one into the other and the passage of time had no meaning. She was scarcely aware of her own feet moving as she followed him in the steps of the dance, although her movements were undoubtedly far from perfect.

And then they were dancing cheek to cheek, their arms outstretched before them as they danced to the far end of the living room, but even without eye contact Devon felt his power, his charisma, like a palpable thing. He twirled her and, once again, his gaze locked onto hers, powerful, magnetic, and...searingly hot. Oh, God! He wanted her. She read that message in the fiery depths of his gaze as clearly as she heard the erotic, pulsing beat of the music enveloping them. Her side tingled as they danced body to body for the span of a turn and Geoff's body heat penetrated his shirt to beguile her. The aphrodisiac scent of his cologne reached out to tantalize her, and his provocative green eyes conveyed silent promises she dared not allow herself to believe.

He dipped then, catching her by surprise, and she clung to him, staring up at him wide-eyed as the music swelled around them to reach one final crescendo before falling silent. The only sounds in the room were those of their own labored breathing, and the snapping and crackling of the blaze in the fireplace. Keeping her suspended, supported entirely by his strength, Geoff slowly, wordlessly lowered his head to capture her lips with his, to plunge his tongue into her mouth, to rob her of what was left of her sanity.

He tasted of wine. Bold, intoxicating and sensual.

Her body felt heavy and ripe, pulsing with life. Desire—no, it was stronger than desire—*need,* throbbed between them. Hers? His? It was impossible to tell, for it had taken on a life of its own. His kiss grew harder, more feverish, searing her with its fiery potency. Excitement coiled within her, impossible to deny. Madness.

Without quite knowing how it happened, she found herself cradled in his arms. Within two long strides, he placed her on the sheepskin rug that lay before the fireplace. A romantic setting, but the sensations raging through her, crackling in the air between them like the static energy of a storm, were anything but romantic.

As he lowered himself to lie at her side, his hand swept down her body, molding her breasts, exploring her body through the constriction of her clothing. Then, leaning forward to kiss her senseless again, he swept his hand down her body until his warm palm lay on her lower abdomen. So close to that secret part of her that still remembered him so very well, and yet...so very far away. Devon arched helplessly, instinctively, in invitation, seeking more. Oh, yes! Why had she never felt this mindless excitement with David?

Oh, no! No, this was wrong!

She tore her mouth from his. "Geoff—" As her heart raced frantically in her chest, she tried desperately to put the brakes on. "We...can't," she murmured. "I have to go, Geoff." Her voice sounded small and uncertain even to her own ears. "Now!" she added more firmly.

He leaned away to look down at her. "You're feeling guilty, aren't you? I'm beginning to believe that what we have here is something...special. Something that may be the best thing that could ever happen for both of us. And you can't see that because you're feeling guilty about spending time with your own husband."

"Technically you are still my husband, Geoff," Devon said as she sat up and hastily adjusted the thin straps of her gown. "I can't argue with that. But that doesn't give me the right to be unfaithful to David." Avoiding his gaze, she smoothed down her skirt and rose.

Geoff was silent for a moment. Then he asked, "Can you honestly tell me that you'll be able to sleep with David again, after what we shared here, and not think of me...of us?"

Devon closed her eyes and swallowed. He was right. What they had was special in a way she couldn't define. She felt more connected to him than ever before. If she were to sleep with David again now, she would feel guilty on Geoff's behalf. "No," she finally responded in a tone scarcely above a whisper.

"So what are you going to do?"

"I don't know." Her tone was almost a wail of despair. Realizing that, she got a grip on her emotions and repeated more calmly, "I don't know, Geoff. Right now, I have to go. I have to be alone to—"

The sound of a vehicle tearing noisily into the yard interrupted her. Geoff frowned, his expression making it clear that he did not look kindly upon the intrusion. "Who the devil could that be?" He began to walk toward to window to check, but before he'd made it half the distance something struck the door with a loud thump. "What the hell!"

Geoff yanked the door open in time to see a pair of red taillights, glowing like two evil red eyes, turn out of the drive onto the main road and disappear.

"What is it?" Devon asked.

"Hmm?" he asked absently, still concerned with trying to figure out who had been in the pickup he'd seen pulling out of his driveway.

"What hit the door?"

Geoff looked down. Two feet away from the threshold lay a grapefruit-sized rock with something white secured to it. Frowning, Geoff cast one more glance in the direction the vehicle had gone, and then bent to retrieve it. "It's a rock," he said in belated reply to Devon's question. Devon came up behind him as he

examined it. Two elastic bands secured a folded piece of paper
to the stone. He glanced at Devon, noting the curiosity and apprehension in her eyes that mirrored his own gut reaction. Whatever this was, it wouldn't be good.

"What does it say?" she asked in a tone barely above a whisper.

Geoff removed the elastic bands and unfolded the scrap of
white paper, holding it up to the light to read the typewritten
words. Devon read over his shoulder.

You were lucky the other night. You've got another chance.
Learn from it. STAY DEAD! Or the next time you disappear, you won't be coming back.

"Oh, my God!" Horror dawned in Devon's eyes as she lifted
her gaze to his. "This means... My God!" Turning away, she
walked to the sofa and then sat down with a plop, as though her
legs could no longer support her.

Geoff closed the door. It meant that Sergeant Kane was right.
The explosion at the Noralco site had been meant for Geoff. But
why? It didn't make sense. He had no enemies. At least...none
that he remembered.

"We should call the police."

He looked at Devon and shook his head. "Kane already thinks
the Noralco explosion was meant for me. If he knows about this,
there's no way he'll want me to leave town tomorrow."

Devon frowned. "He can't hold you. You've done nothing
wrong."

"I don't care. I don't trust cops. We'll keep this between you
and I until we have something more. Some *proof.* All right?"

Fear shone from her eyes like a beacon as she stared at him.
"All right, but...why would someone murder Spencer and Holly,
Geoff? Why..." Her gaze dropped to stare blankly at the win-
dow. "Why would they try to kill us?"

"Us?" he echoed. What was she talking about?

She nodded. "I was supposed to be on that plane, too. Remember?"

No, he didn't remember because he *couldn't* remember a goddamn thing! But...was she right? He'd assumed that the person who'd written the note had simply known of his disappearance. But what if...? He looked back at the note. *Or, the next time you disappear, you won't be coming back.* Whoever had written that line had definitely known him *before* he'd become Jack Keller.

Had a killer emerged from the fog of his past to try again? How could he fight someone he couldn't remember? Feeling suddenly overwhelmed by the enormity of the problem facing him, he swore softly beneath his breath.

Devon must have heard the despondency in the word, for she rose and came forward to place her small white hand on his arm reassuringly. "Don't worry, Geoff. We'll beat him, whoever he is. We'll do it together."

He looked down at the woman standing at his side. The wife he didn't remember who would stand at his side in times of trouble. The wife for whom, he was very much afraid, he was coming to care far too much. The wife who wouldn't make love with him because of her commitment to another man. "Yeah? How? I can't even remember who this person is, let alone why he wants me dead. How do I fight that?"

She frowned. "Well, the first thing we have to do, when we get back to Kelowna, is find out what it is you knew that threatened this person. We'll go through all your papers and things. I'm sure we'll find something that will give us a hint as to who he is."

"I didn't even tell *you* what was going on. Do you honestly think I would have written anything down?"

She met his gaze resolutely. "Yes," she said. "I do." Her hand was warm on his arm, even through the fabric of his shirtsleeve. "You recorded everything. Sometimes in a shorthand that you yourself had trouble deciphering later, but you definitely would have written something."

He considered her for a moment, then said, "I'll drive you

back to Mrs. Wright's.'' Stepping away from her disturbing touch, he moved toward the closet.

Confusion flared in her expression. "Did I say something wrong, Geoff?"

He retrieved their coats without answering because he didn't know how to respond. He was angry and frustrated, and Devon was part of that. Her reassurance of resolving this problem *together* was meaningless to him if she couldn't allow them to be together in the other aspects of their lives as well. But...he didn't want her in danger either. And right now he wanted to get her to safety while he did a little early morning investigating and thinking. He needed to think things through.

"Geoff?"

He looked at her. "You didn't say anything wrong, Devon. It's late, that's all. Almost 2:00 a.m. and we have a long drive tomorrow."

She studied him, aware that he was avoiding discussion. "I don't want to leave you alone, Geoff. Not now. Not with some maniac out there waiting for you."

He was silent a moment and then said, "I'll be fine. Come on. I'll drive you back."

Staring at him with huge wounded and worried eyes, she accepted her coat from him in silence. It seemed that all he had done since leaving the dance had led to hurting her in some way. He gritted his teeth in frustration. Damn!

The noiseless darkness of the early morning still blanketed the region when they stepped outside a second later to make their way across the yard to the Bronco. Their breath hung in the chilled air. Wordlessly, Geoff opened the door for her and handed her in before walking around to climb in and start the vehicle.

Both deep in thought, neither of them spoke until he pulled up in front of the bed-and-breakfast. Then Geoff put the vehicle into park and half turned on the seat to face her, stretching his arm out along its back. "I don't want you to worry about me, Devon. I doubt that there's any reason to be frightened. At least not yet. That note was a warning which probably means we have some time yet before the person tries anything again.''

"Not worrying is something that's easier said than done.''

He nodded. ''I know. Just...'' He broke off and sighed, raking his fingers back through his hair. ''There's something else I wanted to say.''

She looked at him and waited.

For a moment he looked out the windshield in silence and then, finally, he seemed to find the words he wanted. ''I'm sorry if I hurt you tonight, Devon. I never intended to.'' He looked at her then, his eyes shining with some nameless emotion in the darkness. ''But I won't apologize for what almost happened between us either,'' he said in a low voice. ''I'd be lying if I said I was sorry.''

She nodded. ''I know you didn't intend to hurt me, Geoff. It's just that...I'm not ready to deepen our relationship.''

"You say you're not ready.... You aren't still planning to marry David then?''

Stricken, Devon stared into the night. She *had* said that. Did that mean that subconsciously she was planning on being with Geoff? ''I don't know. I need to think.''

"About David?''

"Partly.'' She nodded. ''I have to talk with him, work out where we're going from here...if anywhere. But there are other considerations, too.''

"Like?''

She shrugged. ''Like the fact that I really don't know you anymore, nor you me. My relationship with David is steady, reliable. Whereas this thing between us is...''

"Surprising, unpredictable and exciting,'' he finished for her.

She shook her head. ''I was going to say 'uncertain.' We still don't know where it's heading. And, we still don't know what happened to us, to our marriage, the last time we were together.'' She looked at him then across the darkened expanse of the truck. ''After tonight, I'm beginning to suspect that you were in serious trouble and that you kept it from me in a misguided attempt to keep me safe. And I'm frightened. I'm not sure I can give up something sure and reliable for something uncertain no matter how exciting it might be. Because it might also be dangerous and I have two children to consider.''

Silence enveloped them for a moment, then he nodded and changed the subject, startling her. ''You have a key to get in?''

Devon stared at him. Wasn't he going to argue? Give her reasons why she should take a chance on him? But she answered his question without voicing her confusion. ''Yes, I have a key. Eva thought I might get in late because of the dance.''

He nodded his understanding. ''Well, I'll come by in the morning then, and we can head out.''

''All right.'' She reached for the door handle and then hesitated. She didn't want to leave him, she realized. No matter what he said, she was afraid that the nebulous person who'd stolen their lives from them before would take Geoff from her again before they'd had a chance to even get reacquainted. And so, a little desperately, she stalled. ''If you're taking a leave of absence, and someone else will be doing your job, what are you doing with all your things?''

He shrugged. ''I don't have much. The cabin and all its furnishings go with the position. I've just got my clothing, some books and CDs, and a few personal items. I'll take everything.''

''Oh.'' Devon nodded and swallowed. When he'd told her he was only taking a leave of absence, she'd thought it good that he wasn't completely cutting his ties to Northridge in the event that things didn't work out for him back in Kelowna. But in actuality, she realized, his ties here were not that strong. Nothing that couldn't be severed with a single phone call. Was that good or bad? She wasn't certain. And she couldn't think of anything else to say. ''Well, I guess I'd better get in. I'll see you later then. About nine?''

He nodded. ''About nine.''

Geoff watched Devon go into the house before he put the Bronco in gear and returned home. Halting on the side of the road, he removed the flashlight he always carried from the glove compartment and got out. Had his visitor left any tracks? When

Geoff had left to drive Devon home, he'd been careful to keep the Bronco as close to the other side of the drive as possible, just in case.

Now, he stooped to carefully examine the road in the artificial illumination of his flashlight. The snow had made him hopeful that he'd find something, but it was well-packed on his drive with a layer of solid gravel beneath it. A thorough examination revealed precisely nothing. Damn!

Gritting his teeth in frustration, for a fraction of a moment he considered Devon's suggestion of calling the police, but immediately rejected the idea. There was nothing Kane could do on the little bit of evidence that Geoff had to give him, except ask more questions. Questions that Geoff wasn't prepared to answer yet.

Returning to his vehicle, he pulled it into the yard and went into the house to stand staring at the sheepskin rug where he and Devon had lain together for so short a time. He pictured her as she'd looked with her fair skin flushed with the heat of their passion. Her clear gray eyes glazed with a carnal hunger that swelled his ego along with his heart. God, she was beautiful. He wished the night had ended differently. That they'd made love and had awakened wrapped in each other's arms to face the day and the possibility of a future together. But Devon wasn't ready for that.

It was probably easier for him, he realized. He had entered their relationship with no preconceived expectations or apprehensions. No emotional baggage associated with the bad times they'd had. No ties to other people. He could simply accept what they found together and enjoy it. It was all new to him. Devon was new to him. But, when she looked at him, Devon saw a man to whom she'd already been married for almost fourteen years. A man who not only didn't remember her or any of their time together, but who acted differently than she expected him to. A man whom she didn't trust not to hurt her as he had hurt her once before.

And to earn her trust he had to find out what had happened to them. Somehow. With or without the return of his memory.

He swallowed. He had the feeling that it wasn't going to be easy. Yet, the more time he spent with her, the more convinced he was that they were supposed to be together. He didn't understand it, it was just a feeling, but somehow it felt right. Tonight had pretty much clinched it for him. But Devon was right: nothing was certain by any stretch of the imagination and he couldn't offer her the assurances she needed. There was no sense in even trying until he got back to Kelowna. Hopefully, once there, he could jog some repressed memory and figure out what had gone wrong between them the first time. Figure out who was responsible for all the pain in their lives and stop him before he caused more.

But what if he couldn't?

He hadn't realized until this instant how much he was counting on his memory eventually returning to him once he got back into familiar surroundings. Yet the doctor had already told him that, after so much time, it wasn't likely. Geoff had simply refused to believe him. What would he do if the doctor was right?

He didn't know.

Noting that it was now almost 3:00 a.m., Geoff decided that he'd grab a couple of hours of sleep. He'd undoubtedly be awake by six-thirty anyway, no matter how little sleep he'd had; that was usually the way his body worked. It was a rare day indeed that he slept as late as he had the morning after Devon's arrival.

When he woke, he'd finish his packing and do some more research on the computer. He still had a lot to master after all, a lot of old learning to dredge to the surface. It would keep his mind off the meeting to come in Kelowna, the thought of which was now beginning to terrify him.

It was not the meeting with his parents-in-law that worried him. Nor even the meetings with former colleagues and employees whom he would not remember. No, it was the upcoming meeting with his children he found increasingly daunting.

What if they didn't accept him? What if he was somehow less in their eyes than the father they remembered?

Forcing the unwelcome thought from his mind, Geoff tried to focus on the positive aspects of the meeting to come. Like the fact that, for the first time he could remember, he would be spending Christmas with a family. *His* family. He wouldn't be alone. That meant a lot to him. But from that importance, too, arose fear. For if his children rejected him, the picture that had formed in his mind of a family Christmas would be shattered.

No! He refused to contemplate such things. Catching sight of the sheepskin rug, he eagerly grasped the distraction it offered as a picture of Devon lying there flashed into his memory and fantasies of what might have been insinuated themselves into his mind. He welcomed the torturous distraction. Hopefully, it would keep his mind from inventing ever-more-depressing scenarios about what lay before him the next day.

Devon tossed and turned in her bed, trying desperately to get just a couple of hours of sleep, but it was beginning to look pretty unlikely. Her emotions and thoughts were in turmoil, her mind caught in an endless loop of questions. What if...? How...? When...? But through it all, she had reached one conclusion: she loved David. But the love she felt for him was the love of friendship—a steady, secure emotion for a steady, dependable relationship. What she felt for Geoff was volatile, but more compelling by far. Powerful and hot and oh, so unquenchable. But was it love? Probably, she concluded. In all likelihood, if she was honest with herself, she had probably never stopped loving him.

Having admitted that to herself, could she accept less? Could she settle for the stability David represented when her heart and soul craved the excitement to be found in Geoff's embrace?

No, she couldn't. It wouldn't be fair to any of them.

But what if things between herself and Geoff didn't work out? If she was still in love with her husband, the man she remembered, what if she could not feel those same emotions for the man he had become in the last two years?

It was a risk she'd have to take. She couldn't very well keep David hanging around, a spare man in case the one she had didn't work out.

She swallowed the lump in her throat and faced the truth. She was going to have to break it off with David when she saw him next.

She remembered their last telephone conversation, and how he'd asked her then if she wanted to break off their relationship. Somehow he'd seen it coming before she had. As though he'd been forewarned by some intuitive male instinct, David must have known, or at least suspected, that her coming here would spell the end of their relationship.

Devon closed her eyes and finally allowed the tears she'd held back to trickle out of the corners of her eyes over her temples and into her hair. Damn! She hated the thought of hurting David. Of hurting the children again, for they'd just begun to accept the idea of David as their stepfather. But what else could she do and still be true to herself?

She wanted Geoff in her life again.

Fear knotted in her throat as she recalled the note that had been delivered tonight. Keeping Geoff in her life until they'd had the chance to at least get to know each other again meant foiling the plans of whomever strove to steal him from her. How was she going to do that? Especially with him living alone in an apartment somewhere?

She frowned into the darkness. Only one solution presented itself. He'd have to move in with her and the children. To hell with the idea of him finding an apartment. She had a guest room.

And to hell with the man who wanted Geoff to *stay dead,* because she wanted him alive. And she was going to do everything in her power to keep him that way even if it meant never letting him out of her sight. She refused to lose him a second time.

Twenty-four-hour surveillance. That didn't sound so bad. Not when Geoff was the subject. A soft smile curved her lips as she surrendered to sleep at last and dreamed of better days.

Chapter 8

They'd been travelling for about four hours, although, since they'd stopped in Prince George in order for Geoff to do his Christmas shopping, they hadn't travelled as far as they should have in that time. Recalling Geoff's enjoyment as he searched for gifts, Devon smiled and glanced in the rearview mirror. What the...?

Where had that big eighteen-wheeler come from? And what *exactly* was the driver trying to do? If he wasn't careful—

My God! "Geoff!" Although there was no one to hear her, Devon screamed his name as the Bronco was forced off the road into the ravine on their right. "No!" In panic, she pulled over to the edge and began to stop only to find that the huge semi-truck was now crowding her, pushing her inexorably toward the guardrail.

The driver was deliberately running them off the road!

Reaching the end of the guardrail, with the semi crowding ever closer, Devon had nowhere to go but down...and she went, steering the Jeep down into the ravine as well as possible. Thank God that, although quite deep, it wasn't that steep a drop.

"Are you all right?" Geoff demanded as he jerked open the door of her drastically canted vehicle a few seconds later.

Dazed, Devon tore her gaze away from the sight of the tree trunk crumpling her left fender and raised her eyes to meet Geoff's concerned gaze. "Yes. Yes, I think so. Are you?"

"Yes. Yes, I'm fine. Are you sure you're all right?"

She nodded again.

"Thank God!" he said even as his eyes searched her for confirmation. Satisfied that, although shaken, she was physically unhurt, he finally allowed himself to vent some of the rage that was choking him. "That bastard must have been waiting for just the right moment to force us both off the road. This is the only stretch of road where we were travelling slow enough and close enough together for him to do it."

Devon stared at him with shock whitening her lips. "He said to *stay dead,* but..."

Wordlessly, Geoff offered her his hand and she accepted, sliding from the Jeep. He immediately placed a protective arm around her, willing her to lean on him, to accept his support. "He didn't even stop. We're just lucky that in hitting this ravine neither of the vehicles rolled. I thought for sure you were going to hit that guardrail and be sandwiched there with nowhere to go."

Too shaken to deny her need of his support, she leaned into him as Geoff wrapped his arms around her in comfort. "I was so frightened that I just turned the wheel when I reached the end of the guardrail and drove down into the ravine. But...why would a truck force us off the road?"

Geoff turned his head to look in the direction the eighteen-wheeler had disappeared. "I imagine he was paid to."

Devon closed her eyes tightly for a moment, as though willing it not to be so. "Did you see a sign on the truck or anything?"

With a shake of his head, Geoff returned his attention to Devon. "No. Come on," he said softly. "We'll use the cell phone in the Bronco to call for help and then we'd better get up to the road so that they can find us."

By the time they'd finished with tow trucks and police reports it was nearing 6:00 p.m. and already long dark. Unfortunately, there'd been little they could tell the police about the truck that had run them off the road. Neither of them had received more than an impression of dark-blue paint and chrome as the semi had come up behind them. Thankfully both the Jeep and the Bronco, although damaged, remained driveable and they'd be able to continue on. But they wouldn't reach Kelowna today.

Sitting in the restaurant where they'd had dinner, Devon stared solemnly into her coffee cup. "This will be the first Christmas Eve I've missed spending with the children. They've outgrown setting out milk and cookies for Santa, but still...I'll miss sharing in their excitement."

Geoff studied her but didn't know what to say that would comfort her. "Try not to think about it," he said finally. "We'll drive on a little farther tonight so that we don't have so far to go tomorrow. You'll be there when they open their gifts."

Devon straightened. "Of course. Mom said the kids were fine with it, when I called. Don't mind me, I'm just being sentimental. They're my babies, after all." She smiled, but the gesture was obviously a bit forced.

After a quiet moment, she spoke again. "Geoff—"

"Hmm?"

"There's something I've been meaning to talk to you about." He set down his cup, tensing despite himself. "Go on."

"Well... I know we decided that you'd get your own apartment, but after last night and today...I'd just rather you stayed with us. If you want to that is. I have a guest room that you're welcome to use until we work our way through this tangle. I know the kids will enjoy having you with us."

She wanted to keep him close. She was worried about him. She cared. Maybe not a lot yet, but she cared. "I'd like that," he said.

It was early afternoon when Devon and Geoff arrived in Kelowna. The city had little of the snow they'd encountered farther north; nature insulated the valley against the colder weather. Geoff followed Devon through the city, bright with Christmas decorations, to the long, low brick house that her parents had lived in for more than twelve years. Situated in an older though fairly affluent area of the city, the house had a three-car garage, beautifully landscaped yard, and a pool in the backyard. The pool had been installed for Devon's mother; it had been the only thing Devon could remember her asking for in almost forty years of marriage.

Now, Devon observed Geoff in the rearview mirror as he pulled into the drive behind her and sat gripping the steering wheel, watching her and studying the house. Getting out of the Jeep, she arched her back to stretch out the kinks caused by the long drive, and then turned to look at him. Why was he just sitting there?

Finally, he turned off the ignition, loaded his arms with the presents he'd purchased in Prince George, and got out.

"Hi," she said, offering him a slight smile as she eyed him searchingly. Why did he seem so solemn? She'd noticed when they stopped for lunch that he seemed to be brooding a bit about something. But she hadn't known how to ask him what was bothering him.

Now, Geoff nodded in response to her greeting, but said nothing as he studied the house, scrutinizing the windows, his face devoid of expression. Was he seeking his first glimpse of two young faces? Devon followed his gaze, but the windows were blank.

Clearing her throat, she hitched the strap of her purse more firmly onto her shoulder. "Are you angry about something, Geoff?"

He pinned her with a hard look. "Why do you ask that?"

"You look a bit...stony."

He studied her for a moment and then said, "I'm not angry."

"All right." She still wasn't quite certain whether to believe him or not. "Are you ready?" she asked, turning toward the house.

With a sharp nod, he fell into step beside her as she approached the double front doors which had been crafted of carved cedar. Devon rang the bell, then, without waiting, depressed the latch on the handle and entered.

''Mom, Dad, we're here,'' she called.

The air was immediately permeated with shrill, sharp yapping and the clicking of tiny canine claws on tile. A second later a small red Pomeranian streaked around the corner, caught sight of Geoff, yipped in surprise, and skidded to a stiff-legged sliding halt as he tried to reverse his momentum. Catching Geoff's raised-eyebrow expression, Devon smiled as she bent to reassure the small dog. ''This is Prince Charming,'' she said. ''Prince for short. Mom's only had him a year, and he's a bit of a coward when it comes to strangers.''

''I can see that.'' Geoff set the small stack of presents down on the floor and bent to unlace his boots.

He'd just straightened when a woman came around the corner. ''Thank God you've made it home all right.''

''Hi, Mom,'' Devon said, giving her a quick hug. Then she turned to Geoff. ''Geoff, this is my mother, Honoria Sherwood. You can call her Honey if you like—my father always has. You used to call her either Honey or Mom depending on your mood of the moment.''

Geoff forced a smile to his wooden lips and nodded as he studied the woman before him. In her mid-to-late fifties and slightly plump though not excessively so, she wore a bright green sweatsuit decorated with beadwork and embroidery. With the exception of her hair color which was a light reddish brown, Honoria Sherwood looked rather like an older version of Devon. Uncertain as to just how to greet her, Geoff extended his hand and then hesitated. He didn't feel comfortable calling her either Honey or Mom—yet. ''I'm pleased to meet you, Honoria,'' he said with a nod.

But Honoria Sherwood suffered from no such uncertainty. There were tears in her eyes as she searched his face, and then ignoring his outstretched hand she stepped forward and threw her arms about his neck. ''Oh, Geoff,'' she said. ''It's so good to have you home. They say that Christmas is the time for miracles, but this is the first time I've been touched by one.''

Momentarily stunned by the unfamiliar and unexpected affection from a stranger, Geoff was slow to return his mother-in-law's embrace, but finally he lifted his arms and awkwardly patted her back. "Thank you," he managed to murmur. "Merry Christmas."

A second later, she released him and, blinking back tears, began to bustle and fuss. "Here, let me take your jacket," she said, tugging ineffectually at his sleeves. "Devon, hang up your coat, dear, and pass me a hanger for Geoff." As Devon obeyed and Geoff began to remove his jacket, Honoria quickly went on, speaking to Devon. "Your father and Winston are in the den, and the children are in the guest room playing Sega. They've been anxiously waiting for you to arrive so that they can open their presents." She hung Geoff's coat in the closet.

"I'm glad they waited. I'd hate to have missed it."

"They wouldn't have it any other way," Honoria said. "I was going to allow them to open the ones from us, but they wanted to wait for you.

"Well, come on in," Honoria said, changing the subject and tugging at Geoff's arm as though to pull him inside. Pausing, Geoff bent to retrieve the presents, but she stayed him. "Leave those. I'll have Winston bring them in and put them under the tree. We'll relax and visit for a couple of minutes and then call the children so they can open their presents before dinner." As she led the way out of the foyer, she looked over her shoulder at Geoff. "You must be anxious to see the children."

Anxious, yes. To see them and about seeing them. But before he had a chance to do more than nod, a high-pitched little voice shrieked, "Daddy!" as racing feet—accompanied by shrill yapping from Prince Charming—pounded through the house toward them. Geoff turned toward the sound and barely had time to stoop to catch the little body hurtling toward him. Small arms grasped his neck in a viselike hold while long coltish legs wrapped themselves around his waist, and he looked down into the face of the most beautiful little girl he'd ever seen. "I always knew you'd come back," she said in a soft little voice before hugging him fiercely. "I just *knew* it! This is going to be the bestest Christmas ever."

Geoff's chest suddenly felt tight, and emotion rose up in his throat to choke him. "I'm glad," he managed to say as he brushed a strand of midnight black hair off her face, tucking it behind her ear.

Devon gasped and Geoff looked at her to see tears shimmering in her eyes as she held her hands in front of her face in that praying gesture again. It seemed to be something she did when she was emotional. "What?" he asked.

"What you just did with her hair," she murmured. "You always did that."

"Hi, Mommy," his daughter said, speaking over his shoulder to her mother. "I missed you. Merry Christmas."

"Merry Christmas to you too, pumpkin," Devon replied in a slightly choked voice.

Geoff's gaze returned to his daughter. He didn't want to stop looking at her. She had her mother's eyes, he noticed. And his hair. It was rather humbling to look into the face of this innocent child and see an echo of himself in her, to know that he had had a part in creating her. Would he see himself in Tyler? He looked beyond his daughter's slender shoulder, seeking his son, but the boy was nowhere in sight. "So, Britanny, where is your brother?"

She leaned forward to whisper loudly in his ear. "You used to call me Brie," she informed him. "You can again if you want."

He nodded and said in a low voice, "I want."

She rewarded him with a dazzling smile and then said, "See! I can remember for both of us. That's what I told Tyler, but he said it was dumb." Then apparently remembering the question he'd asked, she added, "Tyler's coming. He said he wanted to finish his stupid game first." She leaned forward to whisper in Geoff's ear again, "He's kind of a jerk sometimes."

"Britanny," Devon said in a warning tone.

Before she could scold the child, Geoff said, "I think most little girls think their brothers are jerks. Don't they?"

Brie shrugged and responded doubtfully. "I guess."

"Well," Honoria said, "we might as well go on to the den. I'm sure Tyler will be along shortly." She led them across a large family room complete with a huge decorated Scotch pine in the corner. Scores of presents spilled out from beneath its sprawling boughs. "Peter, Winston," she called. "They're here."

Almost immediately two men stepped out of a doorway adjacent to the family room. The older of the two had sable brown hair winged with white at the temples and a cleanshaven face. He wore tan trousers, a polo-style shirt and mahogany-colored leather slippers. His piercing blue eyes were his most prominent feature. The younger man, undoubtedly Devon's brother, Winston, had ginger-hued hair worn a bit long and scraped back into a short ponytail at the nape of his neck. His blue eyes were a slightly less piercing variety of his father's. He wore loose-fitting jeans with a baggy black T-shirt on a frame that was lean to the point of thinness.

Devon stepped forward. "Geoff, this is my father, Peter Sherwood, and my brother, Winston."

Geoff shifted Britanny in his arms to set her down. She continued to cling to his left side as though she was afraid he might disappear if she let go, so he hugged her close as he extended his right hand to Peter. "How do you do?"

Peter grasped his hand and stepped close to subject him to a long and penetrating scrutiny. Finally he said, "It really is you, isn't it, my boy?"

What did he say to that? "I believe so, sir."

"Sir!" He looked at Geoff in surprise. "Call me Pete," he ordered, "you always did before."

Geoff nodded. "Pete."

"Well, my boy!" Pete suddenly exclaimed in a booming voice as he pounded Geoff on the back. "It's good to have you home." Throwing an arm around Geoff's shoulders, the older man gave him a jovial squeeze and then looked across Geoff's body at Britanny who still clung to his other side. "Isn't it, little girl?"

Britanny nodded with childish enthusiasm.

A little overwhelmed by the older man's sudden exuberance, and not entirely sure that he liked it—it seemed a bit artificial— Geoff looked toward Winston who, thus far, had been ignored by his father. The younger man was backing away, fading into the background. "Winston," Geoff said, stepping toward him and out from beneath his father-in-law's arm. Winston halted and Geoff extended his hand. "Hi. How are you?"

Slowly Winston reached forward to accept Geoff's hand. "Okay," he said quietly. "You?"

"Fine. Better since Devon found me."

Winston nodded, stuck his hands in the back pockets of his jeans and his gaze slid away. "That's good." He swallowed visibly, his Adam's apple bobbing in his throat. Geoff received the distinct impression that Winston was nervous. Maybe he was just that type of person.

"Britanny, dear," Honoria said into the silence, "run along and get your brother. Tell him I said to come greet his father *now*. We're going to be opening presents shortly anyway."

"Okay, Gram."

"Winston, dear, Geoff brought some presents. They're in the front foyer. Would you mind putting them under the tree?"

"Sure," Winston said, leaving them as Pete moved back into the den. Devon linked her arm through Geoff's and followed while her mother came behind. Geoff felt a bit staggered by the impressions bombarding him. Did Pete's exuberant cordiality camouflage a certain amount of insincerity? Or was he reading things into the situation that didn't exist? Did Winston seem reluctant to make eye contact? A bit leery of him perhaps? Or was he simply a reserved and shy young man more at home with the computers he programmed than he was with people? Geoff was too new to these people to tell.

Devon studied Geoff as they entered the den, trying to see everything through his eyes. It was a cozy room. The outer wall contained a fireplace decorated with stockings for Christmas, flanked by two tall windows screened by lace curtains through which tiny multi-hued lights in the shape of a star flickered in sequence before flashing in unison. In front of these windows sat two upholstered chairs with mahogany arms and trim. Her mother sat down on one of these with a sigh that suggested she was a bit fatigued.

"So, my boy, do you want red or white wine?" Pete boomed from his position in front of the liquor cabinet.

"Oh, neither at the moment thanks. I'm fine," Geoff responded in a low voice.

Her parents immediately looked at Geoff with varying degrees of startlement. "Did I say something wrong?" he asked.

Devon quietly explained. "You used to always drink a glass of wine before dinner. In fact, it was you who got Dad started in the habit. You said it was healthy and aided the digestion."

"Oh—" His gaze swept thoughtfully over her face. "Well, in that case I guess I'd better try a small glass. Red, please."

Pete nodded. "Red it is," he said, but he continued to eye Geoff as he poured. "Have a seat." He indicated the vacant chair set at right angles to the fireplace.

As Geoff sat, Winston returned and seated himself on the sofa on the far side of the room. Devon moved across the room to join her brother. Poor Winston, he'd never measured up in their father's too-critical eyes and, as a result, tended to stay in the background as much as possible, avoiding attention. Pete Sherwood would have been happy with nothing less than a carbon copy of himself in any son, though Devon had never been able to get Winston to understand that.

Of the two Sherwood offspring, Devon had had it easier simply because she'd been born a girl. Her role in life was to look pretty, do well in school, and marry well. All of which she'd done to her father's satisfaction. He wasn't particularly happy with her career choice—too flighty and artsy to his way of thinking—but he overlooked it. She wished he'd been able to accept Winston's career choice in computer programming with as much equanimity. But that was past now, and some things would never change.

At the moment, Winston, like everyone else in the room, seemed to be finding it difficult to take his eyes off Geoff. With the exception of Geoff's introduction to Britanny, so far this visit had been more awkward than she'd imagined it might be.

Perhaps she shouldn't have warned them that Geoff's personality had changed in some ways. They were staring at him as though they thought the changes should be visible. Geoff cleared his throat and Devon thought perhaps he was a bit nervous. Was that why he seemed so cold? Did his expressionlessness conceal a certain amount of reservation and uncertainty?

As soon as she asked herself the question, Devon knew the answer. *Of course.* From Geoff's point of view, he was in a room full of strangers. Strangers who expected him to act, talk, and even think in specific ways. In his place she would have been paralyzed with tension.

Perhaps if she could begin a conversation the tension would ease. "Well, the weather coming back was much better than going anyway," she said into the silence. "I think I mentioned to Mom on the phone that I ran into a blizzard on the way up to Northridge."

"Yes, I believe she said something about that to me," her father responded. "She also said you ran into some trouble on your way home."

Devon nodded. "Yes. I'm going to have to have some body repairs done on the Jeep. I doubt though that the police will ever catch the guy who ran us off the road. We couldn't give them much to go on."

"I'm just glad you weren't hurt." Her father had just begun to distribute the glasses of wine he'd poured when two young faces appeared in the doorway.

"I brought Tyler," Britanny announced. Gripping her brother's hand tightly in hers, she tugged him across the room toward Geoff.

Geoff studied Tyler closely and Devon tried to envision their son the way his father would. Tyler was tall for his age, slender but not thin, and he carried himself with a proud posture that was often lacking in teens. He wore a small gold earring in his pierced ear, of course, but his sable brown, arrow-straight hair—inherited from herself—was nicely styled and shone with clean-

liness. The only thing she would truly change if she could would
be the sullen expression on Tyler's face. It was obvious that this
meeting would not go as smoothly as had Geoff's introduction
to his daughter, for Tyler was clearly not ready to throw his arms
around his long-lost father and welcome him home.

Devon cringed inwardly, aching for both of them. Geoff's face
still looked guarded, expressionless, with the exception of his
eyes. The emotion shining in his dark green eyes could not be
mistaken for anything cold, but neither could she interpret it
completely. A combination of hope, pride, anxiety,
and...something more; it brought a lump to Devon's throat.

Geoff and Tyler stared at each other for a long moment, neither making a move, then Geoff offered his hand to his adoles-
cent son and quietly said, "Hey, sport."

Tyler eyed him with a combination of insolence, wariness and
hope, and for a moment Devon thought Geoff might sweep him
into his arms and hug him. She held her breath. As much as
she'd like to see it, she knew it would be a mistake. Tyler tended
to shun affection rather forcefully; he considered himself too
mature for such displays.

Tyler hesitantly extended his hand—a smaller version of
Geoff's own long-fingered slender hand—to accept Geoff's
greeting. Geoff must have realized that he'd have to content himself with getting to know his son a bit more slowly than his
daughter, for he grasped it solemnly.

"How are you, son?" Geoff asked.

Tyler appeared about to respond and then, abruptly, he tugged
his hand out of Geoff's grasp. "I'm not your son. *You're* not
my father," he said in a rage-filled tone that was hardly more
than a stage whisper, but was strong enough to fill Devon's heart
with dread. "My father's dead." He backed up a few steps. "Just
go away. Go away." Then, turning, he ran from the room, dodg-
ing his grandfather's outstretched hand.

"Tyler!" Devon's shocked call echoed in the room. Geoff's
expression hadn't altered, but Devon sensed his hurt, could imagine the depths of his distress, and her throat closed. Rising, she
began to trail after her son, not knowing what to do or say, but

knowing that there was too much pain in both Tyler and Geoff for her to leave things as they were. "Come back here this—"

"Devon—" Geoff halted her. She met his gaze and saw the concern lurking there. "We need to discuss whatever is wrong, but not now. He needs time."

She considered for a moment. "All right."

Britanny, perhaps needing reassurance as much as Devon herself felt in need of it, clung to Geoff's arm until he lifted her onto his knee. At nine, she was almost too big to be held that way—her long coltish legs dangled down almost to the floor— but for this moment it didn't matter. Then, Geoff accepted a glass of wine from Pete, and they all tried to pretend that everything was fine as they settled into conversation.

"Can we open presents pretty soon?" Britanny's high-pitched young voice asked a few moments later during a lull in the adult discussion going on around her.

Devon smiled at her. "We've made you wait long enough, haven't we, pumpkin?"

Britanny nodded.

Honoria said, "Just let me get the camera ready." And everyone rose to move into the family room. "Britanny, honey, run and get your brother."

"Again?" Britanny asked with obvious reluctance.

Honoria nodded. "Again, sweetheart."

"Okay." With a disgruntled expression, Britanny went off in search of Tyler.

"Winston, I believe you're doing Santa's job this year. Right?" Pete said as they all sought seats near the enormous Christmas tree.

Santa? Curious, Geoff cast Devon a questioning look.

"Every year we draw names for the person who is going to pass out the gifts that are under the tree," she explained. "It helps to lessen the pandemonium."

Geoff nodded and watched as Winston took up a position next to the tree and began sorting through the gifts based on the tags taped to each one. The children raced back into the room and sat on the floor as close to the tree and their Uncle Winston as they could without getting in the way.

"Hurry, Uncle Winston," Tyler prompted, his earlier funk apparently forgotten for the moment.

Winston grinned. "Let's see what we have. 'To Britanny from Grandma and Grandpa,'" he read, handing Britanny a small package wrapped in gold foil. "To Tyler from Uncle Winston," he read next. "Well, now," he murmured with a teasing glint in his eye, "that's got to be a mistake. I could'a sworn the gift I got you was smaller than this. The labels must have gotten mixed up."

"Ah, come on, Uncle Winston."

"Here you go." Winston passed a large package wrapped in red paper to the boy.

Murmuring his thanks, Tyler and Britanny began eagerly ripping the paper from their packages as Winston continued with his job. As soon as the children's gifts were in the open—Britanny had received a doll, and Tyler a model—their grandmother began snapping pictures.

"Geoff, this is for you from Mom and Dad and I," Winston said, presenting Geoff with a large box that, from the way he slid it across the floor rather than carrying it, was quite heavy.

Geoff stared. "Oh...but I didn't expect anything."

Winston grinned. "Don't worry. On the short notice we had, it's not much. And, in a way, you could say you're giving it to yourself."

Both Devon and Geoff stared at him in confusion.

"Just open it already," Pete prompted from his position in his big easy chair on the sidelines.

Feeling himself the center of attention, Geoff rose and began tearing at the wrappings on the large box. When he finally gained access to the contents, for an instant he didn't understand and his bewilderment must have been evident on his face. "Those are your things," Honoria explained, anxiety obvious in her tone. "Things that Devon put into storage when... Well, they're things Devon couldn't bear to part with, so they were in storage here.

We thought seeing them again might help your memory to come back.''

Geoff picked up a stuffed fish mounted on a board. A cardboard tag attached to it with string read, *This is Tyler's first fish. He caught it in Lake Okanagan when you took him fishing for his ninth birthday.* Oh, God! That would have been the last birthday he'd spent with Tyler. The lump in Geoff's throat was so huge that he couldn't speak, the burning in his eyes so intense that he couldn't meet anyone's gaze.

"We tagged everything as well as possible so you'd know what it meant. It's all right, isn't it?'' Honoria asked.

"It's fine, Mom.'' Responding for him, Devon rose to place a hand on Geoff's arm as he lifted a small pair of fur-trimmed moccasins from the box. "Those are the slippers you bought for Brie on her third birthday. She never wanted to take them off.'' Devon looked more deeply into the box. "Your favorite computer magazines are in here, some of the books you'd kept from university, the sweater that Holly made for you for your thirtieth birthday. It's a hodgepodge of stuff, but...for some reason I kept it.''

Geoff nodded and swallowed. Devon's family had given him a box of memories for Christmas. And even though, thus far, the gifts had not triggered any real recollection, they were memories in and of themselves. He could imagine what it had been like fishing with Tyler when he caught his first fish. He could picture a small Britanny enchanted with her new moccasin slippers. And he could touch the sweater made for him, with love, by a sister he could no longer remember, and he could feel connected once more. This was more than he'd ever imagined. Finally, he managed to speak around the lump in his throat. "Thank you,'' he said hoarsely. "Thank you all.''

Chapter 9

"**Y**ou're welcome," Pete said. "Now get on with your job, will you, Winston? Or I'm going to die of starvation before these kids finish opening their presents."

There were "ooh's" and "ah's" as more gifts were opened and hugs exchanged. Laughter and teasing. Crackling wrapping paper and pictures being snapped. Geoff received a silk shirt and coordinating sweater from Devon and a pair of leather gloves from Winston, and a package of golf balls and tees from Pete and Honoria. Presumably, he golfed.

"To Devon from Geoff," Winston called out, handing Devon a package wrapped in green foil.

Slowly, obviously taken by surprise, Devon reached out to take it and then turned to Geoff. "When did you buy this?"

"In Prince George, before I met you back at the car."

"Oh." She looked at the package. "What is it?"

"Open it and find out," he prompted, although he was no longer so sure the gift had been a good idea. He'd purchased it on impulse without taking into consideration the fact that the gift-opening would be taking place at Devon's parents', and that she was a lady engaged to another man.

As the wrapping fell away to reveal a swatch of red satin fabric, Devon's fingers hovered hesitantly.

"Well, what is it, dear?" Honoria asked. "Hold it up."

With an unreadable glance in Geoff's direction, Devon lifted the negligee from the paper. The bodice was predominantly lace with strategically placed swatches of satin, while the skirt was predominantly satin with lace inserts on either side. It was a nightgown designed for seduction. And Geoff had known the instant he'd seen it that he wanted to see Devon in it.

"Oh, my!" Honoria exclaimed with a wide-eyed glance in Geoff's direction. "Well, it is beautiful, but..."

"Cut the man some slack, Honey," Pete said with a grin on his face. "After more than two years alone, what do you think any red-blooded male has on his mind?"

Even Winston chuckled at that as he reached under the tree for the next gift. Geoff felt heat rising into his face; thank goodness he had a dark complexion.

"To Britanny from...your father," Winston read, passing the little girl one of the presents Geoff had brought. Despite himself, Geoff tensed a bit. He hadn't known his daughter's likes and dislikes, so he'd bought what he hoped any nine-year-old girl would like: a Barbie doll and some accessories. He hoped he'd chosen well.

"Oh, boy!" Britanny exclaimed as she finished opening the package. "Thank you! Thank you! Thank you!" she chanted as, Barbie in hand, she rushed over to hug him.

"You're welcome," Geoff said. "I'm glad you like it." Over his daughter's shoulder, he saw the expression on Tyler's face. It was a combination of wistfulness and resentment, and he realized in that moment that Tyler wanted to accept his father into his life as easily as his sister had, but that something held him back.

"To Tyler from your father." Winston handed a large box to the boy. Hesitantly, Tyler accepted it. Placing it on his knee, he looked at Geoff.

"Open it, Tyler," Devon prompted when the boy only looked at the package.

Tyler compressed his lips for a moment. Then, as though coming to some internal decision, he began to tear at the wrapping on the box. "In-line skates!" he exclaimed, lifting his eyes to Geoff's. And, for an instant, before the look was shuttered, Geoff saw the pleasure the boy felt in receiving the gift. It was enough. Then, as Tyler remembered himself and the resentment he wasn't ready to let go of just yet, he said a solemn, "Thank you."

"You're welcome," Geoff returned.

Winston passed the last of the gifts out. "There, I think that's about it."

"Good!" Pete said with gruff good nature. "That means we can eat."

"Wait!" Britanny said. "I have one that I want to give Dad myself." Scurrying over to the end of the sofa she carefully removed a package from beneath it and then came over to Geoff. "Grams helped me make it for you. I hope you like it."

Geoff weighed the package in his hands. It was heavy. "I'm sure I will."

"Open it," his daughter urged.

"All right." Tearing the wrapping from the package, he discovered a scrapbook. A smiling baby girl graced the cover, and in metallic sprinkles the words The Life of Britanny Janine Grayson had been printed.

Geoff swallowed. Ah, damn. His throat was clogging up again. "It's beautiful," he managed to murmur.

Britanny nodded and opened the cover. "See it's got pictures of me from when I was a baby up until now, and copies of my report cards from school, and the ribbon I won for racing, and all kinds of stuff." She turned a couple of pages. "This is you teaching me how to swim. Mom took the picture so she's not in it, but Tyler was standing over here laughing at me. See."

Geoff nodded. "Thank you, Brie. This is very thoughtful."

For a moment the little girl looked uncomfortable. "Well, Grams and me and Tyler kind of all came up with the idea together."

"It was thoughtful of all of you."

Honoria smiled then looked toward Tyler. "Where's your scrapbook?"

The boy shrugged. "It isn't finished yet. I got him something else for now." Dragging his feet a bit, Tyler rose and retrieved a small package.

Honoria looked surprised but said nothing.

"Thank you, Tyler," Geoff said as he accepted the gift. Tyler nodded without meeting his eyes and returned to his spot on the floor where he immediately became involved in examining his own gifts. Geoff opened the box to discover a bottle of men's cologne. "Well, this is wonderful. I've been needing some."

Tyler glanced up, meeting his gaze for a fraction of a second as though to verify Geoff's sincerity, and then quickly became absorbed in reading the box containing his model.

"Can we eat now?" Pete demanded in a disgruntled voice.

Honoria elbowed him. "Honestly! You'd think I never fed you."

"You didn't feed me lunch because you said we were having an early dinner," he reminded her. "Well, it's darned near four o'clock now and I still haven't seen that dinner."

"All right! All right!"

Dinner went reasonably well, though Geoff had some difficulty in refraining from staring at Tyler. What was wrong in that young mind? he wondered. But since he wouldn't discover the answer tonight, he forced himself to focus on the delicious meal and allowed the conversation to flow around him as much as possible while he soaked up impressions like a sponge in the hope that they would provoke some buried memory.

So far, nothing.

It was obvious to him though that Winston Sherwood and his father did not get along. Pete Sherwood apparently resented his son's choice of career, deriding the amount of time Winston spent with his computers, in "solitary confinement." Winston's expression made it obvious that he took exception to his father's pride in Devon, though he did manage to hide it quite well. And

Devon, it seemed, had set herself up as intermediary, continually but tactfully interceding with her father on her brother's behalf, even going so far as to demean her own accomplishments when her father held her up as an example. And through it all Honoria Sherwood sat and ate her meal, throwing out the occasional comment about mundane things, apparently oblivious to the undercurrents surrounding her. It was an interesting family.

What would his own mother be like when he met her? Geoff wondered. He hadn't called her yet although Devon had given him her number. What did one say to a mother they didn't remember? A mother who thought them dead? Still he was going to have to call her soon.

He spooned some dessert into his mouth—a concoction doused in a caramel sauce that Honoria called Carrot Pudding—and watched as the children gobbled the dessert down with three times the enthusiasm they'd shown for the main course. They, of course, finished before anyone else and excused themselves; Brie to take Prince Charming outside before playing with her new toys, and Tyler to play a new Sega game that he'd received. A moment later, Winston also excused himself, disappearing in the direction of the den.

Then, as though by some unspoken agreement, Devon and her mother rose to begin clearing the table. Geoff was about to offer his help when Pete asked, "Do you still like an after-dinner cigar, Geoff?"

Geoff frowned. "I'm not sure."

"Well, come on then," Pete said with a beckoning gesture of his head as he stood. Geoff rose to join his father-in-law and Pete slapped him exuberantly on the back. "We might as well find out, huh?"

In his study, a room that looked more like a library than an office due to the shelves upon shelves of leather-bound books, Pete handed Geoff a fat Cuban cigar and took a seat behind his desk. Almost immediately, his joviality disappeared. He eyed Geoff seriously through the haze of aromatic smoke he exhaled.

Geoff puffed on the cigar and returned his gaze steadily.

"Why did you bother to come back *now,* Geoff?" the older man demanded a moment later without preamble.

Stunned by the question, trying to understand its implications, for a moment, Geoff could only stare. Then he asked, "Is there some reason I shouldn't have?"

"I had to do some fancy footwork to keep Future-Tech alive, when it looked like you'd been killed along with that brother-in-law of yours. Now, if we're not careful, all that work could be undone."

Geoff tried to assess the undercurrents in his father-in-law's tone. "You mean Spencer Loring? You didn't like him?"

"I didn't know him from Adam before this all started, but of course I don't like him now. His stupidity cost Future-Tech dearly. And who the devil else would I mean? Do you have another brother-in-law who was killed?"

Geoff raised an eyebrow. "You tell me."

For a moment, Pete Sherwood didn't seem to know how to take Geoff's comment. Finally he grunted and said, "Oh, yes. Sorry Geoff, but I'm having a bit of difficulty with this amnesia thing."

Geoff shrugged. "I'm afraid there's not much I can do to help you with that—I have difficulty with it, too. To get back to the conversation, tell me why you were so concerned with keeping Future-Tech alive, as you put it."

Pete arched a brow. "Devon didn't tell you?"

"Tell me what?"

"That I own thirty percent of your company. When you started Future-Tech you needed backers. I was one of them." He puffed and blew a haze of smoke ceilingward. "I was protecting that investment."

"Why was it necessary to protect it? I thought Future-Tech had been cleared of the allegations against it."

Pete shook his head. "I was able to mitigate the damage to the company because virtually all the systems that experienced problems were installed by Spencer's company, Fort Knox Security. And Spencer was proven to have made modifications to the systems' software. In fact, he admitted as much to a number of his clients, although he *said* that he'd only made modifications to the reporting systems to improve tracking of access to the systems.'' Pete paused and sighed. ''The man was, admittedly, damn near a genius when it came to electronics.

''Anyway, to get back to the thrust of your question. Some of the companies who experienced losses felt that Future-Tech should have maintained more control over the installation process. I had to make a number of out-of-court settlements for damages incurred in order to prevent the whole story from breaking out and getting blown all out of proportion. But I made damn sure the clients understood and accepted that the settlements were made as a gesture of goodwill, and not an admission of culpability.''

''Does Devon know about these settlements?'' Geoff asked.

Pete shook his head. ''Only that there were a couple of them, but none of the details. She wouldn't have understood the ramifications anyway. Suffice it to say that she knew I was protecting the company to preserve her future. And my grandchildren's. Even without you managing it, Future-Tech has continued to provide her with enough of a monthly income to live on. She would have had some difficult times without it.''

Geoff frowned. ''I don't understand. I was under the impression that Devon had her own business.''

Pete waved a dismissing hand. ''She dabbles in stained glass and interior design. I doubt that it's particularly lucrative.''

''What about insurance? Didn't I have any?''

''Of course you had insurance.'' Pete puffed on his cigar. ''But you disappeared. Without positive proof of your demise—'' he raised an eyebrow for emphasis ''—in other words *a body*,'' he clarified, ''there's a long waiting period for insurance. Seven years to be exact.''

''Seven years! Why?''

Pete shrugged and waved a dismissing hand as though swatting away a fly. ''It has to do with British Common Law which states that a missing person must have been missing at least four years before surviving relatives can seek an order declaring death. The Canadian insurance companies have simply made it a contractual requirement as well, and have extended the waiting period to protect themselves. Basically the contract you signed stated that your beneficiary would have the right to apply to the court for an *Order of Presumption of Death* only after you, the insured, had been missing for seven years.''

Geoff swore under his breath.

''I concur,'' Pete said. ''All that aside, however, I've been able to mitigate Future-Tech's responsibility and preserve the company simply by dint of Future-Tech being the manufacturer and not installer. I have to point out, though, that some clients felt there was evidence of tampering with the software at the production level. Those that accepted settlements will, of course, have to live with what they've received. However, if other clients decide to pursue the matter—'' He shrugged, indicating that there was no predicting what might happen.

''What exactly were the charges against the company?'' Geoff asked.

''Conspiracy to commit corporate and economic espionage,'' Pete replied bluntly. ''But the charges weren't levelled just against the company. They were also directed at you as the president and CEO. Which brings me back to my original point—I think your return *now* could mean trouble. Some of Fort Knox Security's clients were out for blood. They could be again if they discover you've returned. We'll keep it quiet as long as possible. Ensure there are no newspaper articles concerning your miraculous return from the dead, that kind of thing.''

Geoff felt as though he'd been hit in the solar plexus. Despite all of Devon's assurances to the contrary, could he have been involved in something illegal? Would he find himself fighting to stay out of prison without a memory to aid him?

Frowning, Geoff considered what he'd learned about Future-Tech through his own research over the last couple of days in conjunction with what Pete Sherwood was telling him and tried to put together a scenario. ''So some people thought that I, in league with Spencer and Fort Knox Security, was facilitating break-ins for the purpose of corporate spying by...what?''

''In a nutshell, by providing security services preprogrammed with an alternate access. A system that would bypass whatever company security codes were installed by the purchaser of the system in order to grant access to thieves. Once inside the company, the thieves stole sensitive design plans. Some of the stolen information has apparently already made it into competitors' designs.''

Geoff leaned forward to roll the ash off his cigar again. He could see why some companies had suspected that the problem was at the manufacturing level. That was the level at which the primary software routines would be written. Of course, anyone who knew how could have changed them after the fact—just as Spencer apparently had done. ''How much of this does Devon know?''

''Very little. It would only have worried her. I certainly didn't tell her that, had you lived, you could very well have found yourself in the fight of your life. There was no need to hurt her more than she was hurting already.''

''Dad...'' Both Geoff and Pete turned toward the doorway at the sound of Devon's voice. Neither had heard her approach. ''What...exactly...are you saying?''

Pete looked at Geoff and cleared his throat, apparently realizing that he would now have to give his daughter the frightening details of a situation he'd been able to avoid explaining for more than two years.

They'd arrived home from her parents' place only a short time ago, and Devon was putting fresh sheets on the guest bed when she glanced up to see a dark shadow in the doorway. She gasped in startlement before she recognized Geoff lounging there watching her.

''Oh, it's you!'' she said with a faint laugh. She'd thought he was upstairs with the kids, tucking Britanny in and beginning the process of trying to break through Tyler's shell.

''Sorry,'' he said. ''I didn't mean to frighten you.'' Then he smiled slightly. ''They sure are great kids.''

Devon studied him. ''Even though Tyler won't speak to you?'' she asked.

Geoff shrugged. "He'll come around. It's a shock for him."

She nodded and reached for the quilted spread.

"Here, let me help you with that." Geoff stepped into the bedroom, his big body instantly making the room seem small and close. Grasping the edge of the spread, he helped her smooth it over the bed. Finished, they straightened and looked at each other, gray eyes meeting green, clinging as the banked embers of a desire she was not yet ready to acknowledge flared between them.

The intimacy of the moment was more than Devon was capable of dealing with, and she sought desperately for something to say. "Whenever you want fresh bedding, just help yourself. It's in the hall closet. The laundry hamper is in the utility room."

He nodded but said nothing and the silence thickened. For some reason the bed seemed to loom ever larger between them, an object of temptation that made Devon even more aware of the breadth of Geoff's shoulders and the solidity of his muscular chest.

"I...I should go to—" She broke off, unable even to say the word *bed*. She sidled toward the door, trying to appear nonchalant even as she cautiously maintained a safe distance between them.

"Devon—"

Halting, she allowed her gaze to slide toward him, but avoided his eyes. "Yes?"

He stepped forward, bringing his hand up to lift her chin, forcing her eyes to meet his. She was immediately seduced by the tenderness in his gaze as it skimmed her features with gentle understanding. Enveloped by his scent as a tantalizing whiff of his cologne wafted toward her. Taunted by his body heat as he stood closer than was wise. "You can't run from this forever."

She swallowed. "I know, but...good night, Geoff." Quickly, before her waning willpower failed her altogether, she made good her escape.

On Sunday afternoon as Devon headed over to David's, her mind was not on the meeting to come. Rather, it was on the words she'd overheard spoken between her father and Geoff on Christmas day. And on the frightening explanation she'd received. She'd always known that her autocratic father was over-protective, but she'd not suspected to what extent. And now she'd brought Geoff back only to plunge him into an apparent hornet's nest of suspicion, innuendo, and accusation. How could the poor man defend himself when he remembered none of it? And, even more importantly, was he completely innocent?

She'd invariably believed Geoff to be above criminal activity of any kind. But, considering the change in his attitude in the months before his disappearance in conjunction with what her father had said last night, could she be as certain of that as she once was?

She no longer knew what to think.

Pulling into the guest parking at David's condo on the water-front of Lake Okanagan, she looked out over the water. A brisk December breeze had blown away the insulating blanket of cloud that usually covered the valley in winter. The wind stirred a slight froth to the crest of waves still devoid of the myriad sailboats and yachts that would dot the huge lake come summer. And some rare winter sunlight danced on the dark blue waters in a way that should have sparked happiness, an appreciation of nature's beauty, but instead struck a melancholy note in Devon. She felt...alone.

Sighing, she draped the strap of her purse over her shoulder and got out of the Jeep.

David's condo was on the fourth floor of a four-story building. He answered the door almost immediately. "Hi," he said with a gentle smile.

David was a handsome man, there was no question of that; he could have stepped right off the pages of *GQ*. But somehow he now seemed a bit too...perfect. His grooming was impeccable; not a single blond hair was out of place. His clothing was so-phisticated; flawlessly fitted ivory linen trousers and a navy silk shirt clothed his lean form with fashion-model elegance. His hands were perfectly manicured, his teeth perfectly capped. Even his apartment, as always, was perfectly immaculate.

''Hi,'' she returned, stepping over the threshold and slipping off her shoes before stepping onto the rich cream-colored carpet.

David immediately tried to pull her into his embrace, his angry mood of their last telephone conversation apparently forgotten. Devon raised her hands, palms out, to ward him off. ''Please, David. We have to talk.''

He frowned slightly. ''Devon, we can work this out. Now that you're home, we can deal with the problems.''

She walked past him, moving into the living room to stare from the picture window at the fantastic view of the lake. Even the view was perfect. How could *she,* someone for whom clutter was a way of life, have thought that she could possibly measure up to David's expectations? Somehow, in just the short time she'd been away, her perceptions of her life had changed dramatically. Even had she never found Geoff, she realized now that her marriage to David wouldn't have worked. She had...*settled* when she'd accepted David into her life, and she'd settled again when she'd accepted his proposal. She'd been lonely, she'd wanted her children to have a father, and she'd settled. David was a good man, but...he was not the man for her. He never had been.

Looking down, she fingered the engagement ring on her finger. David had chosen it and presented it to her. It was dramatic and beautiful, but...it wasn't *her.* Slowly, she removed it from her finger.

''Devon?''

She turned to face him, to meet his apprehensive blue-eyed gaze. ''David, I...'' She broke off and swallowed. Lord, this was one of the most difficult things she'd ever done. She'd always hated hurting people, hated confrontation.

''You what? Why did you take your ring off?''

She held it out to him. ''I have to return it to you.''

He looked at the ring, but made no move to take it. ''Why? Because Geoff is back?'' His tone was tinged with bitterness.

Devon shook her head and set the ring on the edge of a nearby plant stand. ''No. Because we're not suited to each other. We never have been. I just didn't want to see it.''

"You're wrong, Devon."

"No, David, I'm not. Look at this place." She waved her hand at his immaculate apartment where even the magazines on the coffee-table were fanned out at a precise angle. "Can you honestly tell me that you're prepared to have two boisterous almost-teens in your life? Look at you." She indicated his impeccable sense of style. "Can you tell me truthfully that you're looking forward to having a wife who feels more comfortable in denim than anything else? A wife who isn't exactly the tidiest person in the world?"

David avoided her eyes. "We can work around that."

She stared at him. "You *have* thought about it!" she realized suddenly. "And how exactly did you plan to work around it? Divide the house in half?"

"No, of course not. I thought it would just take...some guidance."

"You planned to try to change us to meet your ideal!"

He met her gaze then, his own heated and angry. "People change for the people they love all the time."

"Wrong, David! People work to overcome small habits that annoy their loved ones, but they don't change their character. Love means the wholehearted acceptance of a person for who they *are*." She turned to look out the window again. "This may be hard for you to understand, David, but I *like* me the way I am."

She didn't hear him approach, but suddenly his hands were on her shoulders, kneading the knots of tension that nested there. "This isn't going the way I'd planned at all," he murmured. "I was going to offer you coffee, and we were going to discuss our situation like two reasonable adults. Then, when we'd worked everything out, we were going to spend the afternoon together. I don't even know where it went wrong."

It had gone wrong the moment he'd tried to kiss her, but she didn't say that. As unobtrusively as possible, she stepped out from beneath his massaging hands and turned to face him.

His hands dropped. "Would you like that coffee now?"

She shook her head. "I think I should go."

"Dammit, Devon! I'm not going to let you do this. You're ruining my life, my career."

She stared at him. He was an attractive man with an excellent career and any number of women who would be eager to date him, or to marry him for that matter. "Would you care to explain that statement?"

It was one of the few times she'd ever seen David agitated. He raked his fingers back through his hair, avoiding her gaze. "Forget it. It was just a slip of the tongue."

"Really, David? Well, a slip of the tongue like that requires an explanation." She studied him for a moment and a horrible suspicion began to surface in her mind. He wouldn't! Would he? "It's my father, isn't it? He said something to you."

His gaze snapped up. "What makes you say that?"

"Just answer the question, David."

He looked away uncomfortably. "Just forget it, will you?"

Ice trickled through Devon's veins as David's words confirmed her worst suspicions. "Tell me."

He shrugged. "It was nothing really. I probably shouldn't even have given it any credence."

Devon simply stared at him, waiting.

He sighed and rubbed his jaw thoughtfully. "Oh, all right. Pete hinted a couple of times that, once I'm a member of the family, a partnership could be coming my way."

Devon's mouth opened but no sound emerged. She shook her head in stunned amazement, unable to form a coherent thought. Finally, she asked, "Did this hinting start before or after you proposed to me?"

David refused to meet her gaze, and Devon believed she had her answer.

She'd forgiven her father for a lot of interference in her life over the years because she'd known that his motivation was love, but this she didn't know if she could forgive. She cared for David, deeply, but she now knew that she had never loved him the way a woman should love the man she planned to marry. Had he ever cared for her?

"You never loved me, did you? You pursued me for the sake

of your career? And you're upset now because you've suddenly lost your ticket to a partnership.''

David said nothing. Was there guilt in silence? She sighed. ''Well, David, I think you should count yourself lucky that you won't be marrying me, because I would not have been the wife you needed.''

He finally spoke. ''I do love you, Devon. I just didn't see any harm in benefitting in other ways from our relationship.'' He looked at her then, and she couldn't deny the existence of the pain she saw reflected in his eyes. The problem was that she didn't know whether it was for the end of their relationship, or the possible loss of the partnership he'd wanted so badly.

''I have to go.''

He grasped her arm, forestalling her departure. ''This isn't over yet, Devon. It can work between us. I'll prove it to you if you'll just give me the chance.''

She looked up into his handsome face. She cared for David. She really did. Just not in the way he wanted, the way they would both need in order to build a life together. She reached up to place her palm against his cheek. ''Let it go, David.''

Sunday dinner, the first real meal that Geoff shared alone with them, was a success. Devon had concocted a meatball stroganoff dish which seldom failed her and which had been, at one time, a dish Geoff enjoyed. Britanny was on her best behavior, helping with the meal and taking pleasure in catering to her father. Even Tyler managed to set the table without complaining, though he spoke little during the meal—and then only to reply in monosyllables to whatever question had been asked of him.

Devon should have known that the smooth sailing was too good to be true. They'd just finished dessert—cherry pie purchased from the local supermarket bakery—when Tyler announced he was going over to his friend's house.

''Have you finished cleaning your room?'' Devon asked him.

''Mo-om!'' he sang warningly in two distinct syllables as he stared at her defiantly with olive green eyes so much like Geoff's.

"Have you finished cleaning your room, Tyler?" Devon re-iterated firmly.

"No! I'll do it when I get back."

"Why isn't it finished?"

"Because it's not, okay? I didn't feel like doing it." His tone was more sullen now than defiant.

Devon flashed a glance at Geoff, but, as usual, she couldn't tell from his expression what he was thinking. She'd hoped he wouldn't have to witness one of Tyler's outbursts. "And do you think that we only have to do what we feel like doing in life? Do you think that I always enjoy doing laundry and cleaning bathrooms?"

"I don't care!" Tyler rose from his chair to stare down at her. "I said I'll do it when I get back. Why isn't that good enough for you? Why can't you just leave me alone sometimes?"

Devon refused to allow herself to be drawn into an argument regarding his right to independence. "Clean your room, Tyler. When you're finished, you may go to Shane's as long as you're home by nine."

His eyes narrowed with rancor and he thrust his jaw out in an obstinate manner. "I hate you," he said in a low voice.

"Hate me all you want as long as you get your room cleaned. Someday you'll thank me."

"Don't bet on it!" Tyler threw the words over his shoulder in an undertone as he turned and stomped off up the stairs. Throughout the exchange, not once had he looked in his father's direction.

When Tyler was out of earshot and the racket coming from the other end of the kitchen suggested that Britanny was making too much noise with the dishes to overhear them, Geoff said, "There's a whole lot of anger in that young man."

"I know. He seems to be getting more and more defiant. I took him to a counsellor at one point, shortly after you disappeared, but..." Devon gripped the bridge of her nose, fighting the sudden urge to cry as past pain crowded too near the surface. The task of explaining to her children that their father was dead had been harder by far than the discussion of divorce ever had been. Dead meant that he was never coming back. Dead meant no more weekend hiking expeditions up to the falls. Dead meant no Dad. And Tyler had blamed her. Even now his accusing words rang in her memory as clearly as they had that day, echoing her own guilt-ridden thoughts. *It's your fault. He wouldn't have gone if you hadn't told him you wanted a divorce. I hate you.*

Devon massaged her throbbing temples. It wasn't true, of course. Geoff had planned to take that fateful plane trip regardless. But guilt had a strange way of making a person second-guess themselves.

And now, despite it all, Geoff was back...alive. Her eyes drank in the sight of him, observing the tilt of his head, the set of his shoulders. And Tyler, so like his father in many ways, was still clinging to an anger she didn't understand.

"Nothing came of the counselling?" Geoff asked, stirring Devon from her thoughts.

She shook her head. "It didn't do any good. Tyler wouldn't talk to him. The counsellor told me that, in his opinion, Tyler was probably angry with his father for dying and angry with me for the confrontation he'd witnessed between us." She shrugged. "I'd figured that much out for myself. What I needed to know was how to reach him. Nobody could tell me that. 'Be patient,' the counsellor said. 'We each have to work through our grief in our own way.'" She sighed and raked her fingers through her bangs, lifting them off her forehead. "I have to confess that my patience is wearing pretty thin."

"Do you want me to talk with him?" Geoff asked.

Devon went still. It was not a question she'd been expecting, and yet she knew she should have. Geoff was Tyler's father. Was she ready for him to assume a more prominent role in the children's lives so quickly? She was afraid that she might start to rely on him, to need him in their lives, and she knew she wasn't ready for that yet. Then again, his primary reason for returning to Kelowna was to try to reclaim his life, and involvement with his children was part of that. Could she deny him that because of her own fears?

Finally, she nodded. "If you want to."

"I think we need to find out where that anger is coming from. Don't you?" His intense green-eyed gaze held her captive for a moment before her gaze drifted to the table where he was fingering the handle of his coffee cup.

Devon swallowed, for she doubted in her heart that Geoff's talk with Tyler would accomplish much. But he was his father, and somehow he was at the root of Tyler's anger. Perhaps... "You're certainly welcome to try. I have some laundry to finish up anyway as soon as Britanny and I are finished with the dishes."

"Sure," Geoff said as he rose. He sounded absent, as though his mind had already moved beyond this room.

Chapter 10

Geoff paused in the hall outside his son's room. The door was open and he could see Tyler sitting at a student's desk situated in front of his bedroom window. He was leaning on his hands staring from the window into the yard next door rather than working.

Geoff knocked on the door frame. Tyler whipped around as though prepared to quarrel, but arrested in mid-gesture when he saw who it was. "May I come in?" Geoff asked.

Tyler stared at him a moment, and then seemed to recover. "Why?" he asked suspiciously.

"I thought you might like to talk."

"What about?"

Geoff decided to regard that as an invitation to enter the room, and he moved in to sit on the foot of the bed, facing Tyler. Meeting his son's fractious gaze, he said simply, "Whatever you want. About me maybe. About school. About cleaning your room. Whatever."

"Cleaning sucks." Tyler scowled and turned back to look out the window.

Geoff followed his gaze to see an attractive blond girl in the neighboring yard. She was sweeping the thin layer of snow that had fallen that day off of a cedar deck. "Who's she?"

"Brandi MacNeil."

Geoff nodded. "Nice. You've got good taste."

"Yeah," Tyler said. And then, apparently realizing what his agreement betrayed, he shrugged and added in a nonchalant tone, "She's okay for a girl, I guess." He picked up a pencil and began tapping the desk with it as he stared out the window.

Geoff doubted that the boy actually *saw* anything; his mind was elsewhere. "So, do you want some help cleaning up?" he asked, wondering even as he did so if his help would be rebuffed.

Tyler took a quick survey of his room, then shook his head. "Naw. I can do it." He was silent a moment, and then asked a question that revealed another direction of thought entirely. "How can a person get hit on the head and forget everything?"

Another doubter. Only this time it was important that Geoff find a way to explain the situation. "Have you ever hit your head really hard?" he asked. "So hard that you see little dots of light dancing in your head for a second?"

Tyler nodded. "Kinda. I got hit in the head with a baseball last year. It knocked me out for a second. But I didn't forget nothin'."

Geoff nodded. "Most people don't. But sometimes when a person hits their head really hard, it hurts the brain. That's called a concussion. If the brain swells too much, people sometimes die because of the pressure in their skull. The doctors say that that's almost what happened to me. Even though I lived, my brain didn't quite heal itself so it doesn't work exactly the way it used to. Do you understand?"

Tyler considered. "Kinda, I guess." Then he frowned. "No, not really."

"All right, here's an example. The first time I saw a truck, I knew what it was, but I didn't know if I knew how to drive it or not. I couldn't remember ever driving. But, as soon as I sat in the driver's seat, somehow I knew what to do. How to start it, how to put it in gear, and how to drive. And it works the same for a lot of things—using a computer, dancing, cooking, and so on. It's like those memories are intact, but stored in a different place and I have to learn how to find them.''

Tyler's eyes widened as though he'd finally heard an analogy that he could understand. ''Like a computer hard drive that got kinda scrambled by a power surge?''

''Exactly.''

He frowned. ''So how come you don't remember people when you meet 'em?''

Geoff sighed inwardly. ''Well, I don't understand it totally myself. Even the doctors don't know everything about how amnesia works. But, from what I understand there are a couple of different kinds of memory. I haven't been able to find my personal memories yet, the memories that tell me who I am.''

''They still scrambled?''

''Maybe,'' Geoff acknowledged with a nod. Or erased. But he didn't want to voice that fear. Not yet.

Tyler started twisting the pencil in his hand. He was silent for a long time, and then he murmured without looking up, ''My dad said he'd be back in a week. He promised me he wouldn't leave us. But...he did. He left us.'' There were tears in those quietly spoken final three words.

A lump rose in Geoff's throat. Since Tyler wanted to talk about his father in the third person, he'd go along with it. Anything to get the kid talking. ''You talked to your dad before he left?''

Tyler nodded. ''After him and Mom had that fight.''

''And that's when he promised you he was coming back?''

Again Tyler nodded.

''Did your dad break a lot of promises?'' Geoff asked quietly.

''Yeah, sometimes,'' the boy whispered. And then he appeared to reconsider. ''But only at the end cause he'd forget. Before that he almost never did.''

Geoff frowned. More evidence that he'd been under some kind of intense strain in his last few months. What the hell could have happened? ''Do you think anything could have made your dad break his promise not to leave you if he'd remembered it?''

The boy was silent for a long moment. His throat worked as he swallowed, and then he shrugged and said, "I dunno," in a sullen tone barely above a whisper. "He was mad at us a lot. I asked him why, but he wouldn't tell me."

Geoff considered the boy and felt tears sting the backs of his own eyes. All this time Tyler had been blaming himself for his father's death, thinking that he'd done something to make his father angry enough to leave them. *Jesus!* Geoff swallowed. What the hell had he done to this family before his accident? No wonder Devon wanted some assurance that it wouldn't happen again. And how, now, did he explain to this young man, the son he didn't remember having, what might have been wrong?

"Tyler, do you know how sometimes when you're really angry with one person it makes you so upset that everyone around you knows that you're angry?"

Tyler thought about that for a second and then nodded a bit hesitantly. "Yeah," he murmured. "Sometimes when I'm mad at Mom, Britanny knows and comes to talk to me to try to make me feel better about it."

Geoff nodded. "Are you nice to Britanny when she does that?"

Tyler shrugged and looked toward the window.

"What do you think Britanny would think if you were rude to her and she didn't know that you were angry with your mother?"

Silence, and then, "I guess she'd think I was mad at her."

"Would she be right?"

Tyler shook his head and then slowly turned to look at Geoff. "Do you think that's what happened with my dad?"

Geoff nodded. "Yeah, I do. I'm sure he wasn't angry with you, or anyone in the family. But something bad was bothering him."

"Then why didn't—" Tyler broke off as his voice broke and he battled back the emotion. "Why didn't he come home like he promised then?" he finished in a whisper.

Geoff swallowed the lump in his throat. "There is nothing on this earth that could make me break a promise to you if I'd remembered it, son. Nothing! You have my word on that.''

Abruptly Tyler lifted his head to level a narrow-eyed look at Geoff. ''My dad died. That's why he didn't come back. My dad wouldn't forget me. Ever! He wouldn't!'' He flung himself around in his chair until he was facing the window again. ''Just go away,'' he said more quietly now. ''You're not my dad. You can't be.''

Geoff considered Tyler for a moment, wondering which direction to go from here. Finally he said, ''I've always been your father, Tyler. Even when I didn't remember. And I'll be your father for the rest of your life. I'd like to be your dad again too— if you'll let me.'' Rising, he moved toward the door.

''Dad—'' The word was hoarse, barely audible, but it was enough to stop Geoff in his tracks. Slowly, he turned to face his son. The boy was standing now, facing him with eyes that begged for understanding, eyes that shimmered with emotional pain.

Sensing that fear of rejection kept Tyler from making the first move, Geoff opened his arms and took a step toward his son. His heart was in his throat, and for a moment he feared that he would be the one to be rejected. And then, as though his gesture was the signal that Tyler had been waiting for, the boy sobbed and flung himself across the room, into Geoff's arms. Geoff closed his eyes and simply held his son. The silent quaking of Tyler's shoulders told him how much his young son had suffered in his absence. It wasn't fair! None of what this family had endured was fair. And, if it was the last thing he did, he was going to find out what or who had been behind it all.

Standing in the hall outside Tyler's room, Devon clutched the basket of laundry and swallowed the painful lump that had risen in her throat. She hadn't meant to eavesdrop, but when she'd heard the nature of the exchange within, she hadn't been able to help it. And, she'd heard enough of what had been said to know that her son had just taken his first step toward bridging the emotional chasm that had separated him from everyone else during the past two years.

"Are you sure you don't want some help cleaning up?" Geoff was asking now. "I actually got pretty good at cleaning up after living by myself for a while."

There was a pause. "Okay," Tyler said. "But I got to give you something first."

There was a moment of silence. "The Life of Tyler Geoffrey Grayson," Geoff read. "Thank you, son. It means a lot to me."

"Sure. You're welcome." Devon heard the nonchalant shrug in her son's voice and recognized it for what it was—male pride.

The sound of toys being put into boxes followed and Devon was about to continue on to Britanny's room to put her daughter's clothing away when Tyler suddenly asked, "Did you ever get lonely?"

"All the time, son. All the time."

Me too, she thought, dragging herself away. *Me too.*

It was Tuesday. She and Geoff had spent the previous evening taking inventory of the items in his home office. This morning, with the Christmas weekend over and business getting back to normal, they'd made arrangements for the private phone line in that office to be reconnected, and then she'd taken him to the industrial park where Future-Tech maintained its offices and warehouse, and reintroduced him to his company. He'd seemed to get along well with the employees he met, though she'd seen more than one considering glance cast his way when his back was turned. Nobody seemed to know quite what to make of him now. Least of all her brother, Winston, who still worked in the programming department of Future-Tech.

Winston had asked Devon about the new coldness in Geoff, the sense that he held himself apart from everyone around him. But, what could she tell him? Yes, she sensed it, too. No, she didn't know where it came from. Somehow the accident had done more than rob Geoff of his memory; it had changed his personality, creating a man more comfortable with *aloneness,* with holding himself apart from those around him, than the Geoff they knew had ever been.

But, she and Geoff had gotten through the first day of his

reintroduction to his past life, and no one had raised the specter of possible criminal charges. She'd had to leave Geoff for a time while she went in to her own office to take care of some of the business that had piled up in her absence and to make arrangements for her assistant to continue holding the fort as much as possible. She and Geoff had agreed to meet back at home for dinner.

Now, she pulled onto the interlocking stone drive and halted her Jeep Cherokee without bothering to pull into the garage. Sitting there for a moment, she studied the house, viewing her home through new eyes.

What did Geoff see when he looked at it?

Flanked by scores of pine trees, the two-story stone and cedar house perched on a rocky bluff overlooking Kelowna and, beyond the city, the winter gray waters of Lake Okanagan. It wasn't the spectacular view David enjoyed from his waterfront condo, but it wasn't bad either. She loved it here. Geoff had once, too. But he'd changed so much in the two years they'd been apart that she was no longer certain how he'd feel about it. In Kelowna, he wouldn't find the kind of solitude that he'd enjoyed in Northridge.

With a weary sigh, Devon gathered up the auto body estimates she'd had done for the repairs on the Jeep and collected the stack of mail she'd retrieved from the group mailbox at the end of the lane, before striding toward the house. It was a warm afternoon in late December. Another mild winter in the Okanagan. In just a few months, the valley would be redolent with the scents of fresh greenery and fruit trees in bloom. The start of the new year was only two days away. It was a good time for a fresh outlook; a new lease on life.

She hoped.

She entered the house through the side door from the garage directly into the kitchen. The smell of freshly made popcorn permeated the air and the distinctive rhythm of rap music drifted down from the second floor indicating that her two children had made a snack. Gayle, the seventeen-year-old neighbor girl that Devon arranged to stay with the kids on holidays and after school on the days that she couldn't be there, began packing up her things in preparation for heading home.

"How were they?" Devon asked as she dug in her purse for the money she owed the girl.

"They were good," Gayle assured her as she tucked the money into her pocket. "Thanks. Call if you need me tomorrow. Bye."

"Bye," Devon said, and then looked toward the stairs. "Britanny, Tyler, I'm home," she called as she dropped the bills on the desk in the corner of the kitchen where they joined a small stack of their counterparts. She wrinkled her nose as she realized that it was almost time to sit down and do the monthly bill-paying. Short of scrubbing toilets, it was her least favorite household task.

"Hi, Mom," Britanny's voice wafted down to her. A moment later the child peered over the oak banister bordering the upper hall and Devon felt a tug of maternal pride. "Grams is coming over to get Tyler and me. We're having dinner at her place, then she's taking us to a movie. Tyler and I are going to stay over at her place again tonight if it's all right with you."

Devon stared up at her daughter in confusion. "Why? You just spent a week with Gram."

Britanny shrugged. "She said she wants to spend some more time with us while we're on Christmas break and that you and Dad need some time to talk."

"Oh." Well, she guessed she couldn't argue with that. "All right, dear. Where's Tyler?"

Britanny shrugged. "He's in his room, I think." And then she was winging her way back to her own room on flying feet. The child never *walked* anywhere.

Devon contemplated going up to check on Tyler and thought better of it. Their confrontations just kept getting worse as her twelve-year-old son strained against the bonds of parental guidance. Devon had no wish to provoke more dissension between them.

She checked her watch. She had a little time before she needed to begin dinner preparations, since it would be just her and Geoff for dinner tonight. *Just her and Geoff! Uh-oh!* Suddenly she desperately wanted to keep the children home, a buffer against emotions she wasn't prepared to face. But she couldn't. Not without revealing too much of her inner turmoil to her too-perceptive mother, and to Geoff. So, she'd just have to concentrate on other things. Like work.

Going into the workroom she'd had constructed behind the garage, she retrieved her sketch pad, charcoal pencils and pastels from a shelf, and moved into the living room where she always found her conceptual creativity performed best. Besides, sometimes work helped to clarify the confusion of her personal life more than countless hours of deliberation could. She had a little more than an hour to devote to beginning work on a new, very promising stained-glass contract and she intended to make the most of it.

Her clients, a wealthy couple from Hong Kong, had a beautiful home with massive two-story windows overlooking a spectacular view. Rather than curtains, the Lings wanted something different for their windows. Something that wouldn't block the light, but enhance it. A stained-glass design in panels on electronically controlled tracks which allowed them to slide over the standard windows would be perfect.

With the Lings' suggestions and her own ideas in mind, Devon quickly sketched a rough idea of what she believed would work best for the stained-glass panels and then opened the case of pastels. Only when she had the design in color could she truly assess whether or not her artistic conception would conform to the medium of glass in the way she envisioned it.

Slowly, an oriental dragon in flight began to take shape on the page, flowing from the tips of her fingers almost magically as the pastels brought its scaly, multi-hued body to life.

Without consciously realizing she was doing it, as she sketched, Devon contemplated the problems facing her. Work always helped her to see things more clearly. This time, though, she wasn't certain that it was a blessing, for when she thought about it, it seemed that almost every relationship she'd ever developed was in some kind of upheaval.

Her son rarely spoke to her except to argue. Her brother blamed her, to a certain extent, for their father's continued censure of him. Her ex-fiancé didn't want to accept her decision to end their relationship. Her husband had unexpectedly reentered her life, but was in so many ways unrecognizable that she no longer knew how she felt about him. And finally, there was her father. She had no idea what she was going to do about his interference in her life, or even if she should do anything, but she was certainly disturbed by it. Perhaps Geoff would have some suggestions.

Geoff arrived at six, just in time to say good-night to the kids before they left with their grandmother. As the shouted *goodbyes* and *see-yas* faded to silence, Geoff's eyes found Devon's. "So it's just us tonight?" he asked in that silk-on-sandstone voice that never failed to caress Devon's nerve endings.

Abruptly paralyzed by the possibilities his words conjured, she could only nod as she began to fuss with the sketches she'd brought into the kitchen with her when her mother had arrived.

"Why don't we order in then, instead of cooking?" Geoff suggested. "Or have you started something already?"

She shook her head. "No, I haven't started anything. I was just thinking about throwing together a zucchini and cheddar casserole. What would you like to order?"

"Chinese?" he suggested.

She smiled, remembering the shock it had been the first time he'd suggested Chinese food. "Sure," she said. "It's been a while since I've had any. I'll just go put my things away and then I'll order."

"Take your time. I'll order and call you when everything is ready if you like."

She hesitated, unused to sharing the responsibility for meal preparations after so much time alone. But there was certainly no reason not to accept his offer. "All right." She began to leave the room, but...it seemed strange to leave everything up to Geoff. "You're sure you don't want me to set the table?"

He met her gaze with an intense unreadable expression and then said, "I can manage."

"Of course." She nodded and left the room.

The first thing Geoff did was order the food. Then he set about making preparations for his evening alone with Devon. In his campaign to get her to let him back into her life, perhaps even on a permanent basis, he'd be a fool not to take advantage of the opportunity that had arisen. Their unexpected isolation for the evening would provide an excellent chance to get to know each other better and to further the developing intimacy between them.

When he called Devon forty-five minutes later, her reaction was everything he could have hoped for. "Oh, Geoff," she said in a choked voice as she stared at the candlelit table with its white linen cloth. "It's beautiful. Like..."

"Like what?" he prompted when she fell silent.

"Like our last anniversary together. You... Every anniversary you arranged a candlelight dinner with wine and soft music."

Geoff frowned inwardly, not entirely certain he liked the thought of competing with the ghost of himself. He pulled out her chair, waiting for Devon to seat herself, but she hesitated. "Is something wrong?"

She looked up. "I feel underdressed."

He considered her, allowing his gaze to roam leisurely over her shapely legs clad in black hose, up to her black denim skirt and over her blue blouse. He liked the blouse. It clung in all the right places. "You look fine to me."

Perhaps his appreciation was apparent in his tone, for she flushed slightly. "All right." Sitting, she pulled her chair forward slightly and then placed her napkin in her lap.

"So," Geoff said as he took his own seat, "why don't you tell me a bit more about some of the things I used to do, or things we did together, so I won't keep surprising myself. What kinds of things did I do that you *didn't* like? Or was I a perfect husband up until those last few months?"

Devon raised an incredulous brow as she considered him, and

then laughed. "Hardly perfect. Do you really want to know about the things you did that irritated me?"

He nodded and reached for the bottle that he'd found in the wine rack and had put on the table to breathe. The Pinot Blanc wine was made at the Calona Vineyards right here in Kelowna, according to the label, and he'd thought it appropriate to the evening. "And, to be fair, I want to know about the things that you did that irritated me, too. You can alternate."

She smiled and held up her glass to accept his silent offer of the wine as the soft dinner music flowed around them. "All right. Let's see." She stared thoughtfully at her wine for a moment. "I think one of the most irritating things you used to do was bring home guests for dinner upon an hour's notice. I can't count the number of times I wanted to kill you for that." She softened her words with a smile. "Now something about me, right?" She looked at him questioningly and he nodded. "Well, that's tougher. It's much easier to overlook one's own faults." After a moment of hesitation she said, "I guess I'd have to say that my housekeeping habits, or lack thereof, irritated you most. My house is always clean, but usually a bit untidy. That bothered you occasionally, though I never understood why. You certainly weren't the neatest person in the world yourself."

Geoff passed her the bowl of beef chop suey. "How so?"

"Well, for example, after a long day at work, you used to love to take off your socks while you were watching television in the family room, but you would just leave them there expecting me to pick up after you. Finally, determined to teach you a lesson, I left them there. At the end of a week when you had no clean socks in your drawer because they were still all lying on the floor next to your chair, you asked me where they were and I told you. You were furious with me, but it was a rare occasion after that when you forgot to put your socks in the laundry."

Geoff shook his head. "I can see where that would have been irritating." Then, he looked at her. "You'll be happy to know that I am now a much tidier person."

"Hmm," she said noncommittally. "Well, I pick up after myself and to a certain extent after the children, but I'm not especially tidy or organized. I have a habit of carrying things around with me and setting them down, then forgetting where I left them." She shrugged. "I'm forever finding mail in the freezer because I tend to read my mail at the same time that I'm trying to decide what to make for supper."

Geoff thought about that for a moment. It was a bit weird, but it struck him as more humorous than annoying. "I can live with that."

She looked at him then, and her eyes brimmed with an emotion that Geoff couldn't interpret. "Can you?" she whispered before hastily averting her eyes. He realized that his inadvertent word choice had made her contemplate the possibility of them having a life together again.

Not knowing what to say that wouldn't seem somehow presumptuous, he poured more wine for each of them and they ate in silence for a few moments. "Tell me what kinds of things we did together...besides dancing. Where did we go?"

Devon shrugged. "We hiked sometimes, and fished, but if you're asking about holidays we never really had one. When we were younger, we couldn't afford one. And, as we got older, you could never seem to take the time away from business."

"What was your dream holiday?"

She smiled wistfully. "I always dreamed of us going on an Alaskan cruise."

Geoff nodded. "Sounds nice."

Devon stared at him. "You never used to think so. Your idea of the place for a holiday was a tropical island."

"I guess I've changed quite a bit, huh?"

Devon nodded. "It's...hard to get used to sometimes. But, it's made me aware of how much we all are the sum of our experiences in life. And, without the memory of those events shaping our perceptions...well, we're different people."

Geoff considered her. "So, if the accident and living alone have changed me, what about you? How have you changed in the last couple of years?"

Devon thoughtfully sipped her wine before responding. "I guess I'd have to say that I'm less dependent on the men in my life. I can change the washer in a tap, clean out the rain gutters on the house, or change a tire. I even replaced the belt in my dryer when it broke—though I almost gave up on that one and I don't think I'd attempt it again.''

Had money been that tight? he wondered. ''Why didn't you call a repairman?''

''Because I'm cheap,'' she admitted with a self-deprecating smile and a shrug. ''I didn't want to pay someone to do something I could probably do myself, so I tried it. If I'd found I couldn't do it, I would have called. But, as it turned out, I managed fairly well on my own.''

''So, in effect, you've gained independence.''

Devon nodded and rose to begin clearing the table.

They were loading the dishwasher when she said, ''I think maybe we should start going through some of the things in your office in more detail. There may be something on some of those disks we found. What do you think? I mean we really need to figure out who this guy is who's after you. Right?''

She seemed very anxious to find something to do that would keep them busy. Aloud he said, ''If you like,'' but he wasn't fooled as to her motivation.

''Oh, damn!'' she said suddenly, interrupting his thoughts.

''What?''

''The sink is plugged again. And I've dumped enough drain cleaner down there in the last month to eat through just about anything. I don't know what's wrong with it.''

If it was the kind of clog that didn't respond to drain cleaner, then the only option was to open the drainpipe under the sink. ''If you have some tools, I'll see what I can do.''

''Would you?'' she asked. When he nodded she said, ''The toolbox is in the garage. I'll get it.''

Half an hour later, Geoff, his once-white shirt grimy and dirty, crawled out from beneath the sink. ''I think that's got it. We'll run some water and see what happens.''

The water ran down the drain without problem. ''Oh, that's wonderful,'' Devon said. ''Thank you.''

''No problem. I'll just go clean up and then we can get to

work in the office,'' he commented. They'd work with just the light of the desk lamp. Maybe he'd put on some soft music. There had to be a way to create a romantic setting in an office; he'd just have to be inventive.

''Sure. I'll bring in some coffee in a moment.''

A few moments later, cups in hand, Devon made her way down the hall to the office only to find that Geoff was not there. His new notebook computer was sitting on the desk, however, its backlit screen glowing, so he must have been there long enough to turn it on.

Frowning thoughtfully, Devon set the cups on a corner of the desk and contemplated going in search of him. If he was still just washing up, she certainly didn't want to disturb him. For more reasons than she cared to acknowledge. But what if he was having another one of his headaches? Ever since she'd witnessed the complete debilitation he suffered when in the throes of one of the headaches that he didn't treat promptly with medication, she couldn't help worrying about a reoccurrence. A moment later, when Geoff still hadn't appeared, worry won out.

The main floor lavatory light was on. ''Geoff?'' she called. There was no answer. She moved toward the lighted doorway, and then froze in her tracks. Geoff was not writhing on the floor, but... She swallowed and stared.

He had removed his shirt and was bent over the sink, dunking his head in a basin of water. Unconsciously, Devon lifted her fingers to her mouth to stifle a gasp as she truly saw the extent of the scarring on his back for the first time and imagined the pain he must have endured.

A livid ridged and shiny scar an inch wide and two feet long stretched across his muscle-sculpted back from left to right beginning behind his left ear, moving across his neck beneath his long hair, and then snaking down across his right shoulder blade. No wonder he wore his hair longer in the back now than he ever had in the past: he wanted to conceal the part of the scar that would have been visible above his shirt collar.

In the next instant, he turned to reach for a towel and caught sight of her in the doorway. Their eyes clashed and held. Despite herself, Devon's breathing quickened as her pulse rate elevated. Of their own volition it seemed, her eyes began an exploration of his body, moving downward to caress his strong neck, tracing the intricate path of a couple of escaping water droplets. Moving down over the firm contours of his hair-roughened chest. Grazing the flat surface of his ridged abdomen. Roaming lower to admire his narrow hips and the rather prominent male bulge in his jeans. Down over his firm thighs. She told herself that she was seeking the man she'd married beneath the layers that characterized this man but, truth be told, she simply liked what she saw...very much.

She always had.

Chapter 11

"Devon?"

She started slightly, met his gaze again, and then moved forward. Grasping his arm, she turned him slightly, and then lifted shaking fingers to examine again the huge, ugly scar that slashed its way across his back. "Do you know what did this?" she asked in a tone barely above a whisper.

He shrugged. "Probably a piece of sharp metal when I was thrown from the plane."

"You're lucky you didn't bleed to death."

He turned to face her then, catching her fingers in his hand before she could lower them. His touch was warm, comforting. "Yeah. Old Bill stitched me up when he found me. Without his help, I would have died. There's no question of that."

Devon lifted her eyes to meet his. "We should send him something. Thank him in some way."

"I already have."

"Oh." The atmosphere between them thickened and Devon suddenly became conscious that she was standing much closer to Geoff than was wise considering the power of the magnetism between them. She tried to tug her fingers from his grasp, but he tightened his hold. A little desperately, she sought a topic of conversation, something mundane to distract him, to distract them both. Her eyes lit on the still dripping waves of his hair. "What were you doing?"

It was obvious that her question had not distracted him in the least, for his reply had a preoccupied tone. "I was starting to get a headache. I took a pill to ward it off, but I thought some cold water might help."

Warily, against her better judgement, Devon lowered her gaze once more to meet his. It was a mistake. Her pulse quickened at the sight of the heat in his eyes, the promise glowing there, and she sought desperately for the thread of the conversation. "And did it?" she whispered.

She never received an answer.

Without quite knowing how it happened, she found herself in his arms. Devon gasped at the almost electric shock of their bodies coming together, the heat of the contact, the texture of his naked flesh beneath her palms. He tangled a fist in her hair, tilting her head, as he captured her lips with his and slowly slid his tongue into the warm wet recesses of her mouth. Devon's heart leapt in response. He kissed her slowly, deeply, with a lazy confidence that made the act as intimate as sex. He was staking a claim without words, telling her with slow, deep strokes of his tongue, that she was his. And Devon, despite the warning bells clanging in her mind, felt desire rising up within her, waging a cunning war against her control.

His embrace tightened, flattening her breasts against the hardened planes of his chest, pressing the evidence of his arousal against her abdomen, and molten heat sluiced through her. She moaned at her body's capitulation. Dammit! What was it about this new version of her husband that made him so impossible to resist?

Of their own accord her hands rose to his shoulders, her nails forming tiny crescent marks in his skin as her fingers curled helplessly. His hands cupped her bottom, lifting her, pressing her gently against the thickened shaft of his arousal and her senses exploded. "Geoff—" She gasped as his mouth released hers to trail gentle kisses over her cheek and temple.

"Hmm?" He lowered his head to nuzzle her neck, to feather soft kisses over that sensitized area. With more finesse than she remembered, he unfastened her blouse and slid it off her shoulders, discarding it carelessly on the floor but she was too far gone in sensation to care.

"Oh, Geoff—" Her eyes drifted closed. *It's too soon,* cried the voice of reason in her mind. *You're not ready for this.* But she ignored it, for once again she found her body holding reason hostage and this time she had no desire to fight its demands. She needed this. More than anything else, at this moment in time, she needed...Geoff.

With that admission, came freedom.

She wanted him. She wanted to feel his heated skin against hers. She wanted to feel his rippling muscles beneath her palms. She wanted to feel his hardness inside of her.

Lifting her hands, she began to explore the oh-so familiar contours of his torso, to run her fingers through the silky hair on his chest, over the washboard ridges of his abdomen until she came to his waistband. His hands were there to halt her progress.

She groaned in protest. What was the matter with him? Didn't he want this as much as she?

In the next second she felt herself swept off her feet, cradled in Geoff's arms as he negotiated his way through the house. And then he was setting her on her own two feet before the bed in the guest room. *His* bed. With passion-glazed eyes he stepped back to look at her clad only in her bra and skirt. "You are so beautiful," he murmured as he reached out to caress her left nipple with the index finger of his right hand. It leapt to attention beneath the subtle caress and Devon gasped at the riotous sensation that rocketed through her.

With a groan he stepped forward to embrace her once again, to kiss her as he slipped her bra off and then he lowered his head to take her taut aching nipple into his mouth. Devon almost screamed at the exquisite agony of it. It had been so long. Too long. And as a great yawning chasm of need opened up within her, Geoff became her whole world.

Somehow, without Devon ever knowing quite how they'd gotten there, she discovered they were on the bed.

And once again, her hands found his waistband. Unfastening his trousers, she pushed them down his hips as far as her arms would extend. He lifted her skirt, bunching it around her waist, as he removed her panty hose. Then, discovering that his own movements were hampered by the pants now clumped around his lower legs, he lifted himself away from her to kick them off, abandoning them in a heap. Devon, aching for his return, fumbled to remove her skirt from about her waist.

And then he was back, gripping her in strong hands grown rough now with the force of his lust, but she was too far gone in her own aching need to care. The passion driving them was too powerful for subtlety. Too hot and raw for lingering.

She felt the furnacelike heat of Geoff's big body pressed to hers as they lay on top of the thick spread, felt him jutting hard against her thigh as he molded her breasts to the shape of his hands, lifting them, weighing them, and a delicious wave of sensual heat overcame her. Her pounding heart accelerated until her pulse roared in her ears. Her breasts tightened, aching for more than the mere touch of his hands. And a flooding, loosening sensation in her loins made her clamp her thighs together.

It had been much too long. Sex had always been good with Geoff. Better than good.

Much better, she thought on the heels of a groan as the pad of his thumb grazed her nipple. He slanted his mouth over hers with an open hunger, a greed that stunned her with its intensity even as it reduced her to the essence of what she was: female. Woman to his man. He caught her chin with one hand, holding her still as his tongue moved deep inside her mouth, a blatant demand for her surrender.

And Devon surrendered body and soul.

She had never been wanted like this before. Never with such swiftness, such fury. She felt certain he was bruising her with the force of his kisses, yet she wanted more. His hand moved down to find her already slick with desire and he growled deep in his throat—a satisfied, animalistic sound. He studied her then with a hard, predatory expression, the tempered fierceness of arousal, and Devon's breath froze in her throat. He was so handsome, so male, so very impossible to resist. And so very passionate. How could she ever have thought this new Geoff to be lacking the passion of the man she'd married?

He removed his hand and her hips arched in silent protest as primal instinct flared to life. But, in the next instant, he was moving over her, kneeling between her thighs and she felt the hardness of his sex pressing against her own yielding softness. Bracing himself on his arms, he held her gaze with his own as he slowly pressed into her.

Devon's breath tangled in her throat and her eyes fluttered closed as she clutched him closer. She was vaguely aware of a roughness beneath her palms as her hands explored his back, puckered flesh which once had been smooth, and in a distant corner of her mind, she ached for the pain he had suffered...without a loved one near. But as his thick sex filled her to bursting there was no more room in her mind for thought. No room for anything but the sensation of being with him again.

His male flesh throbbed within her as he held himself still for just a moment, and then he began thrusting with heavy power. Hard and deep. The impact shook her entire body and she clung fiercely to him as his hips flexed, his rhythm gradually quickening. Her soft moans mingled with his harsh breathing. He reared back, baring his teeth as he pounded into her, pushing her legs higher. Stoking the fires. Elevating the tension.

The end, when it came, was as violent as a prairie thunderstorm, convulsing her body beneath him until she cried out. He echoed her cry—more harshly, a guttural male sound—and with one last powerful thrust shuddered his release into her and collapsed. While the last small quakes rippled through them, while their heartbeats slowly thudded back to normal speed, while the heat of their spent passion slowly evaporated from their perspiration-slick bodies, Devon slowly, mindlessly stroked his hard, muscled body, loving the feel of his heated skin against her palms.

Then, limp with utter contentment, she drifted into sleep.

Two hours later, Devon came awake with a start. The chill of the night had begun to seep into her bones, for they still lay atop the bedspread, and gooseflesh sprinkled the flesh of her arms and breasts. Had the cold awakened her?

She frowned slightly as she listened to the silence. Geoff lay behind her, one arm thrown casually, possessively over her waist, but his big body only kept her backside warm. Still, she didn't want to move, didn't want to let reality in, so she pressed more firmly against him for warmth and allowed her eyes to slowly drift closed again.

A crash, muted and distant, but loud in the silent house jarred her. Her eyes flew open and she jackknifed into a sitting position.

"What! What's the matter?" Geoff demanded as her sudden movement jerked him into wakefulness.

"I heard a noise," she whispered hoarsely. "In your office, I think."

"I'll check it out," he said as he got off the bed and hastily pulled on his pants. "It's probably nothing. Maybe the cat knocked something over."

"I don't have a cat," Devon informed him as she, too, rose and began to dress. "The only pets we have are fish."

A frown drew his brows together as he reached for his shirt. "But there was a black cat at the door this morning asking to come in."

"That's the neighbor's cat, Priscilla. The kids feed her occasionally, and she's taken that as an invitation. You didn't let her in, did you?"

He shook his head as he shrugged the shirt on and opened the door. "I'll be right back," he murmured. "Stay here."

"Like hell," Devon returned in a whisper, not caring if he heard or not. Hastily buttoning her blouse, she trailed after him through the silent house. Thank heavens they'd left most of the lights on. At least they wouldn't have to betray their presence by turning any on.

Geoff reached the closed door of his office and stopped to press his ear to the wood, listening.

"I didn't close the door when I left the office," Devon said in a faint whisper next to his ear.

He nodded acknowledgement and slowly turned the knob. Then, keeping his body pressed against the wall, he flung the door open. There was a bang as the door struck the coatrack within, knocking it over. Then, a loud boom split the night and something buzzed by Devon's ear. Before her confused mind had a chance to identify the source of the boom, or the insectlike buzzing sound, Geoff shoved her away from the door—*hard*—and dove into the room.

Geoff's arms wrapped around the intruder's legs, bringing him down like a rock, but even then the intruder didn't drop the gun. Wrestling him, looking down into the anonymity of a black balaclava that somehow made the man's presence in the house even more ominous, Geoff grabbed his gun arm. He had to gain possession of the gun before the bastard took another shot at Devon...or himself.

Damn! The guy was strong despite his leanness.

Finally managing to get some leverage, he slammed the intruder's gunhand against the floor and the weapon flew from his grasp. That was when something struck Geoff a blinding blow on the head. A thousand tiny lights danced in his brain for a fraction of an instant in time, and then darkness descended.

"Geoff! My God, Geoff, please wake up."

Devon! She was crying!

Wanting to reassure her, he opened his eyes and tried to sit up, but the instant he moved the light seemed to stab through his eyeballs and into his brain with the force of an ice pick. Pain erupted in his skull. Groaning, he closed his eyes and subsided as he reached for Devon's hand. "How long was I out?"

"I don't know. Four...five minutes maybe."

"Is he...gone?"

He thought she must have nodded then, for there was a pause before she responded, but he couldn't open his eyes. "He ran out through the garden door. I think that's how he got in too, because he knocked over my umbrella plant on his way in. That must have been the noise I heard. I guess he didn't know that we never use that door."

She was rambling. Still frightened? "The gun?" he asked when she paused for breath.

"He grabbed it on his way out."

"Are you...all right?" He scarcely recognized his own voice.

"Yes. Yes, I'm fine. But he hit you on the head with the base of the desk lamp. Your head is bleeding." She sounded panicky.

He groaned inwardly. Why did his head always seem to have to take the brunt of everything? "I'll be okay," he reassured her. "My head is used to aches. But...do you think you could get me an ice pack?"

He felt her brush his hair off his forehead with a tenderness that made his heart stumble in his chest. It was nice to have someone care about you. Nicer than he'd ever imagined in more than two years of imaginings. "All right," she answered softly with a slight sniffle. "I'll be right back. And then I'm going to call the police."

Two and a half hours later, after dusting almost every surface imaginable in Geoff's office for prints and leaving a mess of black powder in their wake, the police had left. They'd also removed the bullet from the wall and examined the footprints outside. Unfortunately, since there wasn't much snow at the moment and the ground was too hard to absorb a print, they hadn't been too encouraging about finding anything useful.

Geoff wasn't surprised. He thought that they were probably dealing with professionals. People paid to do a job made fewer mistakes.

Ensconced in bed with his head bandaged, he was now being doctored by Devon, who was a damn sight better looking than old Bill had been on his best day. The cut on his skull, high on the left side above his temple, hadn't looked as though it would need stitches—it had stopped bleeding readily enough—so he'd refused to go to a doctor. He much preferred Devon's tender ministrations.

"Are you absolutely certain you won't see a doctor?" she asked for the fourth time as she removed the ice pack from his head and placed it in a basin beside the bed. "I mean, it *is* possible that you have a concussion, you know."

He shook his head—cautiously—and said, "I don't think so. I've had one before and this doesn't feel anything like that. And *yes*, I'm sure." Having him near, caring for him, was keeping her mind off what had happened here and that was what she needed at the moment. He didn't want her thinking about the intruder and what might have happened, letting her thoughts feed her fears. And more importantly, he didn't want to leave her alone while some doctor kept him in an impersonal room at the hospital *for observation*. "Lie with me for a while?" he asked. The digital numbers on the clock on the dresser proclaimed the time as 1:05 a.m. "You should get some rest."

She hesitated, meeting his gaze for the first time since they'd encountered the intruder, and he saw the shadows in the depths of her eyes. That was when he realized that he'd been wrong. Caring for him wasn't keeping her mind off what had happened; she simply wasn't speaking of it. "All right. Let me just go and check the doors and shut off the lights."

Devon was trying to hide the children in the small space beneath Geoff's desk, shielding them with her own body as she watched the shadow of the intruder, gun in hand, loom ever larger on the wall. He was coming closer! A whimper of fear rose in her throat, but she choked it off. She mustn't make a sound or he'd find them.

She shrank back, trying to conceal her shudders of fear from the children. Who was he, this masked intruder who sought to end their lives? And why did he want to kill them? It made no sense. If only she knew who, then perhaps she could figure out why.

Holding her breath, she cautiously looked over the edge of the desk. The intruder's form looked vaguely familiar, the way he held his head, the slope of his shoulders. She should know this person. If only it wasn't so dark.

Then, as though in answer to her desire the silver light of a full moon suddenly shone through the garden door, spotlighting the intruder...and herself. As though in slow motion he brought the gun to bear on her, and yet she couldn't move for she was held captive by the familiarity of the eyes she found herself staring into. Olive green eyes. Unreadable eyes. Geoff's eyes.

"No!" she screamed. It was a wail of denial more than of fear. The sound of her own voice made her bolt upright in bed.

"What? What is it, Devon?" Geoff asked out of the murky predawn darkness from his position at her side.

But the lump in her throat made it impossible to speak. Leaning her elbows on her upraised knees, covering her face with her hands, Devon merely shook her head.

"You had a nightmare," he surmised.

Hugging her legs, trying to warm the chill in her heart, she nodded. "Yes."

"I'm not surprised," he murmured as he put his arm around her, pulling her back against his chest. "You're cold, too." He began to rub her arms to warm her. "Talk to me, Devon," he murmured. "Tell me about it."

But she could only shake her head. How could she tell him that, in her dream, he had represented the danger in her life, the danger in her children's lives. It would only hurt him. And yet, in a strange way, it was true. For had she never found Geoff, had he never come back into their lives, she was certain that their lives would never have been threatened this way.

"Stay dead!" the note had said. Both she and Geoff had ignored that directive. But at what price?

"Devon?"

"I need some coffee," she murmured. "You want some?"

There was a moment of silence as he tried to read her expression in the gray light. "Sure," he said, finally. "And I could also use a couple more aspirin if you have them?"

Oh, heavens! In her own fear, she'd almost forgotten. "How is your head?"

"A bit of a headache, but otherwise it doesn't feel too bad. Considering."

"I'm glad." She swallowed and rose. "Well, I'll go make the coffee and find the aspirin. You can join me when you're ready."

An awkward silence engulfed them as they shared their coffee at the breakfast table. Perhaps Geoff sensed that she had something on her mind. For her part, Devon knew what she wanted to say. No. What she *needed* to say, but...finding the words was difficult. The terror she'd experienced the previous night had made it clear that she was not ready to accept Geoff back into her life. Not yet. Not when things were so uncertain. She was afraid of being hurt again, terrified of being subjected once again to the emotional agony of losing Geoff to something she didn't understand. To protect herself she needed to prevent a deepening of the emotional bond between them—at least until they'd solved the issue of someone wanting Geoff dead. And she knew of only one thing that *might* work.

"Spit it out, Devon," Geoff suddenly said, startling her.

She glanced at his handsome face. He'd removed the bandage from his head, and showed no outward sign of the confrontation he'd had with the intruder. Then, because she couldn't look him in the eye just then, she fixed her gaze guiltily on her coffee cup and ran her thumbnail down a small crack in the glazing that she'd not noticed before. "I don't know where to start."

"Start. Then, if you need to, you can back up. I'll listen."

Devon nodded and drew a deep fortifying breath. "All right. I don't know how it is for you, or for men in general, but for me to be able to begin a physical relationship there has be some emotional connection in place. And then after..." She made the mistake of glancing up at that point, right into Geoff's too-intense eyes. Hastily lowering her gaze, she sought the thread of her thought before it unravelled completely. "And...when a physical relationship is entered into more...frequently, it seems to serve as a catalyst for deepening that emotional connection. Do you know what I mean?"

Geoff considered her. "Sex makes the heart grow fonder?" he asked bluntly.

Devon felt the heat of a flush rising in her cheeks. "Well, yes, I guess that's it."

"I thought that was the way it was supposed to be. You have a problem with that?"

She cleared her throat. "Yes, actually." Lord, how did she explain this? "I don't want to resume a physical relationship until…"

"Until what?"

"Until we know what it was that tore us apart before, Geoff. Until we know who it is that wants you dead. Until it's…safer," she concluded weakly.

Geoff set his coffee cup down on the table with exaggerated care. "Let me get this straight. You think you can protect yourself, keep yourself from coming to care for me too much, by not making love with me. Is that right?"

Devon shrugged. "I don't know for sure. But I hope so. I just can't do this any other way, Geoff. I'm sorry." Finally, she risked looking at him. "Please understand."

He frowned slightly and the expression was a bit forbidding, but when he spoke he sounded more confused than upset. "I can't say that I understand, Devon, because I don't. I think this must be one of those times when it's simply impossible for the male psyche to make sense of female reasoning. It seems a bit convoluted. But…if that's what you want, I'll accept it. For now."

Devon ignored the *for now* which she wasn't quite certain how to interpret and smiled, relieved that he wasn't angry. "Thank you for at least trying to understand, Geoff.

"And for safety's sake," she added. "I'm going to call Mom and ask if she'll keep the children for a couple more days."

Devon and Geoff spent a good portion of the remainder of the day cleaning the remnants of the black powder out of his office and going through the drawers and files for anything that might help them solve the dilemma facing them. "Maybe we should start with the computer backups," Devon said as she opened the door of his credenza to reveal a shoe box containing some disks.

Geoff frowned as he considered it. "Is that all of them? I seem to remember that box looked fuller when we were going through this office last."

Devon shook her head. "I don't know. It might be a bit emptier than it used to be, but I couldn't swear to it. It's possible that some of them were stolen last night if he had put them in his pocket or something. I know he wasn't carrying anything in his hands when he left though—except the gun."

"Okay. Well, I should be able to tell if there's anything missing when I start working with them."

Thursday morning at seven-thirty, Geoff and Devon pulled into the parking lot at Future-Tech. Devon had insisted that they begin their search for answers together this morning despite the fact that she had an appointment with a client at ten-thirty.

There weren't many vehicles on the lot yet, which was the way he'd calculated it. This company might be his, these employees his, but he remembered nothing concerned with either the company or its people, and it was amazingly difficult to walk into a corporation and try to resume your position as its executive officer in those conditions. He'd felt his self-confidence slipping yesterday when he was here, not to mention his paranoia returning. Surprising questions had begun to occur to him.

Had he ever had a conflict with any of his employees that would have prompted them to seek revenge by attempting to undermine his company and his integrity? Would somebody here remember something, perhaps inconsequential to them, that would help him to explain to himself and to Devon what had gone on in their final months together? How would he know what questions to ask in order to find out?

For the present, however, he was going to content himself with getting to know the company itself again. He wanted to meet his assistant manager, Danson Hart, who'd kept the company afloat for two years. And he wanted to meet Russell Manning, the second partner he'd taken in order to get Future-Tech off the ground seven years ago. "Tell me about Russell Manning," he said to Devon as they got out of the vehicle. "How did we meet?"

Devon looked at him. "You used to work for Russell at *his* software design corporation in Vancouver, Delta Systems. When you were looking for backers to begin Future-Tech he didn't hesitate. He said he knew your capabilities, and he knew that any venture you committed yourself to would succeed. So, he purchased a fifteen percent interest in your company."

"Did he take an active role in the company?"

She shook her head. "Not when you were here. But after...well, when it was necessary, Russell aided Danson with corporate decisions. Dad just handled any legal affairs since he didn't know much about the day-to-day operations."

Geoff nodded. Both Hart and Manning had been in Vancouver on business yesterday when Devon had reintroduced him to the company, so he hadn't yet met them.

Devon. He cast a sidelong look at her as they approached the two-story, unassuming brick building that housed Future-Tech, and he found his thoughts turning back rather than forward. Back to the previous evening, to Devon. God, he wanted her. It had been pure hell, sitting across the dinner table from her knowing that he couldn't touch her. That she wasn't yet his. That he didn't have the right to make love to her, to care for her. But it was the kind of hell he would gladly endure again and again if that was what was necessary to work out the problems that faced them.

He couldn't seem to stop looking at her. Oh, he knew on a perfectly intellectual level that she was not the most beautiful woman in the world. But on a gut instinct level, there was something about her that made her seem to outshine any other woman. It also made him want to kill anyone who tried to hurt her. This protectiveness, this urge to shield a woman, was new to him. At least as far as he could remember, it was.

His gaze dropped to her long, slender jean-clad legs. He wanted those legs wrapped around him, dammit! He wanted the right to hold her in his arms and never let her go. He wanted...*her,* in every way.

Did he love her? It was too soon to tell. But he definitely cared for her a great deal, and he'd already fallen in love with his two children. They were beautiful kids.

Removing the coded card that Devon had arranged for him to have from his pocket, Geoff swiped it and entered the security number. When the locking mechanism flashed a green light, he opened the door, allowing Devon to precede him, and they entered the building. One flight of stairs went up from the entrance, while another went down. They went up.

As they walked along a wide corridor, bright with fluorescent lighting, Geoff studied the production floor on the lower level through the windows on his left. There were a couple of people down there, getting organized for the day's work no doubt, but the floor was only partially illuminated and still quiet. The offices on his right were also dark and quiet. His own office was through the reception area at the end of the corridor. Looking beyond it now, he hesitated as he saw light spilling from his office doorway.

"Who would be in my office at this hour?" he asked Devon quietly.

She shook her head. "I don't know. Danson or Russell maybe."

"Stay here," Geoff directed. Seeing the obstinate set to her chin that meant she was about to argue, he added, "Just in case. Please."

She nodded as he left her to slowly approach the door of his office. A man, his back to him, was stooped over an open file drawer. He wore khaki trousers, a plaid shirt, and brown loafers. Saying nothing, Geoff leaned against the door frame to observe.

The man removed a file, rifled through it, replaced it haphazardly in the tightly packed file drawer, and then pulled another, repeating the procedure. Finally after repeating this procedure at least three times, he removed what looked like a multiple page document from the file in his hand, scanned it, nodded, closed the file drawer and turned toward the door. He jumped visibly when he spied Geoff standing there. Guilt or surprise?

Chapter 12

"Geoff!" he said a second later. "I'd heard you were back. It's good to see you. How are you?" He was lean, with brown hair, brown eyes, and a fair complexion.

"Fine," Geoff said, not moving from his leaning position. He sensed Devon approaching now. Did she recognize the voice?

There was a moment of tension, and then the man said, "Oh, right. I guess you don't know me. I'm Danson Hart, your assistant manager." He hesitated and then stepped forward to offer his hand.

At that, Geoff shifted and shook hands. "Pleased to meet you."

Danson caught sight of Devon then, and smiled. "Hi, Devon."

Geoff nodded to the paper in Danson's left hand. "Did you find what you were looking for?"

He nodded. "Yeah, it's just a contract that was misfiled. I'm afraid it may take me a while to get used to working out of my office again. For administration purposes, it was easier to work out of yours while you were, um, gone. I hope you don't mind."

Geoff shook his head. "No, of course not."

Danson seemed to relax slightly. "Good. Well, I better get back to my office then. I have a meeting to prepare for."

"Problems?" Geoff asked.

Danson nodded. "Yeah, I guess you could say that. Dacc Alarm Systems says they were shorted on the last shipment we sent them."

"Anything I can do to help?"

He shook his head. "I think you'd better take a few days to get back into the swing of things around here before I start dumping problems on you." He headed for the door and then stopped. "Let me know if you have any questions. I'm usually around."

Geoff nodded. "Thanks. Will Russell be in today?"

"He still works primarily out of Delta Systems, you know, but I think he was planning on coming into town today to meet with you. He'll probably be here around ten-thirty or a little later."

"Good. Thanks."

"No problem. See you later, Devon."

"See you, Danson," Devon returned. The thick carpeting in the outer office rendered Danson's retreating steps soundless.

Geoff studied his office. It had a gray carpet—the kind that had a low pile and stood up to heavy traffic—on a thick underpad that cushioned the feet when you walked. The white walls were adorned with two Bateman prints, an artistic-looking wreath fashioned from dried grasses and flowers, and a brass pendulum-style clock. A large window on the wall opposite the door ensured that the room received an abundance of natural daylight despite the fact that the slats on the venetian blinds were angled to keep out direct sunlight.

Nothing looked familiar.

"Do you like it?" Devon asked.

Geoff nodded. "It's nice. Why? Did you decorate it?"

"Mmm-hmm."

Geoff moved across the room to the oak desk, with its attached computer stand, and seated himself in a high-backed leather chair. The desk faced the doorway, ensuring that anyone entering the office was immediately visible to whomever sat there. Two chairs sat angled before the desk. Next to the door, a rather grand fan-leafed palm arranged next to a plump leather sofa that extended along that wall granted an ambience of refinement to the office. It was certainly more welcoming than most offices that he'd seen.

He looked at her now. "What do you think we should do first?"

"Why don't you go through the desk while I go through the credenza," she suggested. "If I find anything I don't understand, I'll ask you about it. Okay? Then, if there's time before I have to leave, we'll go through the filing cabinet together. I'll leave the computer stuff to you."

Geoff glanced at the stand to his right. It held both a personal computer and a networked terminal that would tie into the company's computer. "Sounds reasonable to me."

"If you find anything interesting after I leave this morning, you can tell me about it when we meet for lunch."

Geoff nodded. "Sure." Feeling as though he was trespassing on someone else's personal property, he opened the desk and began examining the contents.

Geoff had just begun sorting through his desk when the woman who'd been introduced to him yesterday as his secretary poked her head around the corner. She was a brunette with hazel eyes, about twenty-three years old by his estimate. "Good morning, Mr. Grayson. Mrs. Grayson."

He nodded and echoed Devon's *good-morning*. "Stephanie, right?"

"That's me," she said with a grin. "Do you want coffee?"

"That would be nice. Thanks."

Gradually, as employees arrived, he heard more and more noise coming from the outer offices, people greeting each other or carrying on conversations, but he ignored it. He felt too disconnected yet from everyone here to try to join them in their discussions.

With the exception of Stephanie who came in occasionally to file something, or put a memo into his basket, or offer them another cup of coffee, everyone pretty much left him alone, too.

Since the credenza was primarily a repository for books, manuals of every description, and blank business forms such as purchase orders, requisitions, fax sheets, letterhead, and so on, Devon had moved to the file cabinet. "Well," she said some time later, "there is some interesting paperwork in here, but I haven't come across anything that looks like it will help us." She dusted her hands off on her jeans. "It looks like some of these files haven't been touched since you last occupied this office." She checked her watch. "Well, I'd better get going. I'll call a cab to take me to the body shop so that I can pick up the Jeep."

Geoff nodded absently as he studied the pages of an old datebook he'd found. "Okay. I'll see you for lunch then."

By eleven, he'd finished exploring every piece of paper in his desk, and was just considering moving to the filing cabinet to take up where Devon had left off when a knock abruptly sounded.

"May I come in?" a male voice asked.

Geoff looked up to see a tall, barrel-chested, silver-haired gentleman dressed in a blue business suit standing in his doorway. Was this Russell Manning? "Of course. Come in," he said.

The man smiled and came toward him with arms outstretched. Before Geoff knew what had happened he found himself enveloped in a hearty, backslapping, bear hug. "Geoff," the man rumbled in a deep voice, "it sure is good to have you back."

"I appreciate that." Geoff returned the hug a little awkwardly. When the man released him, he said, "And you must be...Russell, right?"

The man's blue-eyed gaze sharpened a bit and he gave Geoff an assessing look before responding. "Sorry. This is a bit disconcerting. Yes, I'm Russell Manning. Did Devon tell you anything about me and our association?"

Geoff nodded. "Some. Would you like to sit down?"

With a nod and a weary sigh, Russell sat in one of the chairs before Geoff's desk. "Well, I'm glad Devon told you something at least. I'd hate to have to start from scratch."

"Would you like some coffee?" When Russell nodded in the

affirmative, Geoff paged Stephanie to request a couple of fresh cups and then considered the man before him who apparently had been a close friend. "What can you tell me about the six months before my accident?"

"You don't waste any time, do you?"

"Is there something else you wanted to talk about?"

Manning shook his head. "I just wanted to welcome you back and bring you up to date on things. Let's see...the last six months."

At that moment Stephanie brought their coffee and set it on the desk. "Anything else I can get you?" she asked.

"No thanks, dear," Russell responded. "But close the door on your way out if you don't mind."

As the door closed behind Stephanie, Geoff made a mental note of the fact that Russell felt comfortable taking charge of the staff at Future-Tech. It signalled that his direction had undoubtedly been pretty much hands-on during Geoff's absence, despite his rather small stake in the company. Since Geoff didn't know enough about the way his company had been run in his absence to decide if that was good or bad, he reserved judgement and simply waited for Russell to get around to responding to his question.

Russell sipped his coffee. "All I know about the time before you disappeared is what you told me, and you weren't always particularly communicative during that period. You never are when something's bothering you."

Geoff nodded. "Fair enough. What did I tell you?"

Russell shrugged. "You said that Spencer had come to you with suspicions regarding the alarm systems leaving here with problems."

"Spencer had come to me?" Geoff raised an eyebrow. "That hardly seems the action of a man who was sabotaging systems, does it?"

Russell shrugged. "It's hard to say. He could very well have been erecting a smoke screen to give himself time to clean up the mess he'd made." He frowned. "When he came to you he said he wanted to hire an independent investigator because he was beginning to have some difficulties with some of his clients. Who knows if the investigator would have been legit or not?''

Geoff met Russell's gaze. ''And this investigator was never hired?''

Russ shook his head. ''Nope. You asked him to give you some time to look into it on your own. He probably thought that if he'd refused it would have looked bad.''

Geoff raised an eyebrow. ''That's it?''

Manning nodded. ''Yep. That's pretty much all you told me.''

''And did I find anything?''

''Not that you told me about, and I think you would have told me. There wasn't much we didn't talk about.''

''Did you know Spencer well?''

Manning's eyebrows arched. ''Of course I knew him well. He worked for me at one time, too, you know. In fact, I believe you two first became acquainted at Delta Systems. Frankly, I wouldn't have believed that Spence was capable of something like this if I hadn't seen the proof.''

''Proof of what?''

''Proof that he altered the systems and sold those back-door codes to someone.''

''So he wasn't directly involved in the thefts then?''

Russ shook his head. ''No. But there was a rather substantial cash deposit made to his personal account just before you and he disappeared.''

''Interesting,'' Geoff mused as his frown of concentration deepened. The more he heard about Spencer, the more he realized that all the evidence against his friend had been circumstantial. Could someone have been framing his brother-in-law? But who? And why? More importantly, what had he, himself, discovered in the course of his unofficial investigation? Had he and Spencer been planning to discuss his findings when their plane went down?

Suddenly everything within Geoff went still. Devon's presumption the night he'd received that threatening note, that his disappearance had not been an accident, no longer seemed so unbelievable. If he *had* found something, and whoever was responsible had suspected he had, what would they have done to keep from being discovered? Was it possible that they might have sabotaged a plane? Could it be that the accident that had robbed Geoff of so much was no accident at all?

But for that to be true, the person responsible would have to be someone fairly close to him. Someone who would have known his plans and schedule. Perhaps even a friend, or rather someone who pretended to be. *Jesus!* He stared speculatively at the man sitting across from him: Russell Manning, a friend and colleague, a former mentor. And then, he mentally dismissed his suspicion. Although his amnesia made it easy to suspect virtually anyone because he didn't know these people, he couldn't allow himself to give in to paranoia. What he needed to do was to retrace the steps he'd taken more than two years ago. He needed to rediscover what he'd learned then. He needed to *remember,* dammit!

As though he'd read Geoff's mind, Russell changed the subject and asked, "So what's the medical verdict on you regaining your memory?"

Geoff stared at him. Why did he want to know that? he wondered as suspicion once again seeped out of the deep dark hole in his mind. Was he afraid of what Geoff might remember? And then, realizing that the question was the kind that any friend might ask of him in this situation, he forced himself to relax. The situation was making him more jumpy than usual. "Medically they say there's very little chance of it returning after so long, but I haven't given up hope."

"No, of course not. It's not in your makeup to give up on anything."

Did that comment have a slightly wry tone? "No, it's not." Apparently at least one aspect of his character had not changed. "So then, taking the discussion back to Future-Tech, do we have anything to worry about? Pete Sherwood seemed to think that my resurfacing could present legal problems if certain clients got wind of it."

Russell grimaced. "It's difficult to predict, of course, but I don't think so. Countless investigators for the Fort Knox case

have already been through everything and found nothing con-
crete to pin on Future-Tech or its officers. Frankly, I doubt that
there's anything for anyone to find.'' He raised a brow. ''I hope
you're not going to waste your time trying to rekindle your own
investigation?''

Geoff shrugged. ''I have some questions I want answered,
but...an investigation? No. I don't think so.''

Russell seemed to sag in his chair a fraction. A sigh of relief?
Geoff wondered. Or just a relaxation of worry on the part of a
friend? ''I'm glad to hear it. You need to worry about getting
well again.''

Devon sat at a small square oak table in the center of the
restaurant waiting for Geoff. He wasn't late; rather, she'd taken
off a little early to beat the traffic. Now, she sat there fingering
her napkin and recalling that just a couple of weeks ago, she'd
been sitting in this same restaurant with David, confident in the
course of her life. How ephemeral and mercurial life was at
times.

Abruptly, she shivered and looked around. For the second time
in as many days, she felt eyes on her. Someone watching her.
Yesterday, she'd blamed the sensation on David and dismissed
it, but today, when she looked around, there was no one looking
her way. At least not that she could see. So what, then, accounted
for this strange sensation of being observed? She'd just turned
forward again when she caught sight of Geoff weaving his way
across the crowded restaurant toward her, and all negative
thought fled as a ripple of pleasure coiled through her.

''Hi,'' she said as he pulled out a chair and sat down. ''How
was your meeting with Russell?''

''Interesting,'' he responded. ''How was your meeting with
your client?''

''Good,'' she said with a smile. ''I managed to avert a couple
of minor catastrophes and get one very important contract back
on target. All in all a very satisfying morning.''

He offered her that fleeting little smile that she was coming to like far too much, and then nodded to the menu that lay open on the table before her. "What have you decided on?"

"A small pepper steak with Caesar salad, I think. What are you in the mood for?" Her question was entirely innocent, but the moment the words were out of her mouth something deep in his eyes flared with heat and the air between them charged with awareness.

Finally, he blinked, cleared his throat and said, "That sounds fine. I think I'll have the same."

The waitress had no sooner taken their order and left when a rather high-pitched female voice called, "Devon, how are you?" Devon looked beyond Geoff to see Carla Miles, an old friend she hadn't seen in quite some time, approaching their table. Carla, who had a tall, thin boyish figure, had discovered at a young age that black showed off her beautiful blond hair to perfection and, thus, was clothed in her usual shapeless black dress, black hose, and flats. She accessorized her look with dangling strands of colorful beads, large colorful earrings to match, gold rings on almost every finger, and lots of eye makeup. The result was that she looked a bit eccentric.

In actuality, however, Devon thought the look suited her. Carla *was* eccentric. Devon smiled as Carla stopped at her table. "Hi, Carla. How are you? I haven't seen you in ages."

"Oh, I know, hon. It's been a coon's age. But life is just so—" Carla broke off abruptly as she flashed a glance in Geoff's direction. Her face paled, and she flashed a glance at Devon. "Listen, hon, are you meeting anyone for lunch?"

Devon frowned, not understanding. "Yes, I—" But she got no further before Carla interrupted.

"When whoever it is gets here, I think you should ask them to sit *there*." With a jangling of gold bracelets, Carla indicated the chair at right angles to Devon rather than the seat across from her where Geoff sat.

"No, you don't understand—" Devon tried to explain that Geoff was the person she was meeting, but once again Carla interrupted her.

With icy fingers, Carla gripped Devon's forearm where it

rested on the table, and leaned forward to whisper in her ear. "I'm serious, hon. I don't know how to tell you this, but...well, Geoff is sitting in the chair across from you."

For one second more, Devon continued to consider Carla in confusion, and then the light began to dawn. Carla had not yet heard about Geoff's miraculous return from the dead! Devon smiled a secret smile, winked at Geoff who was looking at Carla as though she'd lost her mind, and said, "I know."

Carla jerked up to a standing position again. "You mean you can see him, too!"

Devon nodded. "Mmm-hmm. But there's a reason for that."

"What?" she asked, staring at Devon with enormous blue eyes.

"He's...alive!" Devon couldn't help teasing her friend. After all Carla had scared the dickens out of Devon on more than one occasion with her séances.

"He's—" Carla started to echo Devon and then stopped to stare openly at Geoff for the first time. Then slowly, she extended her left forefinger to give him a very firm jab in the upper arm. "Well...well...I can't believe it!" she finally managed to get out. "How did that happen?" She looked at Devon as though she expected her to recount some strange new method of resurrection.

"Why don't you give me a call tonight and I'll explain it. Okay?"

Carla nodded. "Sure, hon. I'll call you." And then, still staring at Geoff as though she suspected he might disappear at any instant, she made her way past their table.

After she had gone, Geoff and Devon stared at each other for a moment with lips twitching, and then suddenly Geoff laughed. It was a full-throated, hearty sound, and Devon realized it was the first time since finding him that she'd heard him give in to mirth. For that, she would always be grateful to Carla; Geoff didn't laugh as easily as he once had.

"She thought I was a ghost?" Geoff asked when he could talk again.

Grinning, Devon nodded. "Carla's always been a bit psychic

or something. She says she sees and talks to ghosts quite regularly.''

''So I would have been...just another ghost to her?'' Geoff asked with a smile on his lips.

Devon shook her head. ''Actually I think you would have been the first one she has ever really known beforehand. Poor Carla. I hope she recovers from the shock. I guess I'm going to have to make some phone calls so that your presence doesn't give anyone else who knows us a heart attack or something.'' She reached for a bread stick and tore a piece off. ''Have you called your mother yet?''

Geoff nodded. ''Shortly after Christmas, but her answering machine said she was in Phoenix for the winter, so I just left my number and hung up. I don't think what I have to say is appropriate to leave on a machine. She might think it's just a crank call. If she doesn't check her messages and return my call, I'll try again in a month or so.''

Devon nodded in agreement just as their meals arrived. Over lunch, Geoff told her about his morning and his conversation with Russell. It irked her that no one had ever felt it necessary to tell her any of the details that Geoff had learned, but that was going to change right now. If she and Geoff were to stand any chance of being together in the future, then she had to be part of his life on more levels than just the personal. At least, unlike her father, Geoff didn't try to protect her by shielding her.

She frowned thoughtfully. At least he wasn't doing that *this time*. But had he before? Was that, perhaps, part of the reason for the rift that had developed between them? They'd always communicated up to that time, but it was possible that, whatever had been bothering Geoff, was something he'd felt he had to shelter his family from. But what could have been so sensitive or so bad?

''Devon—'' Geoff called her back from her thoughts.

''Hmm?'' she asked around the bite of tender steak she'd just popped into her mouth.

''Was there ever an investigation into the cause of the plane crash?''

She nodded. "There's automatically an investigation into any accident. Especially one involving casualties. They need to determine if it was pilot error, the weather, or some other cause."

Geoff frowned. "This was a small charter flight, right?" When Devon nodded he asked, "Who was the pilot?"

Devon went still. Uh-oh! This was one more thing he didn't know. She cleared her throat.

"Devon—" he prompted, eyeing her warily now.

"Either Spencer was piloting the plane, or you were. You chartered the plane without a pilot because you both had pilot's licenses."

Geoff froze in midchew and stared at her. Then, he slowly swallowed what was in his mouth. "I'm a pilot?"

She nodded. "You were. Your license would probably have to be updated or something by now. I don't know exactly how it works. But, flying was just a hobby. You and Spencer had taken lessons together for fun a couple of years earlier."

Slowly, thoughtfully, Geoff nodded. "I see." Then, looking down he sliced his steak. "So what was the result of the investigation into the crash?"

Devon frowned. "It was deemed an accident. Some problem with the altimeter compounded by a thick cloud cover." She studied him. "Why? Do you think I may have been right the other night?" The thought that someone might have deliberately tried to murder her husband, along with his sister, his brother-in-law, and herself if she hadn't backed out in anger at the last moment, was staggering. Who would do such a thing?

Geoff nodded. "It's plausible. And I don't want to dismiss the possibility without knowing for certain."

"I'll make some phone calls and see what more I can find out, if you like?"

"Thanks. I'd appreciate that." He looked at her then, his green eyes glowing with male admiration.

She swallowed. "You're welcome," she managed to murmur. Heck, for that look, she'd jump through hoops.

He frowned thoughtfully. "There are a lot of answers I need to find."

And she intended to help him find them, if she could. But first she had to make sure they were looking for the same ones. "What are the questions?" Devon asked.

Geoff looked musingly over Devon's right shoulder as he began to list points. "First, I need to know where that money in Spencer's account came from. Someone was either framing him, or someone was paying him for services rendered. If the latter, then he'd obviously gotten involved in something he shouldn't have. And, if that was the case, then I need to know what it was and *who* was paying him."

Devon nodded. "And second?"

"The second thing I need is the information on the plane crash. And third, I need to retrace the steps I made two years ago. I need to find out what my suspicions were then because, if what I'm coming to suspect is true, and the crash wasn't an accident, then I must have been close to finding some answers."

Almost two months had passed, and the children had long since returned home. There had been only one more ominous occurrence, and that had taken the form of a threatening message left on Geoff's home office answering machine. "If you're smart you'll leave the past in the past," it said. "Or you'll wish you had." The voice had been electronically disguised, which made him wonder if the person was concerned about him recognizing their voice. He hadn't bothered telling Devon about it. There was nothing she could do, except worry, and he was doing enough of that for both of them.

Even with the worry though, their days began to fall into a predictable routine. Since Geoff's presence at Future-Tech was still not absolutely necessary—although he was gradually reassuming more of the responsibilities—he returned home every afternoon to welcome the children home from school and ferry them around to whatever extracurricular activities were scheduled for that day. Those hours before dinner were also the best time for him to focus on rebuilding his relationship with his sometimes difficult and usually headstrong son.

They had made some definite strides. Tyler had finally started talking to him, telling him about his day at school, about misadventures his friends had had, and even occasionally, if Britanny wasn't with them, about girls he was interested in. Yes, Geoff was content with the way his relationships were progressing with his children. He just wished he could be as satisfied in other areas of his life.

Devon continued to hold him at arm's length, and it was driving him crazy. She maintained that she wasn't willing to get close to him, to give *them* a chance, until she knew what had happened before—and they'd made very little headway in their investigation.

He still had no idea what he'd uncovered in his previous investigation of the problems at Future-Tech, or even if they were connected to his strained marriage. Thinking that the money deposited to Spencer's account sounded like a good place to start his current investigation, he'd tried to trace it to its source but had run up against a brick wall. According to Pete Sherwood, it appeared to have been deposited in cash via night deposit.

The net result of all of this was that Geoff was frustrated on two fronts: both at work and in his personal life. That made him jumpy and irritable—especially around Devon, although he'd done his best to hide it. Damn! The only way to ease his frustration was to find the answers he and Devon both required. But how? His memory stubbornly remained in absentia rather than proving to be the boon he'd expected it to be once he was back in familiar surroundings.

Now, as Geoff sat with the other parents and caregivers waiting for Tyler to finish his karate lesson, he decided he was going to have to focus on the office at Devon's again. The first time he'd gone through it, he'd found nothing of particular interest except a series of encrypted disks, and he still hadn't been able to break the encryption code.

Other than the disks, they'd come across only a personal organizer containing nothing of note—although some pages were missing—and a few files: invoice copies, his own bank records and some correspondence.

Damn! There had to be something somewhere. What was he overlooking?

"What's the matter?" Tyler's voice tugged him from his thoughts.

"Hmm? Oh, nothing important, sport. Are you ready?"

Tyler nodded, but continued to eye Geoff from the corner of his eye as they made their way to the dressing rooms.

When these sideways glances continued even as Tyler was dressing, Geoff finally decided to prod him a bit. "What's on your mind, son?"

Tyler paused in the act of putting his socks on and looked up. Then, with a slight grimace, he said, "Nothin'. It's not important."

"Remember what I said the other night about communication being the key to avoiding misunderstandings?" Geoff asked. Tyler nodded, and Geoff continued, "Then let's communicate, okay? Tell me what's up."

Fastening his gaze on the floor, Tyler's face took on a mutinous expression for an instant, then, with a sigh, he shrugged and plunged. "Well...I was wondering, that is...didn't I do good today?"

Geoff frowned. "I'm no karate expert, but from what I could tell, you did just fine. Why?"

Now Tyler raised his gaze to stare accusingly at Geoff. "If I did good, then how come you looked so mad when I finished?"

"Mad?" Geoff's brows arched in surprise. "Tyler, I wasn't mad. A bit worried maybe, but not mad." He saw a dawning expression of confusion in Tyler's eyes and quickly went on. "And I wasn't worried about you. You hardly need anyone to worry about you now, do you?"

Tyler squared his shoulders. "'Course not." Then he frowned. "So what're you worryin' about then?"

Geoff studied the boy, wondering how much he could say without muddling things further. Finally though, he decided to be honest. He couldn't very well demand it of Tyler without delivering it in return. "Well," he said, "before the accident, I left some computer disks in my office that were coded. The program that I used to code them was in a laptop on the plane, and I'm afraid I haven't remembered enough about computers yet to figure out how to read them. I think I need the original encryption program, but I don't know what it was, so,'' he shrugged, ''I'm stuck.''

Tyler frowned. ''Encryption. Is that like when you save stuff so nobody can read it but you on your computer?''

Geoff nodded.

''I still got a copy of that Info-Safe program you gave me to learn how to use. It's on Britanny's and my homework computer. I don't know if it's the right one, but you can use it if you want to.''

Geoff's pulse began to beat just a little faster and he leaned forward to grasp Tyler by the shoulders. ''I gave you a copy of an encryption program?''

The boy nodded. ''I think so.''

Geoff swept him into a big hug. ''You're a lifesaver, sport.''

Tyler stared at him wide-eyed as though he didn't quite know what to think of Geoff's sudden mood shift. ''I am? You mean...you want to use it?''

''You bet I do. As soon as we get home. Okay?''

''Sure.'' Tyler bent to lace his shoes. ''I've got other stuff on there, too. You can look at it if you want to. Maybe it'll help.''

''I appreciate it, son.''

After finishing up the dishes, Devon decided to join Geoff in his office to see how he was doing in deciphering the computer disks. The intense expression on his face halted her in the doorway. ''Is something wrong?''

He glanced up from his perusal of the laptop computer screen. ''I found the missing pages from the datebook.'' He shrugged. ''Maybe I just never printed them off.''

''They were among the encrypted disks?''

''Yeah.''

Devon felt her stomach clench. Whatever he'd found, it wasn't good. ''What do they say?''

He looked at her then with a hard, unreadable expression.

"Come see for yourself, if you like. But I warn you, you're not going to like it."

Hesitantly, Devon moved across the room to stand behind Geoff's left shoulder. The page on the screen was from February tenth, six months before Geoff's disappearance: "Spence says there's something wrong with the security systems. Check it out."

"So Spencer knew there was a problem and approached you!"

Geoff nodded. "It confirms what Russell told me." He depressed a button and a page in late March appeared. Devon read: "Problem is definitely with the software. Looks deliberate. But how? Do more testing."

Geoff depressed another button and a page from April twenty-ninth came up on the screen. "Software has been written with a default access code that shouldn't be there. Winston did most of the programming, but not all. Did he plant the code?"

And on July 29th: "Check records on other programmers."

Devon's eyes widened. "Winston! But...that's not possible! He wouldn't do that!"

Geoff lifted his gaze to stare at her. "And maybe I knew you'd feel that way."

Chapter 13

"You think that...because Winston...?" Unable to finish the sentence, Devon made her way around the desk to plop down in the chair that sat there. "You think that your distance in those last few months could have been because of...your suspicion of Winston?"

He nodded. "If I suspected your brother was guilty of sabotaging Future-Tech's security systems, but I didn't have the evidence, I could very well have felt that I couldn't tell you my suspicions. At least not until I had proof. Look how protective you are of him. From what I've seen, you've always felt responsible for him, and you defend him or make excuses for him even now. Would you have listened to any accusation that didn't have proof to back it?"

Devon felt almost faint. "I...I don't know. Probably not." She swallowed. "Are there...any more entries?"

"There were a few more notes pertaining to the security systems, stuff we already know. There's only one more about Winston."

"What does it say?"

"It was written in late July, too. It says, 'Winston seems to have more money than he used to. Check it out. Anyone else?'"

Devon clenched her fingers together, so stunned she didn't know what to think, let alone what to say. "I...my God!" She rose and approached the window, staring out at the night, at the myriad of city lights below. Then she turned. "Do you believe there's anything to it?"

He met her gaze for a moment, holding it as he tried to assess her reaction, and then said, "I don't know. But I'm not dismissing it."

She nodded and her gaze dropped, moving over the answering machine sitting on the corner of the desk. Her mind focused on the mundane. Blessed normality. "You haven't listened to your messages."

He glanced over. "I hadn't noticed." Devon could believe that. After taking a copy of the program he needed from the kids' computer, he'd been so anxious to see what the disks contained, that he hadn't paid attention to much of anything—even dinner. Now, she almost wished he'd never decoded the disks.

"Are you going to listen to them?"

"Huh?" he asked as he continued to scroll through the pages on his computer screen.

"The messages. Are you going to listen to them?"

"Oh, yeah." Reaching forward he depressed the play button and then resumed his absorbed perusal of a new screen of data.

There was a sound like an indrawn breath and everything within Geoff went still as a premonition of what was to come left him cold. And then an electronic voice blared into the silence. "Your luck won't hold out forever, Geoff. Leave it alone, or you'll disappear for good. I'd hate to see that nice family of yours get hurt all over again." There was a click as the caller hung up, and a whir as the machine rewound itself.

The first thought that raced through his mind was: *How did he, or they, know?* What had he done that had tipped off whoever was watching that he hadn't given up? Had someone heard him talking to his son in the dressing rooms after his karate class? Had someone heard Geoff ask his secretary at work where he could find the complaints that had been filed by clients two years earlier? There was no way to know. He didn't know who was watching.

"Geoff—"

Slowly Geoff forced himself to look up and meet Devon's eyes. She was standing in openmouthed shock. "My God, Geoff! You can't honestly believe that is Winston. It can't be! He wouldn't do something like that."

"Maybe he's working for someone else."

Devon shook her head vehemently. "No! I can't accept that." Suddenly there were tears in her eyes. "It has to be someone else, Geoff," she said in a choked voice.

He rose, wanting to hold her, to comfort her, to protect her from whoever was doing this to them. "You're probably right," he murmured as he enfolded her in his arms.

For a moment, one brief moment of weakness, she leaned on him, fitting her head into the hollow spot on his shoulder that seemed made for just that purpose. And then she was drawing away. "I...I can't do this."

He frowned in confusion. "Do what?"

But she merely shook her head as fresh tears sparkled in her eyes. "I need to be alone, Geoff. Please." She left the room in such a hurry that he didn't get another word out before she was gone. It hurt that she wouldn't let him comfort her. Whether she recognized it or not, she was his woman and she shouldn't have to cry alone. Damn!

He whirled to stare at the answering machine that had multiplied her pain. If he could have gotten hold of the person on the other end of that electronic voice, he was quite certain he could have choked the life from him with his bare hands.

Devon signed the last check, stuffed it into an envelope and leaned back in her chair with a sigh. There! The bill paying was done for another month. There was comfort in routine and she'd been focusing on that ever since last night. But it hadn't kept her from thinking. She'd decided to simply ignore Geoff's suspicions regarding Winston until they found some proof—which she sincerely believed they would not find. But that had been only one of the things on her mind. For an entire day, she'd done nothing but think. And, having finally reached some conclusions, she couldn't put off speaking to Geoff for much longer.

She glanced at her watch. It was eight-thirty. "Tyler, Britanny," she called toward the stairs as she passed them. "Time for you to have your showers and start getting ready for bed."

A minor argument immediately ensued overhead regarding who was going to go first. Ignoring it, Devon went into the kitchen to heat a kettle of water. Some herbal tea would be heaven right now, something to calm her nerves. As she waited for the water to heat, she thought back over the past couple of months and the changes that had been wrought in their lives. So many changes...and now it looked like she would have another one to deal with.

First had been the change in her relationship with her father. He'd stopped speaking to her after she'd finally found the nerve to confront him concerning his interference in her life. She hoped they could work it out, but she refused to be the one to try to bridge the gap between them. He would take that as an admission on her part that she'd been wrong; that she'd accepted that her father always knew best. But she hadn't been wrong and she no longer accepted his judgement as infallible. She was a grown woman, for heaven's sake. And for the first time in her life Devon was determined to weather the strife between them until he understood how important this was to her.

But her relationship with her father was only one of the changes that had occurred. There were the children, too. Each of them had changed in their own ways as they accepted their father back into their lives. They were both old enough to remember their father's personality and realize that he wasn't the same. Both children worked to reconcile themselves to the changes they saw. Britanny seemed to find it easier than her brother. Accepting the changes in her father with her usual pragmatism, she had attempted to explain them to her brother by saying, "He can't remember how to be, so he just *is*." A rather profound statement for a nine-year-old, Devon thought, and so true.

After a time, Tyler had begun to signal his cautious acceptance of this new Geoff in other, more subtle, ways—by talking to him more readily, by imitating the quiet strength of Geoff's new personality in his responses to situations, and, most apparently, by a significant decrease in his sullen behavior. Geoff's talk with Tyler on that first night had been a turning point for their son.

Neither had Devon come through the past weeks unchanged by Geoff's presence in her life. But the changes she'd undergone were emotional and confusing, and she hadn't been ready to examine them too closely. And, because she hadn't been ready to feel them, she'd kept her emotions under rigid control. Tonight, though, she suddenly found herself viewing her situation from a new perspective, almost as though she was standing outside herself.

They had not resumed a physical relationship and would not until they solved their old problems. Devon had been adamant about that. She was still terrified of being subjected again to the emotional agony of losing him to something she didn't understand. She'd hoped that controlling their base urges would prevent a deepening of the emotional bond between them. But she wasn't sure it was working. She couldn't help thinking that these emotions were merely a remnant of the love she'd had for the man she'd married. But…were they? Her physical needs were all wrapped up with her emotional needs to the point where she no longer knew where one ended and the other began.

But it wasn't only her own lust that had become a problem because of Geoff's almost constant presence. She and the children were coming to rely on him, on his being there, in ways she hadn't anticipated they would until she and Geoff had worked out the other aspects of their relationship—if that time ever came. He was becoming an integral part of their lives again before she was ready for him to be, and she didn't know what to do about it.

And then, last, but certainly not the least of her concerns, were the continued threats against Geoff's life. Those made her want to keep him close. But realistically, she knew she was no protection for him. She could continue to help him look for answers without having him so close. That would be best for all of them until...until things were resolved.

Now, if only she could somehow find some way to explain all this to Geoff.

The button on the kettle popped, and she poured water into a small teapot. While the tea steeped, she poured a cup of coffee for Geoff. She was going to take him some coffee and, hopefully, lure him away from those computer disks long enough to have a serious conversation. It was not a discussion that she was looking forward to, but...

Geoff surprised her by entering the kitchen just as she was taking the tea bag from her cup. "Mmm, coffee smells good," he said.

"I was just going to bring you some."

"Thank you." He flashed her that fleeting smile that still had the power to make her heart tremble. He was so handsome, so very masculine. "I decided to take a break. See if I could head off a headache."

"Did you take a pill?" she asked, striving for normality, even as she wondered if she was being honest with herself when she said she needed to keep him at arm's length.

"Yeah," he responded. Then, as though sensing the direction of her thoughts, he reached out a hand to caress her cheek and despite herself, despite all her resolve, Devon leaned into the touch. It felt so good to be close to him.

Dropping the caressing hand to her shoulder, placing the other on her waist, Geoff stepped nearer. The contact was warm, comforting, and as always, she felt fragile beneath his touch, feminine. No other man had ever been able to make her so keenly aware of her femininity. A shiver raced through her as his thumb gently traced the line of her throat. Their eyes clashed and held, and Devon saw the smoldering promise there. Despite herself her heart began to pound, and her breathing quickened.

"Geoff—" She tried to distract him.

She never received an answer.

And then suddenly she was in his arms. Devon gasped at the exhilarating shock of their bodies coming together, seduced by the mastery of his embrace as he tangled a fist in her hair. Tilting her head, he captured her lips with his, slowly deepening the kiss with an expertise that robbed her of strength and reason. The blood throbbed in her veins as he kissed her leisurely, deeply, staking a claim without words, telling her again with slow, expert strokes of his tongue, that she was his. And Devon, despite the alarm bells sounding in her mind, felt a soul-stirring desire rising up within her.

"Mom, can I have a drink?"

Devon and Geoff leapt apart as the high-pitched childish voice doused them with an ice-cold ration of reality. "What, dear?" Devon managed to ask in a tone that sounded reasonably calm as she hastily ran her hands over her mussed hair.

Just then Britanny came around the corner and stopped. She eyed them suspiciously for a moment. Then her face brightened and, with an expression of pure glee, she asked, "Were you guys kissing?"

"What makes you ask that?" Devon hedged, avoiding Geoff's gaze.

Still grinning, Britanny shrugged. "I don't know." Her gaze moved to Geoff. Then she frowned. "How come your hair's all wet?" She flashed a censorious look at Devon. "Mom didn't dunk you for kissin' her, did she?"

"Britanny!" Though, for the first time she noticed that Geoff's hair was damp. She'd been sidetracked by other observations.

Geoff grinned. "No, she didn't dunk me. I had a headache, so I wet my head in cold water."

"Oh." Britanny thought about that for a second and then the frown cleared from her face and she looked back at her mother. "Can I have a drink?"

Devon nodded. "Of course, but only water or milk. Nothing with sugar just before bed. And as soon as you're finished I want you in bed to stay. Agreed?"

Britanny nodded and turned toward the refrigerator, saying, "Thanks, Mom," over her shoulder.

When their daughter had left the room, Devon lifted her gaze to Geoff's face once more. The twinkle in his eyes suggested he was highly amused by their daughter's forthrightness. Devon, on the other hand, didn't know what to think, but she was grateful for the interruption. She backed away, grasping the coffee cup and passing it to him, before picking up her own cup of tea. "I...wanted to talk to you," she murmured. "How are the disk translations coming?"

Geoff eyed her for a moment as though seeking confirmation that the moment of intimacy could not be recaptured. "All right."

He shrugged. "Come on, and I'll show you." Moving past her, Geoff entered the hall and led the way back to the office. "These—" he indicated a stack on the right-hand side of the desk "—are pretty much your ordinary stuff. Letters, a couple of spreadsheets comparing yearly sales figures, that kind of thing. But these," he picked up another smaller stack of disks and waved them in the air, "these contain what look like software subroutines."

Devon frowned. "I don't understand. Is that significant?"

Geoff nodded and waved away her confusion. "It could be. If they're copies of the routines used to program the security systems. And, if they are, they may even show me how the back-door codes were planted."

Devon gave him a stunned look and sat down with a plop on the edge of the chair that sat before the desk. "But...why would you have copies of that kind of programming?"

"I'm assuming I somehow managed to find them. Maybe by copying them from a computer on the production floor if I suspected an employee. I don't know. But since I have them, I'm going to go through them to see if they tell me anything."

Looking faintly relieved by his plausible explanation, though still more than a little floored, Devon sipped her tea. Then she looked at Geoff, "So you're still thinking that it was somebody from Future-Tech who was deliberately sabotaging the systems? What about Spencer?"

He shrugged. "For all I know, everything may still come back to Spencer. I'm simply looking at all the angles, Devon."

"*All* the angles?" she asked.

He nodded. "I can't afford to ignore the possibility that Winston may have been involved."

She sighed and nodded. "I know, it's just that..."

"I know, Devon. But you have to admit that, if the entire problem had rested with Spencer, I should have been able to talk to you about it. Wouldn't you think?"

"Maybe. Unless..."

"Unless what?"

She cleared her throat. "Unless Dad told you not to worry me by telling me and you listened to him."

Geoff stared at her for a moment. "Devon, I know you've been having some problems with your father lately, but...I don't think that sounds very likely. Do you honestly think I would have allowed him to dictate what I could discuss with you and what I couldn't?"

She shrugged. "No, but maybe he didn't give you any choice. Dad can be ruthless in defense of his own, and he does own thirty percent of Future-Tech. Maybe you should ask him if he knows anything about the problems between you and I before you disappeared. I asked him once and he said that he didn't, but I don't know what to believe anymore."

"From what I've seen of the financial statements, Future-Tech was doing well enough at that time that I could have bought your father out if I'd wanted to." The computer beeped and Geoff removed a disk from the drive before inserting another. "He couldn't have influenced me that way, Devon. Though I understand your reasons for preferring to think along those lines."

Devon sipped her tea. "Have you finished deciphering all the disks?"

He shook his head. "There are a couple more. I've scanned most of those that I have decoded looking for anything unusual, but so far nothing has caught my eye. I'm going to go back and read the correspondence more carefully."

Devon nodded, and leaned back in the chair, supporting her cup on the palm of her left hand while holding the handle with her right. She looked preoccupied but said nothing.

Finally Geoff asked, "Is something on your mind, Devon?"

She started, and then with a slight grimace asked, "Am I that transparent?" Geoff didn't bother to reply, and a moment later she rose to begin pacing the office. "I don't know how to say this," she murmured.

Geoff leaned back in his chair, sipped his coffee, and watched her. The more time he spent with her the more fascinated he was. But, he didn't like the sound of whatever was coming. When Devon didn't know how to say something, it usually meant that she feared that whatever she had to say would hurt another person's feelings. Still, there was no sense in him worrying about it until he knew for certain what it was that was bothering her.

Abruptly, she halted, flattened her palms nervously against the black denim of the jeans she wore, and met his gaze. "Geoff, I think we're moving too quickly with this relationship."

Quickly! Everything within him went still. He stared at her for a moment, waiting to see if she'd say something else to clarify her remark, but she just swallowed and stared at him anxiously. He cleared his throat. "I think you'd better explain, Devon."

She sighed and looked skyward. "It's just that you're always here, Geoff."

"I live here."

"That's not what I meant." Seeming to have gathered her courage, she looked back at him. "You're here in the morning for breakfast and to help the kids make their lunches. And now, they expect you there. You're here after school to take them to their karate or music lessons or what-have-you. And they expect to see you. You're here every night for dinner. And even *I* am coming to expect that." He opened his mouth but she held up a hand to stall him before he got a word out. "I know. I know. More than half the time, it's you who's making the dinner. And I appreciate it—I really do. But that's part of the problem, too. I mean the only time you're not here is when you go to work, and you haven't been working full-time yet. Don't you see?"

Geoff stared at her. No, he didn't see, dammit! "Why is that a problem? I thought the idea was to see if it was possible to reclaim our lives together as a family. To see if being together would trigger my memory so that we could try to work things out between us.''

Devon shook her head. ''That would be nice, Geoff, but I'm not sure we're going to find the answers we need anytime soon, and I'm too afraid of...''

''Of what?'' he asked when she broke off. ''Is this about that message last night?''

''No! Well, maybe a bit.'' She winced. ''I'm not doing a very good job of this.''

''So what are you afraid of?''

''I'm afraid of going through all that hell again. Every day, I'm getting closer to you. The kids are getting closer to you. I'm not saying that I don't want you to see them. It's just that I think you should see them a little less often. If we don't slow down now, it may be too late. Don't you see?''

He studied her, taking in her obvious agitation, but try as he might, he couldn't follow her logic. What he did gather made him angry—coldly angry—and he rose to face her. ''So, you've decided that the risk of being hurt is too great. You don't want to give *us* a chance after all, and my being around too much is...what? Putting a crimp in plans you have to get back together with David?'' He knew that David had been calling Devon at work, seeking to rekindle their relationship. She'd mentioned that he'd called a few times.

''I'm not interested in David,'' Devon asserted, and her tone made it obvious that she was telling the truth.

''Then help me understand where this is coming from, Devon.''

''We're starting to rely on you too much, Geoff. The kids are starting to depend on you to help them with their homework, to give them advice. *I'm* starting to depend on you to share responsibility, to be here.''

Geoff's brow arched. ''And that's a problem.'' The statement was half question.

''*Yes,* that's a problem,'' Devon said vehemently. ''Weren't you listening? What's going to happen if things don't work out? What'll happen when you're suddenly not here for us?'' She hammered her thigh with a clenched fist. "Dammit, Geoff. I won't let us all be hurt again."

Geoff frowned. This *was* a result of that message. She was afraid that whoever had left it was going to succeed in making him disappear again. And he had no way to reassure her. Not yet. "Devon, you knew when you brought me here that I planned on being part of the kids' lives, of your life. I'm not going to let anything change that."

"Okay, fine. I believe that you won't intentionally hurt us. But, you may not have a choice. And I can't deal with...*this*."

"*This* being something that threatens *you*," he said in a deadly quiet tone. "It threatens your equanimity. You're thinking of yourself more than you are the children." Moving out from behind the desk, he approached her. "Aren't you?" he demanded. "You're afraid, no...you're *terrified* that what's between us might prove to be strong enough that you'll want to take a chance again even if we never find the answers you need." She started slightly at his accusation, and another suspicion crowded into his mind. "And you're more than half hoping that we won't find those answers, aren't you? Because you're afraid of feeling that strongly again. Friendship is safe, but anything more...that involves emotional risk. And you don't want to invest that much again. I'm right, aren't I?"

"No, if I'd wanted friendship, I would have stuck with David. I want *us* as much as you do. But unlike you, I remember the past. I remember what we lost, and how much it hurt. I..." Devon's eyes widened as he halted in front of her, his proximity making her lose her train of thought. She'd seen Geoff angry many times, but never in quite this way. There was something about his very coldness, the icy calm that enveloped him, that made him seem...dangerous. If only he'd yell, bluster a little bit, at least she would have felt as though she was in familiar territory.

"You're a coward, Devon. And, fool that I am, I've bowed to your wishes, not pursuing this thing between us until we had some security—the security that *you* need. But I'm not going to let you dismiss me from your life, Devon, and I'm through doing things your way."

Devon swallowed. "Wh-what do you mean?"

He advanced another step, until he was standing so close that she could feel his body heat. "I mean be damned to whatever happened before. You keep telling me I'm not the same person as I was then, so what makes you think I'd react the same way?"

"I...I don't know, but..." His proximity was muddling her senses.

"No more buts, Devon. We're going to do things my way for a while. As long as I didn't touch you, didn't try to get close to you, you could forget about this chemistry between us, even fool yourself into thinking that it didn't exist. You aren't going to be able to do that anymore."

Devon regarded him warily. "What do you mean?"

"Don't worry. I'll leave for a while if that's what you want. Not for your sake, but for the kids."

She frowned. "I don't understand."

"Whoever is behind the threats has made it pretty obvious that *I* am the target, but I've been worried that the kids could get hurt inadvertently if there is another break-in or something. If I leave, whoever is following me and monitoring my movements will know that I've left."

"Oh." She swallowed, avoiding his gaze, feeling guilty for forcing him out, but unable to see any way around it.

"But I have to warn you, Devon, that when I come back, the gloves are gonna be off, as they say."

Her gaze flew up to his. "Pardon me?"

"Think about it. And, as for right now, I want you to remember something." He moved even closer. Too near! Much too near.

Devon tried to get her sluggish brain to interpret what he was saying even as it seemed more preoccupied with noticing other things. Like how big he suddenly seemed. And how mesmerizing his eyes were. "What? Geoff, I—" But as the tension in the room became palpable, she broke off, no longer certain what it was she'd been about to say.

The charged air between them thickened and smoldered as he slowly reached one hand up to thread it through her hair and grip the nape of her neck. Without holding her in any other way, without embracing her, he pulled her toward him until she was so close that their breaths mingled. And, while she stood paralyzed in so gentle a grasp, he whispered, "This is what I mean," before lowering his lips to capture hers.

Devon's heart leapt into her throat in response to the touch of his mouth. She sensed Geoff's rigid control, an iciness that told her just how angry he was beneath the surface, and yet the mere contact of their mouths was enough to sear her with the heat of her own carnal hunger.

Damn him! Damn him for knowing me so well! she thought while she was still capable of thought. And then lucidity fled as her lips parted helplessly beneath his and he took instantaneous advantage. Without touching her in any way except for the gentle hold on her neck and the searing command of his mouth on hers, he robbed her of resistance, reason, and recourse. Devon moaned as her stomach performed aerial somersaults. Her lungs constricted; her toes curled; her pulse raced; and she needed...more. She was tired of denying the need to be held, to be touched. She wanted to feel his arms around her. She wanted to feel the furnacelike heat of his body next to hers. She wanted to feel the hard strength of his muscular form cradling her softness. She wanted...him.

If only she could allow herself to succumb to her wants, her desires, without thought for the future. But she couldn't. She had always been the kind of person who needed security above all else, and she couldn't find the ability within her to change. Not now. Not...yet.

She moaned again, in an agony of want and indecision and then moved to break off the kiss. Without opening her eyes because she knew meeting his gaze, seeing its scorching promise, would undo her, she murmured, "No, Geoff. I...can't. Please understand. I need time."

"I understand, Devon," he murmured in return. "You've got

two weeks. After that, whether we've found your answers or not, we do things my way."

Devon had opened her eyes when he began speaking, and now she met his gaze. "What do you mean, *your way?*"

He smiled, but the gesture didn't quite reach his eyes. Devon received the distinct impression that it was designed more to show teeth than anything else. He was still angry.

Moving his hand from behind her neck, he brought it forward to trace the contours of her kiss-swollen lips with the pad of his thumb. "You'll find out," he said. The slight rasp of his baritone voice caressed her nerve endings, sending a shiver of traitorous delight up her spine. "But I guarantee you'll like it."

She frowned as he turned away from her and began packing up the things on the desk. "Geoff, I—"

"Two weeks, Devon," he said, interrupting her. "I'll stay at the office for that long. I've got a comfortable couch there. And then I'll be back." He lifted his gaze to meet hers. *"Full time."*

It sounded like a threat.

It *was* a threat!

Chapter 14

Geoff squinted against the light of a particularly bright street lamp as he drove back to the office. Damn, he wished he could figure women out. Or, at least one specific woman.

He already cared about Devon a lot and it irritated the hell out of him that she seemed to be fighting any reciprocation of his feelings. What exactly those feelings were, he wasn't sure.

Love?

Probably. He thought about her all the time. He dreamed about the scent of her soft skin; about the texture of her silky hair; about the perfect fit her body was for his. And, dammit, he *knew* that she felt something for him too. And yet she fought it tooth and nail.

Why?

Oh, he knew her reasoning. She'd told him often enough. But why couldn't he make her understand that anything *good* involved some risk? That they'd never know if they had anything *together* worth reclaiming if they didn't allow themselves to relax and simply be with each other without fear?

He sighed and shook his head in frustration. He was going to give Devon the room she seemed to think she needed. If she didn't want him around as much, he could deal with it. It wasn't as though he had nothing to do. And maybe, just maybe, she'd realize that having him around wasn't all that bad; that allowing herself to rely on someone else a bit, was not that threatening a situation to be in.

But what about the kids?

Well, she'd said she wasn't telling him he couldn't see them, so he could still stop by to see them after school as often as possible. There was no reason they should be dragged into the situation between himself and Devon.

If it was what she wanted, she could go back to cooking her own meals when she got home after a long day at work. He'd only tried to be thoughtful, and look what it had got him—censure. As though he'd actually been *plotting* to become indispensable.

Women! He muttered a curse beneath his breath.

When he arrived at the office a few minutes later, he unplugged the cellular phone from the cigarette lighter to take in with him. Just in case Devon tried to call him. Future-Tech's phones were on voice mail at night, so he mightn't even hear them ring. Of course the message light on his phone would flash if anyone left him a message, but still...he didn't want to risk missing her call.

Realizing how lovesick that sounded, he almost threw the cell phone back into the vehicle. Then, recalling that he hadn't checked the voice mail service he had on his cellular for a while either, he reasoned he should take it in anyway, and stuck it into his jacket pocket.

Leaving the suitcase of clothing he'd hastily packed in the vehicle, he made his way into the building, juggling the notebook computer on which he did most of his work, and the briefcase containing most of the stuff he'd been working on.

Not in a very good mood at the moment, he flipped on the lights in his office, set down his things, and went into the staff kitchen where he pulled a can of Coke from the refrigerator. Cracking it open, he took a long cool drink and then wished it was something stronger. But there was no help for it now. Since he hadn't had the foresight to stop and pick anything up, he'd have to make do. Slowly, he walked back into his office to stare at the phone. The red light wasn't flashing.

He looked at the sofa against the wall. It didn't look all that inviting so he sat in his high-backed chair and put his feet up on his desk. He might as well check his cellular voice mail, he decided. Taking the phone from his pocket, he depressed a couple of buttons.

There was only one message. After a minute, a woman's voice came on. "Hello, this is Claudette Grayson-Phips. I don't know who you are, but somebody left a message for me to call this number. If you still want to talk to me, you can call me back." She left her number.

Geoff stared at the Robert Bateman prints on the opposite wall without really seeing them. So that was how his mother sounded. Not quite the way he'd imagined. He'd expected her to sound like Sophia Loren; instead she sounded closer to a variation of Candice Bergen as Murphy Brown. She sounded tough and competent, with no hint of an Italian accent—at least none that he could detect. He searched for any hint of a memory of that voice, but once again drew a blank.

After swallowing the last of the Coke, he crumpled the can in his fist. It felt good; a release for some of the anger that still sizzled through him. Then, after setting the misshapen can on the desk, he made his way into the executive washroom that he shared with Danson Hart. Maybe if he dashed his face with a bit of cold water, he'd feel more like talking to his mother.

Mother. He turned the word over in his mind as he ran water into the sink.

A moment later, as he stared at his dripping face in the mirror, Geoff allowed his fingers to tighten on the edge of the basin. He *believed* the woman he was about to call was his mother, but he didn't *know* that she was. Just as he *believed* he was Geoffrey Hunter Grayson—because all the evidence pointed to that being the case—but he didn't *know* that he was Geoff Grayson. In fact, he still had no idea who the man in the mirror truly was. Would he ever *know?* Sometimes he felt lost in a sea of pretense, of trying to be something that he wasn't. And yet what else could he do but try to live the life that evidence indicated was once his?

Reaching for the towel, he dried his face and continued to stare at himself in the mirror. Would his memory ever return? Would he ever be able to look into a mirror and not entertain the shadow of a doubt about his identity? Would the void in his soul ever stop aching? But there were no answers apparent in the countenance that stared back at him.

Finally, he shook his head and made his way back to his office. He had to proceed on the evidence, and the evidence presented him as Geoff Grayson.

Sitting down, he picked up the telephone and dialled. It was time to let Claudette Grayson-Phips know that her son was alive.

Almost twenty-four hours had passed since he'd left Devon's—he still thought of it as Devon's home, not his. Geoff was preparing for another lonely evening spent in his office. Well, at least he had the meeting with his mother to look forward to. She was supposed to arrive on Sunday afternoon.

But he wasn't looking forward to tonight, despite the time it afforded him to do some more digging through obscure files. He was just contemplating going out to a restaurant for dinner when his cellular rang.

"Geoff, it's Devon. I need to see you. Where are you?"

He frowned. She sounded rattled. "I'm at the office."

"Are you going to be there for a while?"

"I can be. What's up?"

"I'll tell you when I see you. Have you had dinner?"

"No. I was just thinking—"

Uncharacteristically, she interrupted him. "I'll pick something up. How about Mexican?"

"Sure." He was starting to get worried.

"I'll see you in a couple of minutes."

By the time Devon arrived carrying a sack of take-out food

and a large tote bag, Geoff was pacing his office in impatience. "Tell me what's the matter," he demanded without preamble.

Setting the bags on his desk, Devon withdrew an object from the tote and passed it to him. It was the answering machine from the main phone line at the house, not his office phone. "Listen to the message on there," she said.

Without comment, Geoff found a plug-in for the machine, and depressed the play button. "Devon, dear, I really wish you would speak to your father. He's been like a bear ever since—" Honoria Sherwood's voice came over the small speaker and Geoff flashed Devon a questioning look.

"It's the next one," Devon spoke over the message.

An instant later a muffled voice came on, recognizable as male, but nothing more. "Mrs. Grayson, do you know where your brother is? I bet he didn't even leave a forwarding address." There was a strange rasping sound, the person clearing his throat behind whatever he was using to muffle his voice. "Tell Geoff to talk to his assistant manager about the latest complaints if he wants to find answers." There was a click as the caller hung up, and the machine shut off.

Geoff stared at it thoughtfully. It looked like they had *somebody* on their side. But who?

Devon's voice came out of the silence. It was tight with strain. "I called Winston and he wasn't home. Tyler heard me leaving a message for him and told me that Winston had come by to see the children yesterday after school."

Geoff looked up. "What did he say?" he asked quietly.

"He told them goodbye—that he was going away for a while. He also told them not to tell anyone unless they were asked."

Geoff's jaw clenched. He didn't like people who put children in the position of keeping adult secrets. "I guess that explains why we haven't seen him since he called in sick on Wednesday. What could have made him run?"

Devon grimaced. "The last time I spoke with him, I mentioned the fact that we were digging into what had happened before. I told him that this time, we were going to find the answers together."

That could have been enough to make him take off. "Did he say anything else to the kids?"

"Just that they shouldn't worry because he'd be fine and that he'd try to come back and see them someday. Apparently he directed them to tell me that, too, when I asked about him." Devon was staring at him with heartbreak in her eyes.

"I'm sorry, Devon."

She swallowed and her gaze slid away. "I know."

He wanted to hold her, to comfort her, but considering the current state of their relationship, he wasn't certain his embrace would be welcome.

She took a deep breath, offered a quick, tight little smile, and began removing the tacos and fajitas from the bag she brought. "I hope you're hungry, because I brought lots."

He nodded, but his thoughts were on the portion of the message that hadn't had to do with Winston. Moving to his desk, he picked up the phone.

"Who are you calling?"

"Danson," he murmured. "I want to hear what he has to say."

Devon nodded. Unwrapping a soft taco, she sat down in one of the chairs before Geoff's desk and began to eat while she waited for him to complete his conversation.

It didn't take long. "Danson," he said, when his assistant manager picked up the phone. "It's Geoff. Can you come down to the office for a few moments?"

There was a moment of silence, perhaps due to surprise, on the other end of the line. Then Danson responded, "Sure, Geoff. I'll be right there."

Not even half an hour had passed when Danson Hart stuck his head around the corner of Geoff's doorway. "Evenin' Geoff." He seemed a bit surprised to see Devon. "Devon," he said with a nod.

Geoff nodded. "Come in, Dan. Have a chair." When the man was seated, Geoff continued. "I understand we're having more problems."

Danson studied him for a moment, glanced at Devon, and then nodded. "Yeah, I guess you could say that."

"Why didn't you tell me?"

"I wasn't sure if you were ready to hear about them. You seemed kind of preoccupied with studying the things that happened before, you know. I assumed you were more interested in trying to get your memory back than in anything else."

Devon reacted with surprise. "You mean you didn't think he cared?" she asked incredulously.

Danson looked uncomfortable. "Well, I wouldn't have put it quite like that."

Geoff studied the man. Danson's body language was telling him that he felt defensive and a bit nervous. "So tell us about the problems."

"All right." Danson cleared his throat. "A couple of our clients are saying that their customers have had break-ins that resulted in the loss of sensitive information. The trouble is that the security systems don't show any breach so there's no real proof except the fact that the stolen plans and designs are, presumably, showing up in their competitors' hands. At first I thought it was just a matter of a company being a bit paranoid, but this is the third complaint now." His jaw tightened. "I thought all these hassles would be over with when everything hit two years ago."

He paused, searching for his train of thought. "Well, it almost seems like the problems never really stopped because this is the same kind of situation we had with Fort Knox Security, except that this time, it's happening with two different installation companies, ComWest Security and Pro-Shield Security. They can't both be at fault."

Geoff's mind raced. "What's the status of their clients—of the companies who experienced the losses?"

"Well, since in these instances the audit trail doesn't show a breach, they're mostly just blustering about having their security systems pulled, not paying the balance on their contracts, and recontracting with one of our competitors. Even that could prove costly though. Especially if word spreads that Future-Tech's systems can't be trusted."

Geoff frowned. "So the difference between what's happening now, and what happened with Fort Knox Security's clients, is that this time there's no proof of a break-in?"

Danson nodded. "That's about it."

"How and why did the proof surface last time?"

Danson shrugged. "According to our techs, the modifications that Spencer made to the systems that he installed provided a more complete audit trail than the one we use."

Devon frowned. "I don't understand. If the modifications Spencer made are what proved there had been security breaches, shouldn't they have realized that it seemed pretty unlikely that he was the one facilitating the break-ins?"

Danson paused, looked at her, and nodded. "You bet it does. I said that at the time. The modifications he made make it damn near impossible for anyone to break into a system without leaving some kind of evidence behind. It's like an electronic fingerprint. But the money they found in his account clinched it the other way. They said he'd probably just made a mistake in his reprogramming that ended up giving him away and wrapped everything up in a neat little package. I think it was just easier to pin the blame on a dead guy."

Geoff silently considered everything Danson had said. "So, if the changes Spencer made to the systems were so favorable, are we implementing them in production?"

Danson's attention returned to him. "Nope. Too costly for the additional programming hours without any demonstrable benefit. At least that's what Russell and Pete decided a while back. Of course, Pete really doesn't know the business and I think he sided with Russ because of Russ's years of experience. Still, the result was that I was outvoted. And, since I don't own any shares..." He shrugged, making it obvious that his voice in the company was not that strong.

"What's your opinion now?" Devon asked.

Danson considered her. "My honest opinion is that we should look at it again. Especially if things like this are going to keep happening. It could get more costly *not* to do it."

Geoff cast a thoughtful gaze ceilingward. "Yes." Future-Tech systems had been deliberately altered and used to expedite corporate espionage. And he didn't think Spencer Loring had had anything to do with it except that, by making alterations to a Future-Tech product in an attempt to serve his own clients more competently, he'd inadvertently made it possible for the thefts that were taking place to be discovered. Geoff's prime suspect now was, of course, Winston Sherwood. But, Winston couldn't have done all the programming on all the systems. And, even if he was responsible for some of the sabotaged systems, who was he working for?

"Danson, do you know who did the original programming on the security systems we sold Fort Knox Security?"

He shrugged. "Not offhand." He glanced at Devon with obvious discomfort.

"We are aware that Winston may have had a hand in this."

Danson cleared his throat. "Well...if I had to guess I'd say Winston probably did a lot of our in-house programming. He was our best programmer. There are other programmers on the floor, of course. And we subcontract a lot too. I can't figure it out. And, believe me, I've tried."

"You've suspected Winston for a while then," Devon asked. He looked uncomfortable again. "Yeah."

Geoff studied Devon. She was looking more angry now than hurt. That was good. There was strength in anger. "Are there any records that will tell me who programmed the individual systems whether it was a subcontractor or one of our programmers?"

Danson nodded. "Sure. In the accounting department. It'll mean a lot of digging though. But, why don't you call Russ? He might know off the top of his head who worked on the subcontracted systems, and that would save you a lot of time. Russ was the one that looked into having all that stuff checked for the cops a while back."

Geoff nodded. "I may do that." He leaned back in his chair a bit and considered the man that, in another life, he'd hired as his assistant manager. "Is there anything else you haven't told me that I should know?"

"No." Danson shook his head. "Not that I can think of. If I remember anything I'll let you know."

"Do that," Geoff responded. It was an order.

"Sure. Well, if there's nothing else, I think I'll get back. I...ah, have a lady friend over for dinner."

Danson was about to close the office door behind himself when Geoff added, "Oh, and thanks for leaving that message, Danson."

The man froze in the doorway. "How did you know?"

"I didn't for certain. But I suspected when you said that Winston *was* our best programmer. You already knew he was gone."

Danson looked uncomfortable. "I wasn't certain you'd take me seriously if I simply approached you."

"I would have," Geoff assured him. "And in future, I'd prefer the direct route."

Danson swallowed. "Sure."

"Thanks for coming in." Geoff waited until the door closed behind him.

Devon looked at him. "Are you going to call Russell?"

He frowned. "Yeah. But I have some thinking to do first."

Devon studied Geoff's set features; they looked as though they'd been carved from granite. He was definitely angry. "Geoff?" He looked at her. "I'm sorry for not accepting the possibility that Winston...you know."

"Forget it, Devon. He's your brother. I understand loyalty. What I don't understand is how he could have gotten involved in something that involves murder. I mean it's pretty obvious now, despite the lack of evidence, that my plane going down was not an accident. Spencer and Holly were murdered to keep this from getting out."

Devon swallowed. "And you and I almost as well. If I had gone...if neither of us had survived...our children would have been orphaned." He was right. How could Winston have become involved in something like that? "Maybe someone was blackmailing him?" she ventured almost hopefully.

Geoff nodded. "It's possible."

"And we still don't know enough to go to the police with

anything. Do we? I mean, other than the fact that Winston has left, what do we have?''

''Nothing yet. But we will have. I'm going to talk to Russell, and then, first thing in the morning, I'm going to start going through the accounting files.''

Devon hesitated. There was so much distance between them. Which was exactly what she'd wanted just yesterday, but now... Now, it felt cold and lonely. ''Tomorrow is Saturday. I'd like to help, if I could?''

He nodded. ''I'd appreciate it.''

Devon looked at her watch. ''Well, I have to get back. I told Mom I wouldn't be long when I dropped the kids off with her.''

Geoff stifled a yawn and glanced at his watch. It was ten-thirty on Saturday morning. Devon hadn't shown up yet, and Geoff had been digging through old records for half the night, it seemed, and the entire morning. His conversation with Russell the previous evening had been all but useless. When Geoff had asked him if he remembered who had programmed the sabotaged security systems that had been subcontracted, Russ's response had been: ''It's been two years since I dug up that information, Geoff, and my memory isn't as good as it used to be. Let me see...no, I just can't remember. I'm sorry. Why?''

Geoff sighed. He liked Russ, they'd visited and had meals together. He regarded him as a friend, but he still didn't know him well. Certainly not well enough to trust him implicitly, so he'd skirted Russ's question. ''Let's just say I have my reasons,'' he'd responded. ''Thanks for your help.''

''You're welcome, Geoff,'' Russ had said, and then he'd added, ''But I really think you should leave well enough alone and get on with your life.''

Get on with his life. He wanted to do that, but he just couldn't do it without answers. And so, he'd gone digging in the storage rooms for Future-Tech's old records to find the information he needed.

It was like finding a needle in a haystack. First he had to find the serial numbers corresponding to the particular systems which had been at fault. Then he had to work backward, through a maze of paper. All of which seemed to be filed in obscure boxes in distinctly different areas of the storage room. He supposed he could have waited and asked for some help from his staff—the people here were, after all, his employees—but now that he finally had a course of action in mind, he didn't want to wait. Besides, until he knew for certain what had happened and who was at fault, he didn't trust anyone.

He still hadn't found anything to tell him who, other than Winston, had programmed the systems, and he was only marginally nearer his goal. The subcontractors who had worked on the systems *not* programmed by Winston were identified as 4839-A and 5621-C.

He'd located the accounts payable listing of corporations and their applicable numeric code and had printed off the list only to find that the company names corresponding to the codes he sought had been deleted and the accounts were inactive.

Now what the hell was he going to do?

He frowned in perplexity, racking his tired brain. The company had to have been paid when it *performed* the work, so all he had to do was find the old accounting records. He'd seen the backups in the storage room.

A half hour later, he leaned over his desk and he began to leaf through the fanfold paper in search of the two codes in question.

There!

He verified the number: 4839-A. Yep, that was it. Running his finger across the page, he sought the corporation's identity.

Manning Systems Ltd. a Division of Delta Systems Inc.

Geoff stared at the page. Maybe there was a mistake. It had to be a mistake. Didn't it?

He hastily began flipping pages, searching for the other code, 5621-C. There it was. More hesitantly now, he ran his finger across the page once again.

Damn!

He stared at the words, not wanting to believe them, yet knowing in his gut that they didn't lie. The words *Delta Systems Inc.* stared back at him in bold black ink.

Slowly, numbly, he sat down. What did he do now?

A knock on his office door startled him. "Come!" he called. It was probably Devon.

But the person who opened the door was not Devon.

"Hello, Russ," he said, hiding his surprise beneath an impassive facade. This visit seemed almost incredibly timely. Did Russ know something? He undoubtedly suspected after Geoff's call. "When did you get into town?"

Leaving the door partially open behind him, Russell Manning strolled across the room and took a seat in one of the chairs before Geoff's desk. "I've actually been in town on other business for a couple of days. Your call was forwarded to my cell phone last night. Unfortunately, this is the first opportunity I've had to stop by."

Geoff nodded and said nothing. He was certain Russ had a purpose here. If he waited patiently, he'd undoubtedly learn what it was.

He didn't have long to wait. "So how's your investigation going?" Russell asked. "I hate to see you cause yourself unnecessary stress, Geoff. But, I assume you're planning on pursuing the matter to the bitter end."

Geoff stared at him, trying to reconcile what he'd just discovered with the concerned demeanor of the man he'd thought to be his friend and partner. He decided that the only way to know for certain what kind of man Russell was, would be to confront him with his suspicions. "Did you hire Winston to plant the back-door codes in my security systems?"

The only hint of emotion that Russell displayed was a slight widening of the eyes. Then, he shook his head sadly. "Once you would never have suspected me of something so heinous, Geoff."

Geoff frowned slightly. He was certain that he'd seen a shadow moving in the outer office. Had Russ brought someone with him? "*Once,* I was blinded by friendship and old loyalties, Russ. I'm not anymore. I liked you from the start, but I barely know you."

"I see." In a relaxed and casual movement, Russell reached

inside his suit jacket. Geoff expected him to pull out his pipe as he had on other occasions. This time, however, Russell Manning pulled out a small black handgun. Geoff tensed.

Without a flicker of emotion, Russell pointed the weapon at Geoff with a casualness that suggested he was very familiar with it. "I tried to warn you, Geoff, but you wouldn't listen."

"Why did you do it, Russ?"

Studying him, Russ ignored the question. "You know," he said almost musingly, "you're much less emotional than you once were. Colder. I have little doubt that, were the tables reversed, you'd be entirely capable of killing me right now. It's odd how a head injury can change a person that way."

Geoff said nothing, preferring to let Russell ramble on if he chose to. It would give Geoff time to think of a way out of this. He hoped.

"Once you wouldn't even have been capable of killing an animal. You never did hunt, you know."

"Most animals don't deserve to die," Geoff observed blandly as his mind continued to race.

Russ smiled. It was the coldest smile Geoff had ever seen. "Touché," he said. "You asked why I did this." Geoff nodded. "For the money, of course. What other reason would there be? I have bank accounts all over the world."

"Does Winston?"

"I would imagine so. Although he's a bit lacking in social skills, he's a very bright boy, you know. Totally unappreciated by his family. I don't imagine he'll be unemployed for long, if he can keep himself out of trouble, that is. Actually that's how we met. He approached me to take care of a small problem for him with a Vancouver organization, which I very kindly did. After that, well, let's just say he was grateful."

Geoff nodded and cast a pointed glance at the pistol Russ held. "So what happens now?"

"I suppose I'm going to have to kill you. I had hoped that I wouldn't have to do it. At least not personally—I've always liked you, you know—but when you disappeared after the plane crash I suspected that one day it would come to this."

There was a faint noise from the reception area. An indrawn breath? Geoff glanced once again toward the door and caught sight of a very familiar head of dark brown hair. Devon! Oh, no! At least, Russell didn't appear to have heard her. He had to keep the conversation going, and pray that Devon got out of there. "You knew I was alive?" Geoff asked conversationally.

"Oh, not for certain. Not until the day I saw you in Northridge. But, I suspected."

"You saw me in Northridge! When?" Geoff strained his ears toward the outer office.

"Delta Systems supplies customized software for the entire Noralco corporation. I had to go to Northridge one day—to maintain customer relations, you know—and I almost bumped into you. You, however, showed not the slightest hint of recognition, so I asked the Noralco foreman who you were. After I had your assumed name, it took a bare minimum of probing to learn Jack Keller's story. That's the nice thing about small towns—everyone knows everything about everyone. I also learned that even in the kind of job you had up there you maintained a schedule. That's one thing that hasn't changed. You were always a creature of habit, Geoff."

Geoff frowned. "You arranged for that Noralco explosion?"

"Of course. I couldn't risk your memory returning, or someone who knew you discovering your new life. I figured, with a little careful planning to get as many men as possible out of the way, I could have you taken care of without risking any personal connection to you or your death. I even found a man who had a strong personal motive to do the job, an ex-employee with a grudge. But as usual, you came out alive and a hero on top of it."

Geoff stared at him. Russ's own plan had backfired. "It was the news coverage of the warehouse explosion that allowed Devon to finally find me."

Russell shrugged. "Oh, well. Even geniuses make mistakes. And the unpredictability of human action and reaction is virtually impossible to prepare for. For example, I had no way of knowing that Devon would cancel out of the plane trip two years ago either.''

''The plane trip that *you* had ensured would be one way.''

''You're very perceptive.''

''Was it you making the threatening phone calls?'' he demanded.

''Hardly, Geoff. There are employees available for that kind of work. Though they're not as reliable as they used to be.''

''The break-in,'' Geoff said. ''What were you trying to steal?''

Russ grinned. ''Not quite as smart as I gave you credit for yet, are you? The break-in was designed to make you think a theft had occurred while the true purpose was to plant a listening device. It worked quite well too until Devon decided she didn't want you around. Women can be so fickle, can't they? So hard to figure.''

Keeping the muzzle of the small black gun trained on Geoff, Russell rose and moved to the side as though preparing to leave. Of course! He couldn't kill Geoff here in the office. The number of people with access to the building was too small. Russ would immediately be on any list of suspects.

''Why did you have to plan to kill everyone on the plane when it was me you wanted?'' Geoff asked. The shadow was still moving in the outer office. Dammit, Devon! *Get out!* he wanted to yell.

Russ shook his head, as though in disappointment at Geoff's lack of understanding, and then explained. ''Not just you. Spencer, too. If I hadn't done it, you and Spencer would have ruined everything. But, I gave the investigators a fall guy when I deposited a hundred thousand dollars to Spencer's personal account. There is a fortune to be made in industrial espionage, you know, Geoff. And I'm among the best in the business simply by having the foresight to have a back door installed into all of my security systems that allows my clients to easily circumvent specific systems without that infiltration being detected. I have clients all over the world. And, I'm rich.''

He indicated with the muzzle of the gun that it was time for

Geoff to rise. "Let's go. It's time for you to disappear again, only this time...you won't be coming home."

Shaking with a combination of shock, fear and fury, Devon stood in the reception area just outside the partially open door to Geoff's office. She'd been about to knock and join them when she'd heard Geoff ask Russell if he'd hired Winston to sabotage the security systems. Fury at Russell Manning had almost blinded her to how dangerous he was, how desperate Geoff's situation was, but she'd checked her impulsive response at the last moment. Somehow, she had to help Geoff.

She could see the gun in Russell's hand. Russell had only to take a half step forward and, if he glanced in her direction, he'd see her. She had to do something quickly. But what?

She didn't want to leave long enough to place a call and try to explain the situation. Russell was already on the verge of forcing Geoff to leave. If they left, she might never see Geoff again. The thought almost choked her, but she shoved it aside.

Reaching across the secretary's desk, she lifted the receiver from its cradle, dialed nine for an outside line, and then quietly but hastily dialed 9-1-1. She couldn't risk talking, but hopefully it would bring help. Quietly she dropped the receiver onto the secretary's chair, out of sight.

Now what could she do to stall Russell? Disarm him?

Devon looked around the receptionist's office for something with which to hit him, something to knock the gun from his hand. There wasn't much to work with: a heavy-duty hole punch, a stapler, an electric pencil sharpener, a couple of phone books, a note spike, and some rolls of fax paper on the stand beneath the fax machine. She'd never realized before how unsuitable offices were to yielding up weapons. She eyed the note spike and nervously opted for a combination: the note spike, with the heavy old hole punch as backup. Sidling back to the door, she listened for a moment.

"Did Winston know about the plane being rigged?" Geoff was asking.

Russell shook his head slightly. "Don't be a fool, Geoff. Winston is a behind-the-scenes man. It's what he excels at. He might have had his suspicions I suppose but I never told him any more than he needed to know to get his end of the job done.''

Devon took a deep breath and closed her eyes for a second in relief. Thank you God, she sighed. At least her brother had not been a part of all of it.

''Now come on,'' Russ said, with a wave of the gun. ''It's time to go.''

God help me, she prayed. She had only seconds left in which to act!

Chapter 15

Gripping her makeshift weapons tightly in her hands, Devon girded herself with every scrap of courage she possessed and burst into the room. Focusing with single-minded determination on her objective, she didn't even glance in Geoff's direction as she raced toward Russ, her right hand raised high with the note spike at the ready. Within two giant steps she was upon him. He'd just looked her way, his cold blue eyes registering faint surprise, when she struck without giving herself time to think. Plunging the note spike into his shoulder, she brought the hole punch down on his gun arm with as much punishing force as she was capable of delivering in a left-handed blow.

It worked! With a howl of rage and pain, Russell dropped the gun.

Peripherally, Devon was aware that Geoff launched himself over the corner of his desk and scrambled toward them. But before she knew what had happened, before Geoff could get close, Devon found herself trapped in an iron grip, her arms trapped at her sides and her jaw clasped in a painful, viselike hold.

"Another step and she dies," Russell warned Geoff in an arctic tone that was at odds with the warmth of his breath as it fanned over her ear and cheek. Somehow Devon had expected someone so cold-blooded to be totally devoid of human warmth.

Geoff halted. "You wouldn't."

"Oh, I assure you I would. I was a good soldier, you know. Killing is nothing new to me, nor is it as abhorrent as some seem to find it. But, if you want to put me to the test, go ahead. I promise she won't feel a thing when I snap her neck."

Geoff stayed where he was and Devon sensed Russell relaxing slightly. "You married a smart man, Devon," he murmured in her ear. "Too bad he wasn't smart enough to leave things alone, don't you think?"

Since the grip on her jaw prevented her from speaking, Devon assumed he did not expect a response.

"Now then, Geoff," he said in a conversational tone, "I want you to back up behind the desk again." Geoff didn't move. "*Do it!*" Russ shouted. Devon jumped and cringed at the cold rage she heard in those two words.

Slowly, carefully, Geoff eased back.

"Devon," Russ said, "I'm going to loosen my hold enough for you to bend down and pick up my gun. Can you do that?" He spoke in the gentle coaxing voice of one speaking to a child and loosened his grasp on her jaw enough for her to respond.

No! she wanted to scream. Giving him back his gun was the last thing she wanted. But what choice did she have? She looked at Geoff, searched his face for some sign of what he might want her to do, but his expression was glacial and unreadable. Finally, defeated for the moment, she nodded.

"Good girl." Russell's tone was so condescending that Devon would have liked nothing better than to shove his words back into his throat with her fist. But, taking a cue from Geoff's impassivity, she concealed her emotions. As Russell loosened his hold slightly, Devon bent to grasp the gun. "Easy now," he cautioned. "Pick it up by the barrel. That's it."

As soon as he had his gun in hand again, Russell shoved Devon forcefully toward Geoff. She wanted to fling herself into

Geoff's arms, to hug him in case it was their last opportunity, but, not wanting to get in the way, she stood at his side feeling ineffectual and useless. Thanks to the failure of her poorly conceived plan, they were now *both* captive. If only she'd gone for help. All she could do now was hope that the police arrived to check out that open line to 9-1-1. Damn! How could she have been so stupid? She'd only made things worse.

She studied Russ. Blood from the puncture wound she'd inflicted on his shoulder stained his light gray suit, but it didn't seem to affect him much. He was having no trouble holding the gun.

He noticed her perusal. "Oh, don't worry, my dear girl. Other than a rather painful bruise on my forearm and a slightly annoying affront to my shoulder, I'm quite all right."

"Too bad," Devon replied, unable to contain her rancor. "I hope you get blood poisoning."

Russell smiled. "Well Geoff, at least your poor wife won't be left wondering what happened to you this time. She'll be joining you." Then his smile disappeared. "Move it. Both of you. We're leaving." When neither of them moved, he looked at Geoff warningly. "I want to make this look like an accident, but it isn't absolutely necessary. My own disappearance has been planned for some time now. So, if you try anything, the first bullet is for Devon. You understand?"

Geoff nodded.

"Good. Then, put on your jacket, hold your wife's hand and walk out of here side by side."

Geoff's hand warmed her icy fingers as they made their way to the main door with Russell right behind them.

"How did you know I'd be here today?" Geoff asked.

"I've had you watched for some time now, Geoff. You *and* Devon. I couldn't trust you not to regain your memory, or, as it turns out, not to meddle. So, there isn't much I *don't* know about you."

As they stepped onto the tarmac of the parking lot a couple of minutes later, the sun was high in the sky, the cloud cover that had settled in earlier already gone. Devon looked at the huge expanse of blue sky overhead, and wondered if she'd live to see another day. It was early March. In another few weeks, the fruit trees would be in bloom. Spring was her favorite season; she'd hate to miss it. But, at the moment, it looked as though they needed a miracle.

There were no police in sight yet. But then, despite the fact that it seemed much more time had passed, it had probably been less than five minutes since she'd dialed.

The parking lot was empty except for Geoff's Bronco and Devon's Jeep. The Bronco was the nearest.

Where had Russell parked?

Glancing at Geoff she saw him scan the parking lot, too. Their eyes met and she perceived some powerful emotion that she was incapable of interpreting in the depths of his eyes.

Had he learned to love her again? she wondered. He'd said once that he wanted to see if he could reclaim his life in its entirety. He'd wanted to see if he could fall in love with her again. Suddenly the answer to that question seemed very important. Oh, Lord! Why had she wasted so much of their time together? If only God would grant her one more miracle, she'd never waste another moment of her time with Geoff on analyzing their relationship. She'd live it to the fullest. If only...

But she couldn't allow herself to think about that now. The thought of losing something so newly found, so precious, would be her undoing, and she wouldn't allow herself to lose control.

So, she focused her attention on the empty parking lot. Russell had probably parked around back to ensure that no one saw his vehicle, she concluded. That way there'd be no witnesses to tie him to the area.

Witnesses. Oh, God! She was going to be killed. A jolt of icy terror raced through her veins.

"Open the driver's door, Geoff," Russ directed as they approached the Bronco. Geoff obeyed. "Now unlock the rear door." When Geoff had once again done as directed, Russ prodded Devon with the muzzle of the handgun. "Get in front. Slide across to the passenger side."

As soon as Devon had complied with his orders, he stepped

back slightly in order to grip the rear door handle. Keeping the gun carefully trained on Devon, he opened the door and got in to sit on the edge of the rear seat. Then, looking at Geoff, he said, "Get in and start it."

The vehicle roared to life. Devon automatically put on her seat belt. The incongruity of the action struck her a moment later. How odd that she would cling to habit even in a moment like this, but perhaps she needed the normalcy of the act. "Okay, now what?" Geoff asked.

"Go to Westbank and take 97-C west," Russell ordered, referring to a roadway carved out of the mountains that had shortened the distance to the west coast considerably. "I'll let you know when to get off."

They had just left the parking lot when Devon noticed the police turning in. Too late! She prayed that they'd noticed the Bronco leaving and would follow, but her prayer was in vain.

Geoff drove in silence while Devon stared at the passing traffic. So many people going about their daily business without any inkling that only feet away from them two people were at the mercy of a killer. A police cruiser passed and she prayed for a miracle, but it didn't materialize.

As they turned a few minutes later and began to climb up into the mountains where patches of snow were more plentiful despite the warm weather they'd had recently, Geoff spoke for the first time since starting the Bronco. "Where are we going?" He looked at Russ in the rearview mirror.

Russell stared at him and then shrugged. "There's a turnoff up here. The road leads to a place that overlooks a romantic little waterfall. It's probably just starting to thaw a bit at this time of the year."

"I'm not in the mood for romance," Geoff said, striving for a tone of indifference as he struggled to keep his rage at bay. He had to keep Russ talking. He needed to know what he had planned.

Russell smiled. "No, I don't imagine you are."

A few minutes later, Geoff took the turn that Russell indicated.

The road was gravel and obviously a lot less traveled. "So what's going to happen when we get to the waterfall?"

Once again Russell eyed him consideringly. "Planning ahead Geoff?" he asked.

Geoff held his tongue.

After a moment, Russell spoke. "There's a rather sharp corner in the road just where that waterfall is. You're going to have to be extremely careful. Nobody likes to see such an idyllic scene marred by a tragedy. Unfortunately, it happens all too often. Don't you think?"

Geoff thought it through. An accident? "So how are you planning on getting back to civilization without the truck?"

"Do you think me totally lacking in foresight? I have a rental vehicle waiting for me, of course."

But the more Geoff pondered the possibilities surrounding an accident, the less likely it seemed. Russell wasn't telling him everything. Maybe an accident had been his plan when he'd had only Geoff to contend with. He could have struck Geoff, knocked him unconscious, and then put the Bronco in drive to shove it off the road. But, it was unlikely that Russ would be able to do that with both Devon and Geoff. If Russ struck Devon, Geoff would have time to react. If he struck Geoff, Devon would try to do something, although her smaller size and lack of strength made success less likely. Still, considering Geoff's disappearance the last time Russell had tried to take him out of the picture, he was pretty certain that Russ would want to make absolutely certain that both Geoff and Devon were dead. No mistakes. No more problems.

That meant that Russ probably planned to shoot them both. By leaving their bodies in such a remote location, he ensured that discovery would take a while and he'd have time to put his own plan to disappear into action. No doubt he planned to retire to some tropical island and live on the money he'd made betraying others.

Geoff searched for a solution to their predicament, frantically coming up with plans, examining them and discarding them.

Devon's presence made things more difficult; he'd be willing to take more risks if she wasn't there.

A small wooden sign at the side of the road proclaimed Crystal Falls, 4 km. That was probably the place Russell had in mind. There wasn't much time left.

If only he could get the gun away from Russell. Somehow. Maybe.

Geoff studied the area. They weren't really that far from civilization, but it was remote enough that there wasn't likely to be any help unless they happened upon a hiker or camper. He looked for something that could give them an advantage. There was forest on the left, and had been for quite a while which meant that it might last for another four kilometers. The best plan of action he could come up with was to slam on the brakes. Hopefully the action would throw Russell off balance long enough to allow Geoff to grab the gun. If that didn't work, the contingency plan would be to make for the cover of the forest. It was a desperate plan conceived out of desperation, and their chances of success weren't great, but anything was better than doing nothing. Now if only he could somehow let Devon know what he had planned.

He glanced at her. She was sitting stiffly, her eyes directed straight ahead, her hands clenched in her lap. Geoff reached across the space separating them to grasp her hand, cradling her icy fingers in his warm palm. He heard Russell tense where he sat behind them, but he said nothing so he probably assumed that Geoff was simply trying to offer reassurance to Devon. Which he was—just not the way Russell would imagine. Somehow, wordlessly, Geoff needed to convey the message to Devon to be ready.

He squeezed her hand slightly. She glanced at him. He met her gaze, held it for the space of a second, and then signalled with his eyes toward the floor where he stepped very lightly and casually on the brake. Her gaze flew back up to his face, questioning.

She knew something was up.

He stepped back on the gas, speeding up gradually so that

when he did slam on the brakes the effect would be greater. Then he squeezed her hand gently again, and this time tried to indicate the forest. She glanced beyond his shoulder, knowing that he tried to communicate something. Whether she understood or not, he didn't know, but it was the best he could do.

"I thought you said you weren't in the mood for romance, Geoff?" Russ said as he eyed their clasped hands.

"There's a big difference between romance and reassurance, Russ. But you probably haven't had much experience with either one, so I won't hold your ignorance against you."

Russ's eyes glinted coldly at him in the rearview mirror. A minute later he said, "It's just ahead. Start slowing down."

That was the signal Geoff had been waiting for. He slammed on the brakes. *Hard.* The Bronco fishtailed on the gravel road. He heard Russell swear, but he was too busy fighting to keep the truck on all four wheels to pay him any attention.

The vehicle was still rocking when Geoff leapt up onto the seat and plowed a fist into Russell's jaw as he was trying to pick himself up off the floorboards of the Bronco. Now for the gun. Where was the damn gun? Geoff searched frantically, but couldn't see it. Russell was getting up again, and there was an icy look in his eyes. That's when Geoff realized that the gun was still clutched in his hand and this time the muzzle was pointed at him. Damn! Reaching behind himself, he threw his door open. "The forest," he shouted to Devon. He reached for her hand intending to pull her after him only to discover that she'd already unfastened her seat belt and had thrown open her own door. She had further to go that way!

Geoff waited to ensure she made it around the vehicle and then turned to race for the trees. Her footsteps crunched on the gravel behind him, and for a moment he actually thought they'd make it. And then he heard Devon scream. The sound held a combination of pain, fury and frustration.

"Stop right there, Geoff!"

Geoff halted and slowly turned.

Russell had overtaken Devon, and was holding the gun to her

throat as he backed toward the sheer edge of the canyon on the other side of the road.

"Get back in the truck, Geoff."

"Or what?" Geoff demanded. "You're going to kill us anyway."

"There are a lot of different ways to die, Geoff. Some are much faster than others. Now, if you don't get back in that truck, I'm going to throw your wife over the edge here." He indicated the sheer drop into the ravine with a motion of his head. "Then you can listen to her scream all the way down. Hell, it's only a hundred feet or so. You might even hear her hit bottom. Have you ever heard bones snap?" Russ kept backing away, drawing ever nearer the edge of the ledge.

Geoff saw the fear on Devon's face, but ignored it for it would only cloud his thinking. Determined not to get back in the truck while Russell was in control, he sought an advantage. If only he could get close enough, maybe he could tackle him. It would endanger Devon, but then she couldn't be in much more danger than she was already. They didn't have many options left.

Geoff gritted his teeth, controlling the almost overpowering urge to rush Russell, to drive his fist into the man's face and see him go down. Instead, he moved forward very slowly, hoping to convince Russ that he was, once again, going to comply with his orders. If he had to die, he was damn well going to do it on his terms, and he sure as *hell* was not going to allow Russ to make their deaths look like an accident of any kind. Or a murder-suicide. Or whatever he had planned.

"That's close enough."

But Geoff kept moving slowly forward.

"Get in the vehicle, Geoff. Now!"

"I don't think so, Russ," he said almost conversationally.

Russell shrugged. "If that's the way you want it, Geoff. I'll have to walk a ways to retrieve my car, but, other than that, this place is almost as good as the next." Keeping his left arm pinned tightly beneath Devon's chin to hold her, Russ aimed the gun at Geoff and began to squeeze the trigger. "After all, it could take months for your body to be found in this ravine anyway."

"No!" Devon screamed. She was about to lose her husband all over again, and this time she was going to be forced to watch him die. She couldn't stand it! She wouldn't!

Kicking back as hard as she could, she struck Russ's shinbone with the rock-solid heel of her ankle boot. What happened next happened so quickly, in such a lightning-fast series of events, that it was almost impossible to determine the sequence.

The gun went off, its report echoing and reechoing through the canyon even as Russell thrust her away from him, swearing and shouting, "You goddamn bitch!"

Terror raced through her. Had Geoff been shot? But she seemed unable to regain enough equilibrium to search him out properly. That was when she realized that she was teetering on the edge of the ravine. Oh, God, she was about to fall!

Whether Russell had forgotten how close they stood to the edge of the precipice or not, Devon didn't know, but his action had thrust her onto the edge. Perhaps it had been deliberate, for he watched impassively as she fought for her life.

Then, in the final second before she completely lost her balance, she saw Geoff running toward her. Pure joy burst within her. Geoff was alive! The gunshot must have gone wild.

She reached toward him, and...fell.

Geoff's fingers grasped only air. "Devon!" he shouted. Oh, God. Please, no! Steeling himself, he looked over the edge. Hope and worry surged through him. Devon lay unmoving below, but she'd fallen only fifteen feet or so to a narrow ledge. As long as she hadn't struck her head, she could be alive. But he needed to get help as soon as possible. Pain and worry and rage fought for supremacy within him. He grasped the rage, used it to gird himself, and turned on the man who had robbed him of so much that mattered in his life.

Ducking to put himself below the path of Russell's extended gun arm, Geoff charged. The gun flew from Russ's grasp as they crashed to the ground. Both men rolled and fixed their gazes on the weapon, reaching for it as it skittered toward the edge of the cliff. Neither caught it. It disappeared over the edge, falling into the ravine.

Geoff cursed silently. Okay, so he'd have to do this the hard way. And he'd have to do it fast in order to get help for Devon. He focused on winning, not even considering that the barrel-chested old soldier whom he fought not only outweighed him but had more experience.

He reared back as Russell reached for his throat with his huge meat-hook hands. Evading the man's grasp, he drove his fist toward Russell's jaw and heard a satisfying crack. But the blow only stunned Russ for a moment. He tried to roll, planning to pin Geoff beneath him and Geoff couldn't allow that. Drawing his arm back as far as possible, he drove his fist into Russell's soft belly, leaving the man gasping for air. Still, it wasn't enough to force Russ to slacken his hold. And this time, catching Geoff by surprise, he managed to roll.

With his hands around Geoff's throat, leaning into the hold, Russ began to strangle him. Frantically, Geoff gouged at the older man's face and arms, trying to cause him some injury that would force him to release his hold. Nothing worked. Time was running out. Geoff could feel the blood roaring in his ears.

If he lost, who would help Devon?

He dropped his hands to the ground, feeling around for a weapon. Any kind of weapon. And finally, his fingers closed on a stone. It wasn't large—only about the size of his fist—but it was heavy. Gripping it in his palm, he brought it up and struck Russell on the temple with all the force he could muster.

For a moment, Russ only stared at him. And then slowly, as blood trickled from the wound on his head, he toppled to the side—unconscious.

Geoff gasped for air, too weak for a moment even to move from beneath Russell's sprawled legs. And then, remembering Devon, he scrambled to his feet, dug in Russell's jacket pocket for the cellular phone the man always carried, and raced to the edge of the ravine. She still hadn't moved.

Growing more frantic by the second, Geoff placed a call for help, praying all the while that the cellular would connect, that the mountains wouldn't block his reception. Then, with help on the way, he studied the nearly sheer rock face edging the ravine for a way to reach her without rope. Nothing. Damn! With no way to aid her himself, he could only wait.

While he waited, he made certain that Russ—who was, unfortunately, still alive—would not be able to cause them any more problems that day. And hopefully for a long time to come. Using Russ's own jacket, Geoff ripped strips to tie the man's hands and feet until the police could take him into custody.

Devon opened her eyes to a sunlit room painted in pale yellow and white. For a moment, confusion creased her brow. Where was she? And then as she slowly turned her head and saw the rails on the sides of the bed, she realized she was in a hospital. Three huge vases of flowers sat on the stand beside her bed.

She lifted her hand to brush a tickling hair out of her face and froze, staring at the cast on her arm. Had she broken her wrist?

As she brushed the hair back from her face, she searched her memory for the circumstances that could have resulted in such an injury. A car accident?

Memory returned with an abruptness and cold clarity that left her head reeling. Russell! He'd pushed her into the ravine.

Slowly Devon sat up and took inventory of her physical condition. She discovered that, in addition to the cast, both her head and her right leg were tightly bandaged. But she was alive.

Alive. Geoff! Was he…? But she couldn't even allow herself to think the word. Slowly, she pulled back the bed curtain to examine the rest of the room.

That was when she saw him.

Geoff, clad in jeans and a black T-shirt that hugged his tall form and broad shoulders like a second skin, stood staring from the window, his back to the room. Devon had never seen a more wonderful sight. He was alive!

"Geoff—" Her voice cracked on the single syllable, rusty with disuse. Still he must have heard, for he swung around so quickly it was a wonder he didn't get whiplash.

"Devon!" For an instant he only stared at her as though uncertain as to whether to believe his eyes. His expression was as impassive as stone, but it no longer bothered Devon for she'd learned that his impassive expression was only a mask designed to hide the emotions of a very tender and considerate man. He came forward to grasp her cold fingers in his large warm hand.

And now, before another minute passed, she could say the words she'd wanted to say through that whole terrifying drive into the mountains with Russell. "Geoff, I...I love you." He opened his mouth to speak, but she held up a hand to forestall him. "Please. I have to say this *now*."

"All right."

Her gaze slid down to the bedcovers. "I think sometimes that I love you...the new person you've become, even more than the man I married. The feelings are so strong sometimes that they're frightening. But I was wrong to try to deny them. And I was wrong to keep us apart. Will you...will you forgive me?"

He said nothing, and hesitantly, nervously, Devon looked up.

Suddenly his jaw clenched and he lifted his hand to gouge at his eyes with his thumb and forefinger as his face twisted with emotion. "Damn," he whispered.

Then, with a choked sound, he bent to clutch her in an urgent embrace. "There's nothing to forgive, Devon. I love you. And when I thought...God! It's a miracle that that ledge was there to catch you. But even so, you can't imagine how I felt seeing you lying so still on that ledge. I was so afraid...." He swallowed and then simply said, "Thanks for coming back to me. And don't you ever scare me like that again." His voice cracked with the strain of the emotion he struggled to contain. For a long moment he simply held her close, as though his next breath depended on her.

"Mom!" At the joyous shout, Devon and Geoff separated and looked toward the door. "You're awake!" Britanny sprinted toward the bed with Tyler following. A smiling Claudette Grayson stepped quietly into the room behind them.

"You've finally met your mother," Devon said to Geoff.

"Yes." It was a simple word, but there was a wealth of meaning in it as he smiled at his mother. "She refuses to let the fact that I don't remember her affect our relationship in the least."

In the process of leaning over to kiss her daughter and hug

her son, Devon smiled. "Well, she's had longer to gain wisdom than I have."

"Hey!" Claudette interjected. "Don't make me sound like an old crone."

Geoff smiled and walked over to hug the woman he'd accepted as his mother. "You'll never be an old crone."

"That's a good boy!" she said, patting him on the back. "You see, Devon, it only takes thirty-odd years, give or take, to train a son."

Devon cast a look of mock horror Tyler's way. "It's not going to take that long, is it?"

The boy shrugged. "Sure. I wanna be just like Dad."

Devon smiled. She'd waited a long time to hear those words. "And I'll be very, very proud," she said, squeezing his hand affectionately. She was taking advantage of the fact that he was accepting affection. Who knew how long it would last? Probably only as long as she was in the hospital.

"Well," Claudette said as she made her way into the room, "I'm glad to see you finally decided to wake up." She sounded like a mother scolding her child for sleeping too late when there was work to be done.

Devon smiled and looked at Geoff. "How long have I been unconscious?"

"A couple of days." She saw the reflection of the worry he'd suffered in his eyes. "The doctors kept you sedated. You gave us quite a scare."

"Russell?" she asked.

"In jail where he'll be for a very long time if I have anything to do with it."

Devon picked at the fabric of the blanket and then, seeing Britanny's wistful gaze, patted the bed beside her in invitation. As her daughter settled onto the bed at her side, Devon considered the other question she needed to ask. It was one of the most difficult. Finally, she cleared her throat. "What about Winston?"

Geoff searched her face. "Apparently he's already left the country, but I couldn't leave him out of the statement I gave the police, Devon. If he comes back, he'll be arrested. I'm sorry."

She shook her head. "No, don't be. You did what you had to do. I love my brother, but I guess it's time I let him fight his own battles."

Geoff took her hand in his.

She forced a smile to her lips. "How are Mom and Dad holding up?"

Geoff frowned thoughtfully. "Your dad's hard to read. He's angry with himself for not seeing Russell for what he was. And, I think he's disappointed about Winston, but he hasn't said much. Your mother is pretty hurt by everything, but she's strong. They've both been coming by to see you every evening."

She nodded, wondering if her father had forgiven her for telling him to stay out of her life.

As though he sensed the question that weighed heavily on her mind, Geoff continued, saying, "Your father said to give you a message."

"Oh? What was that?"

"He said to tell you that he'll never interfere again unless you ask him to." Geoff studied her face.

With a soft smile, Devon draped her arm over Britanny's shoulders to hug her close. "That's wonderful." And, with the exception of Winston's betrayal, everything was wonderful, for the first time in a long, long time. She refused to allow Winston's problems to inhibit her happiness. Life was too short and uncertain not to rejoice in every moment. "When can I go home?" she asked.

"Soon," Geoff promised.

Soon was actually four long days. But, by the time the doctors released her, she felt almost like herself again. Her leg and her arm were still a bit sore, but she was happier than she'd been in a very long time.

Geoff arrived alone to take her home. "The kids are staying with your mother for the rest of the day," he explained.

"Oh." Devon felt faintly disappointed.

"They wanted to come, but I asked them to give us some time alone."

"Oh." Well, that was different. A thrill of anticipation raced through her as she contemplated exactly what Geoff must have in mind. It had been a long time. Much too long.

When they arrived home, Geoff carried Devon into the house and all the way upstairs, so she wouldn't tax the healing ligaments in her ankle. Once in the bedroom, he very gently helped her to undress.

Devon smiled. "I've missed this," she said. "I've missed *you*."

"I'm glad," he murmured in that silk-on-sandstone voice that tantalized her nerve endings. Then, turning away for a moment, he withdrew the sexy red negligee he'd gotten her for Christmas from the closet.

Devon frowned inwardly. What was he doing? Weren't they going to make love? Then thinking that he must have just wanted to see her in it, she allowed him to drop it over her head and shoulders, and then she smoothed it into place.

"There," Geoff said. "Now you get into bed and rest, and I'll be back shortly."

Rest! Her disappointment was crushing. "I've just spent a week in bed, Geoff. I hardly think I need to rest again so soon."

"I'll be back," he assured her. "I have to check on our dinner."

"Dinner?"

"Mmm-hmm. And you are not to set foot outside this room. Do you understand? It's a surprise." And then, mysteriously, he left.

It was almost an hour later when Devon heard the tinkling noise of dishes rattling gently against each other. A moment later, her bedroom door opened to reveal Geoff carrying a serving tray laden with food. A single red rose in a crystal vase occupied a position of prominence on the tray.

"Oh, Geoff," Devon murmured as he folded down the legs of the tray to create a small bed table. "You've gone to so much trouble. Thank you."

"You're welcome," he said with a smile as he leaned forward

to place a gentle kiss on her lips. "But wait until you see dessert."

Ah, dessert, Devon thought with an inward smile. Now *that* was what she was looking forward to.

They shared a delicious meal of tossed salad, lasagna, bread sticks, and wine while Geoff told her about the trials and tribulations of running a household and caring for two children without her. Finally, Devon dabbed her lips with her napkin and smiled. "Mmm. That was absolutely delicious," she said.

Geoff nodded. "Thanks. My mother refused to allow me to let any more time pass without learning how to cook 'decent Italian food,'" he said with a grin. "She's quite a lady."

Devon smiled. "Yes, she is. Now, if you're finished, why don't you set the tray on the floor and give me my dessert."

"All right." With a secret smile, he lifted the place mat on the bed table and removed a large white envelope. "Dessert, my lady," he said as he presented it to her with a flourish.

"Wh-what's this?" Devon asked in confusion.

"Open it." Smiling, he removed the tray of dishes and set it on the floor out of the way.

Opening the envelope, Devon slid out the contents. "Why, it's...tickets!" she exclaimed. "For an Alaskan cruise! When do we go?"

"The end of May. That should give you time to heal completely."

"Oh, Geoff!" Devon said as she threw her arms around him. She was too choked up to say another word. And suddenly she knew the main difference between this Geoff and the old. This Geoff had learned to treasure life, and the relationships that were forged.

And, so had she. Finally. It had taken Russell and his wicked actions to teach her, but she had learned.

When she could speak again, Devon lifted her head to stare into the face of the man she loved. "And now, Geoffrey Hunter Grayson," she murmured. "Will you get into this bed and make love to me? I've been waiting...forever."

Geoff smiled. "Your wish is my command, my lady."

"Hmm," Devon mused as she watched him begin to remove his clothing. "I'll have to keep that in mind for future reference."

And then, as Geoff joined her in her once lonely bed, the only words spoken belonged to the language of love.

Epilogue

Three months had passed since the day death had almost claimed them both. They'd returned from their spectacular Alaskan cruise only two weeks ago. Geoff had suffered no further ill effects from his confrontation with Russell. And, with the exception of the occasional twinge in her wrist, Devon claimed she'd made a complete recovery.

Life had taken on the predictability of normal family life, and Geoff rejoiced in it. It was everything he'd wanted and more. Every day was new and exciting, and somehow the fact that he might never regain his memory no longer mattered quite so much. He'd fallen in love with his wife for the second time. He found new delight in his children on a daily basis. Tyler spent an incredible amount of time emulating his father's mannerisms. And Britanny never tired of telling him that she loved him and love was what had brought him back.

Who was he to argue? Geoff thought with a wry twist of his lips as he left his office to go in search of another cup of coffee. As he passed the entrance to the garage, he noticed that the sound of Devon working on her newest stained-glass contract had ceased. He opened the door to ask her if she wanted to join him in a cup of coffee only to find that she wasn't there.

Frowning slightly, he went in search of her.

Minutes later, he found her standing on the deck looking down on the twinkling lights of Kelowna. Something about the scene, perhaps the way she was standing or the tilt of her head, stopped him in his tracks. He'd seen her like this before—serene, a bit wistful, and...oh, so beautiful. A vision of her turning with a smile to face him, holding a champagne glass out to be refilled, flashed in his mind as clearly as he saw her now. "Happy birthday, darling," he remembered saying. "How does it feel to be thirty-two?"

Geoff swallowed. He hadn't met Devon until she was thirty-four.

The brief flash of memory faded as quickly as it had come upon him, yet it left him shaking with emotion.

He *was* Geoff Grayson.

It was no longer a conclusion drawn from evidence, but knowledge that came from within himself. The proof had come from the shadowed recesses of his own mind. If he never regained another memory, at least he had been granted that certainty.

Taking a deep breath to calm his racing heart, he opened the patio door and stepped out to join Devon. She turned at the sound, stretching a hand toward him in welcome. "Hi," she said softly. "Isn't it pretty?"

He looked down on all the twinkling lights and the gleaming swath of moonlight reflected on the night-blackened waters of Lake Okanagan. "Mmm-hmm," he said. She shivered slightly and he stepped closer to wrap his arms around her. "You should have a jacket," he admonished.

"I just stepped out for a breath of fresh air and the view captured me. I was trying to figure out a way to recreate it in stained glass."

Geoff smiled. "If there's a way, I'm sure you'll find it." He rested his chin on top of her head and luxuriated in simply holding her.

"Geoff—" she said a moment later.

"Hmm?"

"How would you feel about being a father again?"

"I think I'd like that very much." She said nothing more and the silence gradually became fraught with possibility. Was she...? "Devon? Are you...pregnant?"

"Mmm-hmm."

Geoff's heart leapt into his throat. Another child! "When?"

"Around the first of November, I think."

Releasing her, he gripped her shoulders and turned her to face him. "You're sure?"

She nodded and smiled. "I'm sure, Geoff."

He wanted to say something. Anything to express the incredible feeling of pure delight he felt, but somehow the words escaped him, so he settled for wrapping his arms around the beautiful woman who was his wife. Inhaling the intoxicating scent of her soft hair he decided that life was very good indeed, for they'd experienced an entire season of miracles. First Geoff's return, then their escape from the clutches of a madman, and, now, the miracle of new life. But...there was one thing lacking. Geoff had no memory of the vows he had made to this wonderful woman, and he needed to say them again.

"Devon?"

"Yes?"

"Will you marry me?"

She reared back to stare up into his face. Then, stroking the premature strands of gray hair at his temples, she smiled and said, "I'll marry you any time you want, any place you want, Geoffrey Hunter Grayson. I love you."

"And I love you."

* * * * *

Take 2 bestselling love stories FREE

Plus get a FREE surprise gift!

Special Limited-Time Offer

Mail to Silhouette Reader Service™

3010 Walden Avenue
P.O. Box 1867
Buffalo, N.Y. 14240-1867

YES! Please send me 2 free Silhouette Intimate Moments® novels and my free surprise gift. Then send me 6 brand-new novels every month, which I will receive months before they appear in bookstores. Bill me at the low price of $3.57 each plus 25¢ delivery and applicable sales tax, if any.* That's the complete price, and a saving of over 10% off the cover prices—quite a bargain! I understand that accepting the books and gift places me under no obligation ever to buy any books. I can always return a shipment and cancel at any time. Even if I never buy another book from Silhouette, the 2 free books and the surprise gift are mine to keep forever.

245 SEN CH7Y

Name	(PLEASE PRINT)	
Address	Apt. No.	
City	State	Zip

This offer is limited to one order per household and not valid to present Silhouette Intimate Moments® subscribers. *Terms and prices are subject to change without notice. Sales tax applicable in N.Y.

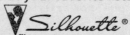

Bestselling author

LINDSAY McKENNA

continues the drama and adventure of her
popular series with an all-new, longer-length
single-title romance:

MORGAN'S MERCENARIES

HEART OF THE JAGUAR

Major Mike Houston and Dr. Ann Parsons were in the heat
of the jungle, deep in enemy territory. She knew Mike's
warrior blood kept him from the life—and the love—he
silently craved. And now she had so much more at stake.
For the beautiful doctor carried a child. His child…

Available in January 1999, at your favorite retail outlet!

Look for more **MORGAN'S MERCENARIES** in 1999,
as the excitement continues in the Special Edition line!

Silhouette®

PSMORGMERC

COMING NEXT MONTH

#901 MURPHY'S LAW—Marilyn Pappano
Men in Blue

Detective Jack Murphy and psychic Evie DesJardien had been in love—until the night Jack was told she'd betrayed him. They were passionately drawn back into each other's lives when Jack enlisted Evie's help to catch a killer. Could the two learn to trust in their love again…before it was too late?

#902 CODE NAME: COWBOY—Carla Cassidy
Mustang, Montana

When Alicia Randall and her six-year-old daughter answered Cameron Gallagher's ad for a housekeeper, she knew that she could never let him discover the truth about her. Then she found herself immediately attracted to this sexy stranger. Was this the happiness she had been searching for, or would her past catch up with her and ruin her future?

#903 DANGEROUS TO LOVE—Sally Tyler Hayes

Sexy spy Jamie Douglass knew she was falling for her strong and irresistible instructor Dan Reese. He was a difficult man to get close to, but Jamie was determined to break down his barriers. Then a routine mission turned deadly, and Jamie was forced to admit just how much she felt for this tough, sensual man. She trusted him with her life…but did she trust him with her heart?

#904 COWBOY WITH A BADGE—Margaret Watson
Cameron, Utah

When Carly Fitzpatrick's determination to find her brother's killer brought her back to the McAllister ranch, she met Devlin McAllister, the son of the man accused of the murder. Torn between her growing feelings for Devlin and her desire to discover the truth, Carly found herself falling in love with this strong, sexy sheriff—but what would he do when he found out why she'd really come to town?

#905 LONG-LOST MOM—Jill Shalvis

Stone Cameron thought life was moving along nicely for himself and his daughter—until Cindy Beatty came to town. Deeply distrustful of women after his long-ago love abandoned him, Stone tried to resist her sensuous appeal. But there was something oddly familiar about this beautiful stranger that made her impossible to resist…and he knew that it was only a matter of time before he gave in to the attraction.…

#906 THE PASSION OF PATRICK MacNEILL—Virginia Kantra
Families Are Forever

Single father Patrick MacNeill's time had been consumed with caring for his son, leaving him no room for a social life—until he met Dr. Kate Sinclair. Suddenly he began to remember what it was like to feel…and to fall in love. So when Kate tried to deny the attraction between them, he planned on showing the lovely doctor his own bedside manner!